THE CAVES OF KIRYM

THE TOKEN BEARERS — BOOK ONE

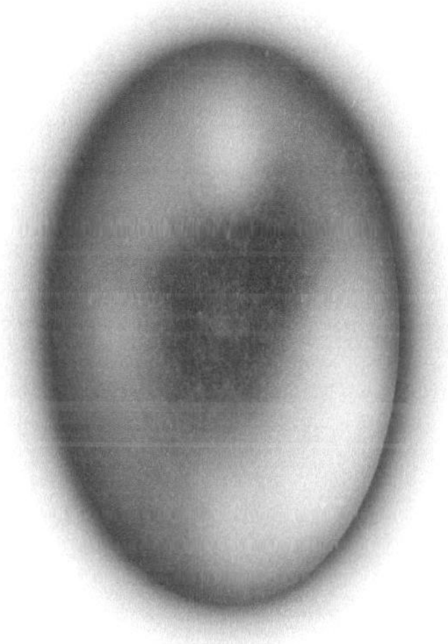

The Caves of Kirym

Derin Attwood

The Caves of Kirym

A Wordly Press Publication
Ashhurst, New Zealand
Phone 64 6 326 8066

Published by Wordly Press in 2014

Set in 12/18/24 Adobe Garamond Pro
This text uses English (UK) spelling.

ISBN 978-0-9941108-0-0

A catalogue record for this book is available from the National Library of New Zealand.

Wordly Press
www.wordlypress.com

Acknowledgements

No book is written in isolation and many people supported me as I wrote. I can't acknowledge everyone, those who are not mentioned are certainly not forgotten.

Those who have helped include Craig Attwood who maintains my computer. Llyvonne Barber assisted me with the weirdest research, never questioned my need to know of twenty ways to decapitate and poison people, and designed the amazing cover. Michelle Elvy has been an amazing friend and has inspired me to be a better writer.

My husband Ron gave me his total support through everything and my son Garreth who is always enthusiastic and supportive in what is a very solitary occupation.

Characters on this Adventure

Name   *Relationship*

From the Land Between the Gorges — Veld's Family

Name		Relationship
Armos	M	Boatbuilder
Bokum	M	Hunter
Cindra	F	Natia's twin, joined to Grenin
Danth	M	Tarjin's Papa, joined to Jinda
Grenin	M	Joined to Cindra
Halse	F	Kirym's eldest sister, promised to Teema
Harby Jnr	M	Son of Armos, known as Young Harby
Harby Snr	M	Papa of Armos, known as Old Harby
Jorlenta	F	Daughter of Armos
Kirym	F	Veld and Loul's youngest daughter
Lantiah	F	Widow of Slynd
Loul	F	Kirym's Mama, joined to Veld
Mekrar	F	Kirym's sister, twin to Mekroe
Mekroe	M	Kirym's brother, twin to Mekrar
Peet	M	Eldest son of Armos, joined to Harnita
Tarjin	M	Son of Danth
Tarl	M	Kirym's oldest brother, joined to Zhins
Teema	M	Hunter, promised to Halse
Veld	M	Headman, joined to Loul, Kirym's Papa

Name		Relationship
Yanda	F	Zelriff's sister
Zelriff	F	Oldest woman of Veld's family

From the Hill's — Raffs Family

Name		Relationship
Bildon	F	Orphan
Kamdra	M	Joined to Tindra
Raff	M	Headman, joined to Soojee
Salcan	M	Kamdra's brother
Soojee	F	Headwoman, joined to Raff
Tindra	F	Joined to Kamdra
Zeprah	F	Flatlander, joined to Raff's son

The Lake Settlement — Finlow's Family

Name		Relationship
Findlow	M	Headman, joined to Natia
Lyndym	F	Findlow and Natia's daughter
Natia	F	Twin to Cindra, joined to Findlow
Rathay	M	Aligned to Findlow's family
Sundas	M	Adopted by Natia, Findlow's Family

Raider's — Slynd's Gang

Name		Relationship
Arbreu	M	Slave owned by Slynd
Bextan	M	Slynd's right-hand man
Lanshere	M	Slave
Pelak	M	Warrior
Slynd	M	Head of the Raiders

1

Kirym Speaks

My first visit to Raff's hill settlement would be my only visit. This was an important trip for me, my first away from our land. We would check that our neighbours had wintered well, and return with my eldest and favourite sister, Halse, who had spent the winter with them.

Mama woke me just before midnight, clicked the life token on her forehead to mine and laid out my travel clothes. The drab green and brown material was warm and soft, and would be needed in the cool spring air.

Mama had a hot meal ready for us, a thick stew and fresh bread, and I joined my siblings on the large porch that surrounded our dwelling. We ate as we waited for those who were travelling with us to arrive.

My brother Mekroe played his pipe, the notes echoing in the darkness.

"Save your breath and energy, Mekroe," Mama said softly as she came to the door laden with cloaks, shawls, and scarves. "You'll need it for the journey." She handed Papa a pack filled with gifts for Raff's family. "Travel safe, Veld, and take care of the young ones."

Papa smiled, pushed her hair behind her ear and clicked his token to hers. "I will, Loul. We'll be home in five days, no time at all."

There was a sudden increase in noise as a crowd of people burst into the open area in front of the porch. Shoulders were slapped and hugs, kisses and smiles exchanged.

Mekroe, who had pushed his pipe into his belt, pulled it out again and added shrilly to the noise until Papa looked sternly in his direction. He slipped it back into his belt, grabbed his cloak and threw it around his shoulders. He picked up two packs and handed one to his twin sister. Settling his onto his shoulder, he took a quiver of arrows from the storage chest my eldest brother Tarl had carried onto the porch and tied it to his hip. Then he chose a bow and stood waiting expectantly for everyone else.

Papa raised his voice above the noise. "Are you ready to leave, friends? I want to be at the lakes by sun up."

Heads nodded and there was a hum of acknowledgement as packs and weapons were shouldered. Thirty people would make this trip out of our land, and I was the youngest. I was so excited.

Mama hugged me. "You mind your Papa. Do exactly as he says, no matter what!" She wrapped a shawl around my cloaked shoulders and handed me an old shoulder pack.

I slipped into the line of people as they walked up the path, but looked back to wave to Mama. I rounded the massive elm tree and she was lost from my sight. Then I ran to join my sister, Mekrar.

"Don't walk with me," she hissed. "You shouldn't even be on this trip. You're far too small. You'll hold us up. I'll be sooo embarrassed when someone has to carry you. I don't know what Papa is thinking of, allowing you to come along."

"If I'm such an embarrassment, don't walk with me. You're only annoyed because you didn't get to go to Raff's until you were much older than me. I practised hard for this." The look she gave me as she fell back to walk with her friends was far from sisterly.

She added to their soft chatter and occasional giggles, while further back I could hear the low murmur of the men who walked at the rear.

Teema slowed down and joined me. I liked him; he would become my brother during the summer when he'd join with my sister Halse.

The low lake was a major landmark on our trip and we arrived there just as the sun rose. I'd visited the lake many times. Each summer we fished, swam, and sailed the small boats that were the pride of Armos, our closest neighbour.

We stopped here to rest and share a meal, although Papa didn't allow us long.

Armos joined him as he shared his food with me. "We're making good time, Veld. With your permission I'll take Tarl and Young Harby to guard the rear."

Papa nodded. "Can you add Mekroe to your group? And Tarjin, I think. They're past the age of playing on these trips."

Armos nodded. "Will Mekrar join us? It's hard to keep her and young Mekroe apart."

"Not this time, she's happy with the older girls. The twins can't expect to be together all the time." Papa paused. "They're all growing up, Armos. We're becoming old men." They both laughed as we scrambled to our feet. Papa strode out again and I followed closely behind him.

Within a few steps, Teema joined me again along with his best friend, Bokum. The terrain was far rougher now as we walked across country aiming for our second landmark, the great waterfall. It sat on the northern gorge that divided our land from Raff's.

The path to the waterfall was steep and soon we were all gasping for breath. Just over halfway up the cliff, we entered a maze of rocks and tunnels, catching up with Papa and some of the hunters who had gone ahead. We ate our midday meal here, which left my pack empty. I volunteered to lighten someone else's pack, but they all declined.

It was warm among the rocks. They protected us from the wind and the spray of the waterfall.

Papa made me remove my shawl and cloak. He put them into his pack and brought out a harness and ropes. I climbed into the harness and Papa tied it around my chest and over my shoulders. Teema put a harness on also, but when Papa picked the third one up, Bokum took it.

"You've enough to do leading us," Bokum said, and put it on.

A strap from the back of Bokum's harness tied onto the front of mine and two more went from the sides of my harness and back to Teema's.

Papa hunkered down beside me. "Follow Bokum closely. You'll have to watch you don't walk into him. You won't be able to talk to him or Teema, but they'll keep you safe. Don't look down." He smiled. "You'll be all right?"

I nodded. "It's exciting, Papa, just as you said it would be."

We set off again, in single file this time. Papa and the hunters went in front, Armos and the young men he was training in the rear. The noise of the waterfall got louder and the spray settled on my hair and face. The rocks were wet and slippery, but there were plenty of handholds. Then the rock wall on the river side suddenly disappeared and we walked on a wide path with the water thundering past us. Ahead of us was a sheer cliff with deep handholds on the rock face, but Bokum turned left between two large boulders and in behind the waterfall.

It was loud and I could understand why Papa had said I wouldn't be able to talk. Even if I had shouted, I'd not have been heard.

Teema and Bokum held on to a rope that hung well above my head. The path was very narrow and towards the middle of the fall it narrowed further and sloped towards the outer edge. The river thundered past my shoulder. I tried to cling to the rock face, but slipped and hung over the edge, terrified, supported only by the ropes attached to my harness. The wall of water hit my left shoulder and my pack slipped off, instantly swallowed by the swirling maelstrom below me. I looked down at the water and rocks, but knew I was safe. I took a deep breath and reached out for the path again.

The path stayed narrow, but soon the incline was towards the rock face and I felt a lot safer. Again and again, I was showered with cold water, but the path widened and we moved faster. Soon we were out from under the water flow.

When the path turned away from the waterfall, we removed the harnesses. I helped Teema roll them up. Bokum disappeared around the rocks.

"I dropped my pack."

"Happens to everyone on the first trip," said Teema, grinning. "That's why we gave you an old one and we emptied it before you entered the fall."

I was cold and wet.

I wrung out my clothes as well as I could.

Teema rubbed my hands to warm them up.

There were paths and tunnels leading in many directions. Teema turned into one and then another and another. Soon the thunder of the water was muffled by the enclosing rocks. It was warm in between the rocks and my clothes started to steam.

Papa waited at a junction in the paths, helping Harby and Tarl throw packs up to Peet. Harby gave Bokum a leg up. Then Bokum leaned over the edge and Papa and Teema hoisted me up to him. At the top, there was a gentle incline to a warm grassy area where those ahead of us waited.

"Wasn't that exciting? I'm never truly relaxed with it though," Bokum said, as we sat down.

Horan snorted. "If you ever appear to be, lad, I for one won't go through with you," he said. "Things go wrong. Remember when the rope broke and —"

"Horan!" Teema interrupted. "That's scare tactics for no reason." He turned to me. "The intrinsic danger of the trip is offset by our safety precautions, Kirym. Armos and Young Harby came up ten days ago to renew the ropes and anchor points. Any hint of danger and we don't cross."

Lantiah helped me lay out my boots and jacket so they could dry. "The path is exposed and it'll be cold, but we've time to dry out before we leave, and we have extra boots if they're needed. We've a long way to go, but the path is easy from here on."

Mekrar sat beside me. "That was sooo exciting. I did it without a harness," she said. "I'm never going to wear one again. It's only for babies like you."

Papa came up behind her as she was speaking. "You'll wear a harness if you're told to," he said gruffly. "On these trips you'll be obedient or you won't come. Everything everyone does is evaluated. Remember that."

Mekrar went red and hung her head. "I'm sorry, Papa."

Papa ruffled her hair. "Never take it for granted. When you think it's fun, you stop taking care. That's when things go wrong." He picked up some food and a flask of water and went to talk to Armos.

We followed a narrow rocky path from our rest area. The air was cooler now and I was thankful for my cloak. Again small groups formed as friends settled in to walk together. My brothers, Mekroe and Tarl, slipped to the back of the group with Armos. It was late afternoon now and I was tired, although I'd never tell anyone.

"It'll be warmer when we get into the trees, but it'll be nearer dusk so you'll need your cloak even then," said Teema as he, Bokum and Peet joined me.

"We'll soon hit Raff's path," Peet said. "Mind you, this early in the season, it won't resemble much of a path."

Bokum grunted. "It'll be easier than breaking a track as we are now. I think it's time we set up an all-weather path from the rocks. Creating a new one each spring makes the trip so much longer."

"This is serious," said Peet. "You want a fast trip? Why? Surely the trip is part of the adventure."

"Bok, are you snuggling up to Raff's crazy grandmamma again?" asked Teema, with exaggerated seriousness.

Teema and Peet roared with laughter. Bokum went red, but laughed with them.

Teema turned back to Peet. "If we let Bokum lead, the trip'll be quicker. It seems he has the most incentive."

"You're a great one to talk, Teema. What about Halse?" asked Bokum. "Has a winter alone given you second thoughts on joining with her?" They laughed again.

"Come on Bok, who's the girl?" asked Peet. "Do I sense a

joining here? Will you be living with us, or will you become Raff's ma...?" He stopped talking as Papa raised his hand for silence.

Papa turned us back the way we'd come for a short distance. "Questions later," he said. "The path is open. There are tracks in both directions and the stellon is missing."

Young Harby's eyes widened. "But it's been there for — forever. Could Raff have taken it to the settlement?"

"I doubt he'd do it without telling us. It's happened recently, possibly earlier today. He knew we were due to visit. If he'd done it he'd have someone here to explain. There are none of Raff's signs, so I have to assume something's wrong. We need to get there quickly," said Papa. "The younger ones will need help and so make your decisions for your families please." He hunkered down and pulled me close to him. "We must run child, you'll not keep up. I'll have —"

"You need to move fast, Veld," interrupted Teema. "She'll manage. I'll help her if she needs it. I'll protect her as my own."

Papa looked at him for a brief moment and nodded shortly. "You're a good son to my family, Teema. Thank you." He turned back to me. "Obey Teema as you would me! Keep up with him and don't make a sound! Even if you're hurt, make no noise. Be brave, make me proud of you." He turned away, readying the men for battle.

Mekrar clicked her token to mine. "Don't worry, Kirym. It'll be fine. If Papa didn't think you could cope with this, he wouldn't have brought you along." She shrugged. "All of this, it's just a precaution." As bright as she sounded, she looked scared.

The men had their bows and knives ready and, flanked by Tarl and Bokum, Papa moved us quickly back to the path. Once there he stopped and waited, not moving for a long time. Birds and insects began to sing again. He stepped onto the path. Armed men ranged behind him and to the rear with Armos. Everyone was quiet and watchful.

Keeping to firm ground on the left side of the path, Papa set off at a quick trot. After about nine hundred steps, he held up his hand. We stopped. Papa, Tarl and Bokum moved forward and knelt by something on the path. Papa pointed to Teema and me and beckoned us forward.

A pack with two arrows in it lay on the ground. There was a bloody spear beside it.

Papa rubbed the sticky blood between his thumb and finger and nodded. "From this morning – not a fatal injury though." He pointed to footprints on the path. "He was helped away and carried some of his own weight. Not the pack however." He stooped and picked up something almost hidden in the mud. He rubbed it against his tunic and held it out. It was a token, similar to those we wore.

It belonged to Halse, although not as I remembered it. Formerly pale yellow, it was now almost grey.

Papa patted Teema on the shoulder. "It may not mean anything," he said. He clicked the token to mine, watching me closely.

I suddenly felt very tired and would have fallen had Teema not grabbed me. Everything went misty and I just wanted to sleep.

Papa frowned. "That's not right, it's never done that before." He handed me two harkii nuts. I chewed them slowly and felt better, although still very tired. Papa looked down the track. "We go fast. Everyone must keep up." He picked up the pack and thrust it at Lantiah. "Can you manage that?" he asked. Not waiting to hear her answer, he turned away and continued down the track.

Once again, we ranged behind him, the more experienced men with Papa, Armos and his young men and boys at the back, the rest of us in the middle. It was dark in the trees, making it difficult to see the detail of the path ahead. I felt more tired than ever and had trouble keeping up. Teema tightened his grip on me and took some of my weight.

Papa signalled again and we stopped.

Teema led me off the trail and knelt beside me. "You need to stay here," he said. "Lie down and keep still. I'll come back for you, I promise. No matter how long it takes, Kirym, stay here — stay still."

He clicked his token to mine and helped me curl up with my cloak around me, his pack under my head. He placed my shawl over my face and tucked my cloak around my feet. "If you don't move, you won't be seen." His footsteps faded away and I was left with the forest sounds around me. I was warm and tired. I slept.

2

Teema Speaks

A body lay across the path.

I looked for a place to leave Kirym. I hated leaving her, but really I had no choice. It seemed obvious that something bad had happened at Raff's settlement.

I spied a big oak tree a little way off the path. Kirym would be safe here. I nestled her between the massive roots.

She was pale and tired after contact with Halse's token and that worried me. Tokens didn't do that to people. Still, it would keep her sleeping while I was away. Her clothing was good camouflage, the mottled greens and browns concealed her among the old leaves and debris of the forest floor.

Before she lay down, I clicked my token to hers. This was usually done only to close family members and I couldn't yet claim the kinship. The connection it created though, would let me know if she was in danger and would make finding her easier when I returned. It would possibly worry her mama, but Loul would understand.

I looked back at the tree and memorised the roots. With the leaves I had strewn about, even I had trouble seeing where she lay.

I returned to the path. Almost everyone had gone on, but Grenin, Danth and Tarl had stayed to hide other younger ones. I stood on a bush so it leaned onto the path. With its roots intact, it would grow straight within a few days. If we weren't back by then, it wouldn't matter.

Bokum had checked the body. "It's Ranot, Raff's youngest. We'll collect him later. I wonder what happened here." He shook his head, frowning. "Veld wants us to come into Raff's from the ridge. It makes good sense approaching from two directions."

We cut across a shallow valley and after a short hard climb, worked our way along the ridge and around a rocky outcrop. Finally we got a view of the settlement below.

It was no longer there.

There was a smoking mess that had been the circle of dwellings. The ragged remnants of smoke blew northward, the reason we hadn't smelled it as we travelled here. There were no people in sight.

"This wasn't an accident," I muttered to Bokum. "I hope everyone escaped, but where are they?"

Bok grimaced. "They'll be somewhere nearby if they survived."

We edged our way down to the outskirts of the settlement, waited and watched.

I nocked an arrow into my bow, and waited, ready for anything. I stiffened when I saw a flicker of movement in the trees.

Veld, Armos and Peet approached the centre of the

settlement, weapons ready.

No challenge.

The three men walked west towards the area where Raff's dwelling had been. The light was almost gone and it was getting hard to see. I was relieved when Veld returned and signalled us down to him.

We met in the open area between the burned dwellings.

"Raff's dwelling is fine," said Veld. "Some of them are up at the grove. Quite a few are dead though. Let's see how we can help."

We walked through the devastated settlement. Raff's dwelling was the only one standing intact. It was strange stepping onto the large porch without the welcome ceremonies he enjoyed so much.

Raff sat by the door, grey with exhaustion and thankful when offered water and the food we had brought with us. I was shocked at how few people were there.

"Halse is at the grove with others," said Veld. "Bokum, take some men and get them. Teema, Tarl, you collect the young ones. It'll dark before you get there. Take Zeprah with you, she knows the path. There shouldn't be any danger, but be prepared. Peet, Walf, go and get Ranot's body."

Raff looked devastated when he realised his son was dead.

As I grabbed my weapons, Raff's daughter-in-law Zeprah approached me. "I've spoken to Grenin, I know where the little ones are," she said. "Halse didn't tell me you had a child, or does she not know?"

"Not my child. Kirym, Halse's sister. She took ill on the path, so ..." I paused. "The twins are there also and a few others. Is Halse all right?"

Zeprah frowned. "She was hit on the head as she tried to protect Sarel and Arlanquee. She sleeps deeply." She grabbed a hooded lantern and stepped off the porch.

Joined by Armos and Tarl, we took the path this time. It was longer, but safer at night. Even so, it didn't take us long to get to the signal bush. We separated to collect the various hidden children. Zeprah came with me.

I was concerned Kirym may have panicked and shown herself, but the ground was smooth and as I watched, there was no movement. I knelt, brushed away the leaf debris and lifted her cloak. Instantly I felt the prick of a sharp blade at my throat.

She recognised me and lowered the knife.

I helped her up, hugged her and again clicked my token to hers.

"Four people ran past, going east," she said as she stood and slipped the knife into its sheath.

I looked up at Zeprah. "Veld sent guards to the waterfall and the top pass. Just a precaution."

We joined the others at the path. "Can you manage, Kirym?" I asked. "I can piggyback you."

"I'll walk — I've had a good rest."

Despite her reassurance, I thought she still looked tired.

Mekroe grumbled about being left with the children.

"A good warrior does what his leader demands, Mek," said Armos, "even if it is to stay behind. Obedience is important."

"People who say that generally get to go," Mekroe mumbled.

Armos chuckled. "We all have to obey, lad. Do you think I want to always guard our rear? There are plusses though. I get to teach all o' the young men, get to know you and train you to the high standard your Papa needs."

"But I missed all the fun," Mekroe muttered.

It was peaceful walking through the trees and the darkness hid the worst of the devastation in the settlement. We arrived back at Raff's just as a meal was laid out.

Raff's eldest daughter Sojaff handed each of us a rug. "Some of the men are collecting the dead, others are digging a grave. We'll bury everyone in the morning. Veld wants us to return with you until we can decide what to do." Tears slipped down her cheek. She looked exhausted.

Just then Bokum arrived back from the grove. Most of those he brought were women and children and there were fewer than I thought there'd be. The attack had taken a huge toll. Three people were on stretchers. Halse was one of them. Deathly pale, she had an oozing wound on her temple. She looked strangely naked without her token.

I was pleased when Veld placed the holder on her forehead and slipped her token into it. It glimmered just a little as it settled. I stood, intending to click my token to hers.

Veld shook his head. "Where's Kirym?"

"Here, Papa." She stepped out of the shadows.

"Have you eaten?" he asked.

She shook her head.

"Eat first, child." He raised his voice. "Come friends. Eat, keep your energy up." He took my arm and led me over to share a platter of food with Kirym.

Raff sat opposite us. "What if they return tonight, Veld?"

"I've set guards on all of the paths, Raff. If they return, we'll know long before they get here. You're safe for now, and tomorrow we'll get you over the gorge," said Veld. "Tell me about the attack. What happened? I thought it was only a game you played with the Flatlanders. You raided them, they raided you."

"With the Flatlanders, yes, that's all it's ever been. A game we played every summer. They'd take a few baskets of our produce and a bit of meat. Mostly it was tied up with one of our daughters being taken for a joining — and we did the same to them. Goodness, that's how I joined with Soojee. Generally we knew in advance when they were coming, and the worst that happened was a few bruises and an occasional sore head." He laughed dryly. "Often we'd have a hunt prior to their arrival so there'd be extra meat for them. We'd chase them back to their settlement and join the celebrations. There are many family links between us."

"So what changed?"

Raff shook his head. "I didn't recognise these men. They came from the east, over the mountain. They attacked at midnight and set fire to our dwellings. They used weapons against people who were asleep. It was fortunate they were seen quite early in the attack."

"How come they were seen? I mean, you don't have guards at night, do you?" asked Bokum.

"No we don't, and I know you've warned me about being so complacent, Veld, but we've always been so safe here. Last night, Soojee was called to help with a birthing. She saw a fire and screamed. There was a lot of smoke — made it hard to see. My men were attacked as they ran from the dwellings. Some didn't get out at all. Bludgeoned in their beds! We tried to get the women and children to the safety of the grove." He shook his head. "We fought. Our women fought also. It was bloody. Then they left. Why?" He shrugged. "If they'd stayed, they'd've killed us all." He took a deep shuddering breath and wiped his eyes. "Pointless. Old people, children, our babies — all gone." He paused, frowning. "They robbed us. They raided the dwellings as they burned. They seemed to know where we kept our treasures, although to be honest it wasn't much of a secret. Our valuable things sat on the stellon." Raff leaned back on the set and closed his eyes. Within moments he was asleep.

I looked around the room. All of Raff's family slept.

Veld nodded. "Leave them. There's little that can be done tonight and they'll need their strength."

Kirym slipped off the set and took Halse's hand, leaned

down and clicked her token to her sister's. She went white and slipped to the floor. Her token dimmed.

Veld reached her moments before I did. He leant forward to connect his token with hers.

"Veld, you can't!" I said, hauling back on his collar. "You can't compromise your health, even for this. We need you at full strength."

"But it must be family!"

"You're not the only family she has, Veld," said Armos, "and before you do anything, let's decide who would be the best person for this. You have to lead us. If we use Tarl or one of the twins, they may no longer be able to care for themselves. They'd become a big liability. So we leave her as she is and sort it out when we get home, or you go along the path that's already been taken. Let Teema do it."

Veld looked up with a frown. "What do you mean? Teema's not family."

"Veld, you've called him son. He'll join with Halse when the time's right. Anyway, you gave Kirym to him earlier. The connection's already there."

Veld looked troubled. He sat thinking for a long time. The room was silent as all of those awake watched. I remembered back to when we discovered the loss of the stellon and Veld's words — 'you're a good son to my family'.

Veld gave a quiet laugh and said almost in mimic. "Yes. You are a good son to my porch, my family. She's yours, Teema. Take her."

"She'll always be your daughter, Veld, but she is my friend." I hoped it would be enough.

Veld thought for a while longer, and then nodded. "I hope you're right. Yes, do it."

I lifted Kirym off the floor and laid her on a set, clicking my token to hers. I felt my energy drain away for a brief moment and watched with amazement as her token flashed and connected to mine. As my energy returned, her eyes flickered open. Her token, normally gold, her family token colour, darkened to a deep vibrant blue.

Veld gasped. "I thought those sorts of connections were myths. What does it mean?"

"It means it was the right decision, Veld," said Armos.

Veld gripped my shoulder. "Thank you, my friend. Look after her for the rest of the trip. After that, well, we'll see what Old Harby and the Council of Women come up with. I have no worries for her future though." He sighed. "Get some rest. We'll rise early." He lay on the floor, closed his eyes and was immediately asleep.

I sat beside Kirym and watched the blue token pulse slowly in time to her breathing. The sight settled me and I too slept.

I woke to movement. It was dark outside, but the hearth glowed, lighting the room. Zeprah, Lantiah and Mekrar were helping the injured and young to eat.

Veld strode in with Raff and a few others. "A quiet night," he said, "but I want to move fast now. We'll take the deer path. It's harder, but there's less chance of being surprised on it." He looked around at who wasn't busy. "Peet, find out who needs assistance and who can help carry the wounded. Lantiah, make sure everyone eats. Zilpan, help Raff get the possessions sorted."

"I think Sojaff's already done it, Veld," said Zilpan. "There's little to take with us. Most of it was burned or stolen by those monsters."

Kirym woke, pale but alert. I searched through my pack for three harkii nuts, crushed them and gave them to her. She ate half and fed the rest to Halse.

Halse stirred slightly and moaned, then settled back as she had been.

"What else can I do for her?"

"You've done all you can for now. The rest'll be decided by others. Let's eat and see how we can help."

We assembled on the lamp lit porch. A trench had been dug on the northern side of the dwelling. The shrouded remains of the dead lay next to it.

Raff stood beside the trench. "We can't bury our dead as we normally do, there isn't the time. We have small memories from each of them to take with us and when the time is right, we'll use them ... when it's the right time." Raff's voice drifted to silence as he brushed away his tears.

Sojaff stepped up beside him. "Because our headwoman, my mama, is injured, I'll take her place if there is no objection." There was silence and a few nods. She guided Raff to the top of the trench, and stood beside the first body.

Raff started speaking, his voice breaking with grief. "Sarel, my darling daughter. Sister, wife and mama. Gifted to us from the land between the gorges. Sister to Lyndym and Veld, joined to Tiber. Mama of Zeplar and Arlanquee. We'll see you no more, but you will stay in our hearts and on our stellon."

Someone started to sob as Peet and Bokum laid Sarel in the trench. Raff and Sojaff moved to the next shrouded body. "Ranot. Son, brother and husband. Son of Raff of the Hills and Soojee of the Lowlands. Brother to Tiber and Sojaff. Joined to Zeprah. We will see you no more but you'll stay in our hearts and on our stellon."

One by one, the bodies laid in the trench were acknowledged, their families and associations mentioned.

It was heart-wrenching as more than half of Raff's family were buried.

It was hardest to say goodbye to the children and babies. The youngest was laid in the trench last and nestled between his parents. Raff broke down completely, so Sojaff talked of him.

"You were our future and our hope. This is where our memory will linger. Though the smallest, the youngest, the newest of our family, you Arlanquee, will begin a new stellon. Arlanquee, child of the family, son, grandson, brother. Future denied. You will remain in our hearts. You will forever be remembered."

By now, almost everyone was sobbing. Everyone from our family had tears in their eyes. Many of these people were related to us also.

I worried about Kirym. She leaned against me, pale with grief. With an aunt, uncle and a number of cousins dead, and Halse at death's door, she appeared to be beyond tears.

I didn't think that was good. I felt nauseous at the sights I had seen. I knew the memory of the bodies Veld had pulled from the burned dwellings would remain with me forever. I wondered what it would do to Kirym.

The trench was quickly filled in and Veld allowed us a few more moments with our thoughts. He took Raff's arm. "Come, Raff. Bring your memories and let's go home."

The sun had scarcely risen when we left the settlement. There was none of the laughter and chat of yesterday. The deer track was narrow and steep and everyone carried more than they should. We shared the carrying of the stretchers and made good time despite having to stop to tend the wounded. The only person looking happy was Mekrar who had a baby to care for.

The baby's parents lived, but her papa, Kamdra, was one of the severely injured and her mama, Tindra, was helping care for him.

Halse had not moved other than the momentary stirring when given the harkii nut. Still, she showed no sign of pain, which was a relief.

I helped with a stretcher that carried Kirym who was still weak, although she would have walked uncomplaining. It was also loaded with possessions from the settlement. I continued to be mystified by the pulsing blue token Kirym wore and noticed frequent glances from others who must also have wondered what had happened.

As we approached the waterfall everyone became more apprehensive. The path here was exposed and we felt vulnerable. I was pleased when we finally climbed down into the jumble of rocks and laid down our loads.

Veld organised us quickly. "Take the children and young ones through first with a few to care for them while we get the rest through. Then we'll take the wounded. Those with harnesses and the knowledge to use them can help get everyone through."

The children and young ones were easy. Young Harby and I helped Kirym walk through and left her in Lantiah's care while we helped others. Harnesses were adapted for the walking injured, but the people on stretchers posed a big problem. It just didn't seem possible for two men to walk through carrying a stretcher.

After a lot of discussion, we threaded ropes to sit alongside the stretcher poles and tied them to the harnesses. Bokum and Young Harby carried Halse through and it worked for Soojec also, although they were both heavy loads for the men.

We faced a more difficult problem next. Kamdra was a

massive man and two of us couldn't carry him. We left him until last, discussing our options. By mid-afternoon, Kamdra was the only person left to carry through the waterfall and we began to relax.

Armos and Peet had gone to the top pass to collect the guards Veld had sent there last night. They all returned out of breath and scared.

"There are men coming over the pass," said Armos. "Sixty or seventy, more than attacked the settlement."

"Thank goodness we've left the settlement then." said Raff. "They'll not know what happened to us. The deer path was a good choice, we left no track to follow."

Peet grabbed Veld's arm. "One of them was Slynd!"

Veld frowned.

"I recognised him, too," said Armos. "He's older, but it's him."

"Are you sure?"

Armos and Peet nodded.

Veld exploded into action. "Get everyone across, NOW!" he said. "Raff, we have to destroy this path. I'll not allow these men to attack my family."

Raff looked devastated. "But that'll mean we can't return, ever. Our memories, Veld. Our history is here. We'll lose that."

"Better to lose your history than your lives. Slynd! He knows the path. You've seen what these men do. Do you want that for the rest of your family?" He raised his voice. "Let's go! Now!"

The stretcher was ready for Kamdra. We had doubled the ropes and lengthened two of them so there could be two men at the front and two at the back. Even so, it was an awfully hard lift.

Tindra, Kamdra's wife, and his brother Salcan had stayed back, helping to care for him. Raff took Tindra through first, and they were followed by Salcan.

Peet and Young Harby carried the front of the stretcher with Armos and me at the back. Armos, walking behind me, was followed by Bokum. Veld brought up the rear, bringing the rope with him. Bokum walked through backwards, watching the path behind Veld, his bow and arrows ready.

I didn't think I could have done that.

We crossed the most difficult area under the waterfall. I began to relax, but suddenly Kamdra started to vomit blood and thrash about.

We stopped, and I held tightly to the rope above my head, desperately trying to keep my balance as the ropes jerked and pulled. I felt rather than heard the stretcher begin to rip, and froze with horror as he began to convulse violently. His body gave a huge lurch, the strain was too much for the stretcher and it split down the centre. Kamdra plunged over the edge, crashed onto the rocks and disappeared into the thundering turmoil below us.

Harby must have felt the movement. He turned to check on Kamdra. His eyes widened with horror and he lunged for the falling body, ripping one of the ropes from Peet's grip.

"No!" I screamed, although no one could have heard me. I darted forward, feeling the rope loosen as Armos followed me.

I missed Harby, but the rope twisted and flicked around his chest. He hung over the edge with no other support. Peet and I pulled back on the ropes and Harby was able to grab the path and hoist himself back up. I held my breath as he crawled to safety. When the path widened, he vomited and collapsed.

Peet helped him up and they walked unsteadily around the rocks.

I felt the hand rope slacken. The path was wider here and I turned to watch for Bokum and Veld.

Armos squeezed my shoulder as he passed me. He looked as stunned as I felt. He picked up the remains of the stretcher and walked unsteadily along the path.

"Kamdra?" Tindra brushed past me looking for Kamdra, not grasping what had happened. She swung round, horrified as she realised he was no longer there. She backed away from me and, before I could react, she bumped into Bokum.

The hand rope was no longer taut and they both overbalanced.

I lunged for them, missed Tindra but knocked Bokum to his knees. Veld dived forward and grabbed Tindra by the wrist.

She hung over the edge, looking terrified.

I hauled Bokum out of the way and grabbed Tindra's other arm. Veld and I lifted her to safety. She came sobbing and clawing at the stone path.

Veld took her in his arms, helped her to her feet and out into the sunshine.

He handed her to Lantiah and Zeprah and motioned Bokum and me to return to the path with him. "A long time back, we prepared for this." He pointed to one of the big rocks we walked around to get to the path. "If we dislodge the big one at the bottom, there's a pile of rock behind it that will fall across the path, blocking it. We may be able to clear it later."

Armos approached carrying a solid tree branch. He pushed it in behind the rock and started to lever it out. Bokum, Veld, Young Harby and I added our weight and it inched forward. It seemed to take a long time, but suddenly it rolled out and we were enveloped in a cloud of dust. When it settled, the path looked impassable.

3

Arbreu

It was dawn when Arbreu heard the fighters coming up the hill. He listened carefully, trying to work out if the raid was a success. A victory meant celebration, plenty of food and maybe a rest.

Then he heard Slynd snarl, and scrambled to his feet. Had the attack gone as planned, Slynd would have stayed at the settlement dividing the booty. His return meant it must have been a disaster.

Arbreu struggled to hoist the huge load he'd been allocated onto his shoulders. Some of the men had been ordered to carry the trinket covered pole Slynd found. It was heavy, and while none of Slynd's mercenaries would oppose him by objecting, they wanted their own possessions carried also. All but the fighters were overloaded.

"Ambushed!" Slynd screamed as he burst into the clearing. "They were waiting for us." He kicked out at Lanshere who was still attempting to hoist a pack to his shoulder.

Slynd didn't stop, but stomped through the clearing and continued up the hill towards the mountain pass. The men fell into line behind him. The fighters rounded up the slaves, and ensured that no one escaped.

The sun was well above the horizon when Slynd finally stopped for a rest. By then, whispered conversations had told the story. No ambush, but the unguarded settlement responded quickly and fought back fiercely. Although Slynd had the upper hand, he quailed visibly when, having attacked an unarmed young woman trying to protect her baby, another came at him with a scream of outrage and would have killed him had Bextan not stepped between them, allowing Slynd to escape. Bextan paid a dear price for that, a spear embedded deep in his shoulder. On the path back, he'd dropped the pack of stolen treasures he'd grabbed as he raided one of the dwellings. He was still in need of support to keep up with them.

A cold meal was prepared. Slynd and his fighters ate most of it, leaving only scraps for the slaves.

Arbreu was lucky this time, Bextan passed on some of his food.

Bextan didn't do this because he liked Arbreu, but Arbreu carried his pack and if he was unable to, no one else would. Poverty in this group was a sin, and the wages of that sin was slavery. Slynd would not make any allowances just because Bextan saved his life.

Usually a battle meant they would feast. Over the winter, feasts had been further apart than most of them wanted. The unsuccessful attack meant little booty. Arbreu suspected that many had grabbed items during the attack, but these had been hidden. Mainly they were concealed from Slynd, who would demand a portion of everything. When he was angry, his portion was large.

They were headed for the mountain pass. The terrain got

steeper and it was obvious they wouldn't make it over the pass with the loads they carried.

Eventually Slynd was convinced to stop and strip the pole of the valuables embedded in it. He demanded a fire and food. Fuel was scarce here, so as the jewels were dug from the pole, it was pushed onto the fire.

Arbreu watched the carved top of the pole burn and had the notion that something of value was being destroyed. For the first time ever, he regretted not having the prestige of a fighter, able to demand that part for himself. The wood was relief carved, the top curved and grooved with strange holes and symbols. He was surprised at how fast it burned, especially when the rest of the tree only smouldered reluctantly.

As the fire spluttered and died, Slynd, angry at being thwarted by people and fire, ordered them to move on. By evening they had crossed the low pass and were half way down the short slope before the final rise to the high pass. There was no wood for a fire and everyone was cold and unhappy.

Slynd's mood was foul. He gave details for their next attack, a small wealthy settlement on the far side of the two mountain passes.

The suggestion of spending more nights on the mountain this early in spring was not received well. The paths over the passes were short, but dangerous. Three slaves had fallen last time they did it. Slaves weren't important, but they carried the possessions. While most fighters divided their property between two or three slaves, any loss altered the balance of power.

Everyone wrapped up as best they could, and fell into an uncomfortable sleep as the moon began its trip towards the western horizon.

Morning came early, but most of them slept on, soaking

up the warmth of the sun.

By midday, they were awake and bickering. Only the cold and hunger kept the fighting to a minimum.

Slynd sat to one side watching warily. He stood abruptly and walked back the way they had come. The slaves were hurriedly kicked to their feet and everyone followed. The western side of the pass was now warmer than the eastern and Slynd increased his speed.

This was battle mode.

Just below the tree line, Slynd allowed them a brief rest.

"A few nights ago," he said. "I found a path across the gorge. It's risky but quicker than the passes. Not as dangerous. I strung a rope to help y'all use it. It's a door to the land between the gorges. We have two communities to attack. Then I'll own the richest land on the coast. I'll retrieve my birthright and have my revenge on those who stole it from me."

He led them into a maze of rocks near a waterfall. The tunnels were narrow and they had difficulty getting the massive loads through.

Slynd was annoyed when they fell behind. "Leave the packs," he yelled. "We'll get them later. No one knows this path, they'll be safe."

The packs were dropped and Slynd led them to where the water thundered over the cliff.

Arbreu was scared and, looking at the faces of the other men, he realised they were too. Especially when they understood that the path went under the waterfall.

There was no rope.

Pelak turned to Slynd demanding an explanation.

Slynd hesitated and there was a loud bang. The path fell

away, rocks cascading out around their feet.

Slynd jumped back in shock and pushed his way through the line of panicking men. Eventually, they found their way back to where the packs had been left.

"The vibrations from the water must have detached the rock I hammered the rope into," Slynd said as he threw himself on the grass. "We'll have to go over the pass now. There's another way into that land. I built a bridge over the other gorge a long time ago. We'll attack the settlement on the far side and then cross the gorge and take back my land."

From behind a rock, Pelak pulled out a bundle of bloody bandages and an old platter with a hunk of bread, half chewed, and the browning remains of some fruit on it. "I thought no one knew of this place," he snarled.

Critical eyes turned on Slynd.

"No one does," screamed Slynd, jumping to his feet. "The bandages are Bextan's, and I gave him the food. He needed it, he's wounded. He showed his loyalty. I reward loyalty." He grabbed his spear. "Move out," he yelled. "I want to be there tomorrow."

4

Kirym Speaks

Everything was different. Teema's token had changed. Now it was dark blue and I was aware of his emotions and thoughts. It was strange. I saw Kamdra's death and Tindra falling much as he must have. I knew Armos had collected the stretcher and brought it out with him. I watched him fold it and put it in his pack.

"There's an explanation," he said, when he saw me watching him, but he refused to say more.

After we had come through the waterfall, I walked.

Everyone wanted to get away from there, so we spent the night on the eastern side of the lake. We were all unsettled and unsure, and few hungry enough to do justice to the hastily prepared meal.

"Veld, shouldn't we send someone to warn Loul we're coming?" asked Lantiah, as she packed the platters away.

"That would do little but worry her."

"She'll be worried anyway. She'll know from Kirym's token

that something's wrong."

"I have no idea what Kirym's token will have told her, Lantiah. We'll be there soon enough. We're not expected for another three days. A messenger will imply problems that don't exist."

I wondered what she meant about Mama knowing because of my token. I fell asleep waiting for Papa to be free to ask about it.

Everyone was very quiet. Most had questions, but were too tired or traumatised to ask.

By midmorning, we were again using the paths we had walked along so happily just two days earlier.

The moon had risen when we finally reached home. We rounded the elm tree and saw the dwelling lit up, Mama standing serenely at the door.

She ran into Papa's arms. "What happened to Kirym?" she asked. "I felt I'd lost her."

I pushed my way through the crowd.

She hugged me tightly, and then held me at arm's length staring at my token. She looked up at Papa.

He shrugged and shook his head.

By morning everyone was rested, fed and had their wounds tended to. We sat around the large gathering porch where we generally had our family celebrations.

Papa welcomed everyone before turning to Raff. "We need to acknowledge Kamdra, Raff. Would you like to start your ceremony now?"

Raff moved to one side of the open area in front of the porch. "Kamdra. Husband, papa, son and brother. Son of Jalkam and joined to Tindra. Death is different now. With no stellon and in an unknown land, we can only promise to remember you with love, and keep you in the place we hold you dearest. In our hearts. It's the only place we have now."

Raff spoke words that had never been used before in their burial ceremonies and there was a buzz of disturbed comments. He looked so unhappy.

Papa went and stood beside Raff. "Your traditions can't be identical now you live in a different land. However you are welcome here, and can make this your home. Things change, and you'll need to adapt. But you're alive, and your family will carry on. New traditions will grow, and we will help you retain as many as possible."

"Veld is right. We have to accept that things alter. Kamdra is the beginning of this. His memory will never go back to the land he grew up in." Raff paused. "And nor will we." He scooped a small hole in the soil near one of the gardens and dropped in a seed. He filled in the hole and placed a roughly carved stick beside it.

"This seed is all I have for Kamdra. At any time, we can remember our family here." He turned away, tears in his eyes.

Papa waited as people chatted quietly and then stood. "Now my friends, we'll talk of what happened to Kamdra. Armos, can you start? Then any questions can be answered."

Armos explained what occurred under the waterfall and Peet added what he'd felt and seen. Tindra listened, her eyes shining with tears. At the end of the narration, Papa asked if there was anything to add.

Kamdra's younger brother Salcan stood up.

"I see you, Salcan. What do you wish to know?"

"Kamdra was my brother. He's dead. His child has no one to care for her. His wife is without support. Who's responsible for them? Who'll care for them now? Who killed my brother?"

Raff stood slowly. "Salcan, you saw Kamdra attacked by the raiders. They killed him. Are you suggesting we send Tindra into their care?"

"The raiders left. Kamdra still lived. I walked under the water and my brother followed. I came out but he didn't. The men with him weren't his brothers. They owe my family. They owe his wife and they owe his child."

A shocked angry buzz erupted around the porch.

Armos stood. "Salcan, we understand you're hurting, but I'll not have accusations made against men who risked their lives to bring you here."

He picked up a pack and opened it. "I collected Kamdra's stretcher. As you see, it's ripped, but it would probably have stayed together had Kamdra not thrashed about so much."

Soojee struggled to her feet. "That didn't happen during the walk from the hills."

"You're right, Soojee, but there's a lot of gore on the stretcher. Such a blood loss would have caused a massive convulsion. He lost too much blood to have survived."

Soojee nodded. "Yes, it makes sense, I've seen it before." She turned to Salcan. "You've had a great loss, Salcan, more than many. Our hearts are with you. These men did everything they could to save Kamdra's life. They put their own lives in danger, and almost lost Young Harby to the waterfall. Teema and Veld risked their lives to save Tindra."

Salcan closed his lips tightly and lowered his head in thought. Everyone was quiet, waiting. He finally looked up. "In my sorrow, I'm a fool. Armos, Veld, I thank you for trying to save my brother." He sat down beside Tindra, but neither of them looked happy.

Raff stood again. "Our lives are different now. We've all suffered loss, but no one is without support. We're now one family and everyone is cared for." He turned to Papa. "Someone said you saw the stellon."

"No. It was gone. They must have carried it away, we saw no drag marks."

Armos stood. "Veld, I saw it — well, the remains of it. It was near the top of the pass. All of the memory stones and shells were gone. It'd been put on a fire and the story tip was burned." He turned to Raff. "I'm sorry. That's when we spotted them. We couldn't save it."

"Nothing is worth another life, Armos," said Raff. "The stellon is only a thing. Memories can't be taken away, they live in our hearts. It's different, but our lives are different, and we'll manage." Everyone was silent as Raff's family thought about his words.

"Papa, what's a stellon?" I asked.

"The young ones should know this, Raff. The stellon was yours. Can you explain it to them?" said Papa.

"I've never had to, Veld, I've always shown them."

He sat beside me, and others from our family gathered around.

"Your family has a memory box. In it your papa writes everything that happens. He writes the births and the names you choose, the joinings and the deaths, the visitors and the harvests. He writes what's important so your children and the children belonging to your children will know who you are. So they'll know what's happened in your life. I'm sure he'll soon write about the trip you've just made and of our coming here to live. The stellon held our memories. It was a pole, big, taller than three men, and made of wood, a strange wood, very heavy. Our history was engraved into it. The top, which was carved hundreds of season cycles ago, told the old stories. Those stories have been lost in the mists of time, but legend says it told of the travels of our ancestors. Below that we recorded the lives of our people. With each birth, joining and death, we added a memory to it, a small thing generally, like your token. Not necessarily a thing of value but something that would remind us of the person, often a pretty stone or shell. Sometimes at death it was a thing they'd carried through life or had made themselves. The birth, the life and the death were connected. There was a section for each season cycle, some large, some small." Raff paused and drank from his flask. He looked sad and tired. "I don't have a memory here for Kamdra, but I'd have used something green. He grew food for our family. He was a big man, so I planted an acorn to his memory here. If I've made the right decision, it'll grow to show the size Kamdra was, and it will bear his name. Our stellon was very old and we had filled it up. Arlanquee's birth was to start the new stellon and we planned a big ceremony this summer. Now we'll have to find a new way of doing it. I'm not sure how though. Stellons need to stand together to connect. While I remember what was on it, I need to find a way of saving it all for our future generations. There's a lot I have to add to our history now."

"You could use a memory box like ours," I said.

Soojee smiled. "We haven't the knowledge of making parchment as you have."

"We could teach you, it's not a secret. Then you can write down what was on your stellon before you forget and you can begin the new memories at the same time."

Papa nodded. "That's a good suggestion, Kirym. I should have thought of it. I'm forgetting my obligations as host."

"Raff, you're now part of our family," Mama said. "We've no secrets from family and we'll do our utmost to save your history. Now Veld, there's a lot of work to be done. The sun's high and everyone must be hungry. Then there are new dwellings to be planned."

Everything had changed. More people, more noise, but my friends treated me differently also. I knew my token had changed. Tokens were pale colours, but Teema's was dark blue, and Mekrar told me mine was also.

I missed Teema. I realised I hadn't seen him since early morning, and when I thought of him, my token throbbed and I felt he was a long way away. I asked Papa where he was.

"I've sent him to the lakes, Kirym. Findlow and Natia are aligned to Raff's family as well as ours. They need to know what has happened," he said. "Grenin and Young Harby are with him. They'll return soon and bring Findlow's family with them."

By then everyone was ready.

Papa stood up. "Friends, let's eat and build some dwellings. There's still much to talk about, but we've plenty of time."

5

Teema Speaks

I woke well before light. I was surprised I'd been able to sleep for so long. Veld had set extra guards and I settled down to sleep soon after we arrived home, thinking he'd call me to join them. So it was nice to stretch out and relax for a short time, knowing he'd allowed me to sleep the entire night.

I was staying with Loul and Veld. The single men's dwelling where I normally slept was one of those given to Raff's family until new dwellings were ready.

There was movement through the large fireplace that divided and heated the two rooms. I wrapped a rug around my shoulders and wandered through to see where I was needed.

Kirym lay on a set watching Loul feed Tarl's daughter.

"Morning, Loul." I leaned down to kiss her cheek and click tokens, and then clicked Kirym's.

Veld passed me a warm drink. "Did you sleep well, son?"

I nodded. "I thought you'd want me for guard duty, Veld."

"I had another job in mind for you, if you're willing to take it on," he said. "Come son, I'll tell you what you'll need to know."

We stepped onto the gathering porch. He handed me my tunic and cloak as he took the rug from my shoulders. "I need someone to travel to the Lakes. Findlow and Natia need to know what's happened, to know they're in danger too. I thought it may be better coming from family."

"Danger? Raff and Soojee were just unlucky weren't they?"

"Oh, no! The attack was carefully planned, Teema. Findlow is in great danger, and I want him and his family here, no matter what objections he may have." Veld gave me a message for Findlow.

I was shocked at how gaunt Veld was looking. He appeared to have aged considerably over the last few days. I wondered if I too had similar lines on my face.

Grenin joined us carrying bows, arrows and my knives. I lashed one to my thigh, the other to my hip and took my bow and a quiver of arrows. Veld handed us each a pack of light, nourishing travelling food and a water flask.

A pile of travel packs we had dumped against the wall when we arrived back from Raff's suddenly heaved and parted. Young Harby pushed his way out, and smiled awkwardly. "Ahhh, slept here last night! Big argument and Siba chucked me out. Again!" He chuckled. "But it's good this time. I get to go with you two. Yeehaa!"

"You'll have to move fast, Harbs." I said, laughing. "I'm not sure you can keep up?"

Harbs punched me playfully on the shoulder, but stopped when Veld frowned at him. "Do you really want to go? It could be dangerous, Harby. You have a family."

"So does Grenin."

"You'll have to do precisely as you're told, by both of us," said Grenin, smiling.

"Not a problem, I'll even carry the packs," he said enthusiastically.

Veld frowned. "It could help to have three of you go, but this is deadly serious, Harby. More people may die if we get this wrong."

Harby settled immediately.

"I've told Teema what he's to say and do," said Veld, "but Teema. Be guided by Grenin. He has great experience. Make sure all of Findlow's family return with you. The danger is immense. You all have strengths, work with them. Now please, go fast and go with care. I expect to see you on the eve, in four days' time." He clasped each of us by the hand and clicked his token to mine.

We swung our packs over our shoulders and set off at a jog. It was still dark, but we knew the path well. The journey to Findlow's was easy and there were shortcuts seasoned travellers used.

The trip over our land was uneventful and we made excellent time. It was early afternoon when we reached the gorge that marked the southern edge of our land. We looked for signs that would let us know something was amiss, but all appeared normal and we crossed the bridge and jogged on. We followed the small valleys southwest until we came to the valley where Findlow's lodge was.

The sun had set, but as yet there was no moon and we travelled more cautiously now. Grenin was in the lead and because of the gloom I had little warning when he suddenly stopped.

"Let's wait for the moon," he said. "I feel ill at ease blundering about in the shadows."

We settled in the dark of a tree. It was pleasant here; we

were sheltered from the wind and able to rest and quietly chat. Grenin and I took the opportunity to eat and drink. Harby slept.

Grenin chuckled quietly. "That one seems able to sleep anywhere. I don't know how he does it. I like my home comforts, warm rugs and Cindra to cuddle at night. He must spend half his time bedded on the ground, under a tree or in with the animals. Yet he seems happy enough."

"It takes all sorts. Maybe it's his absences that keep him and Siba together. I think she'd rip his throat out if they were in each other's company more. It's a weird balance they've created. I'm with you though, I like to be ..." I paused.

I heard an odd noise, one that wasn't part of the night. I leaned forward and put my hand over Harby's mouth. He was instantly awake and I could see his eyes shining in the gloom. The moon peeped over the horizon and we strained to see what had caused the sound.

On a path below us walked a column of men. They were unnaturally quiet for the number, almost as if they were hunting.

We watched, trying to figure out who they were. As the leaders of the column walked into the moonlight, Grenin touched my arm. I turned to see him shake his head and beckon us back into the shadow of the tree.

The men walked west and out of sight.

Grenin waited a long time, listening carefully. He spoke in a low voice. "Four autumns back Findlow abandoned the lower settlement because of the dam. Few know about that." He thought for a few moments. "Did you recognise anyone in that group?" I shook my head. "The second in the line was the man named Slynd. I'm sure of it," he said. "He wouldn't know of the new settlement site, but he'll make a guess and I imagine the path between the two will still be easy to follow."

"Well," said Harby. "We'd best move it. We've a lot to do tonight." He turned away and started jogging.

Grenin smiled broadly and followed.

The moon had moved almost a hand span from the horizon when we came to the perimeter of the lake and could see the long building Findlow's family lived in. We watched carefully as we jogged towards the dwelling, but all appeared normal. As we got closer, we called a greeting and identified ourselves.

The big door of the dwelling opened and a huge man appeared. He raced towards us with surprising speed for his size and grabbed hold of Harby whom we'd left in front. He picked him up and gave him a big hug, then dropped him.

Harby managed to keep his footing, but looked shaken.

Grenin and I roared with laughter and thumped Sundas on the shoulder.

He beamed at us. "Come in, come in, come in," he said.

We walked into an enclosed porch and stepped down into a large room. The fireplace glowed in one corner, but I was surprised to see packs spread across the floor.

Findlow stepped forward. "Welcome, Grenin, Teema," he said stiffly. "I didn't expect you this early in the season."

"Had we come later, it seems you wouldn't be here, Findlow. You leave early in the season. Surely the hunting's not yet that good? Or is there another reason you pack your hearth?"

"Ah Grenin, this isn't the time and you ask too many questions too early in your visit. We've made plans, and I suggest you go off and fish for a few days. We'll meet and talk after that. Far far better." He nodded, agreeing with himself, stepped to the door and opened it.

Grenin, Harby and I turned to watch him but didn't move towards the door as manners dictated.

"If we'd wanted your fish, we'd have come with fishing

spears and nets, and we wouldn't have come in the dead of night," said Grenin. "We came with an invitation from Veld, and a warning of danger. Veld invites you to visit. Your whole family."

Findlow looked at us. "You speak of danger? And you're here. Could you possibly be the threat?"

"Oh yes," said Harby sarcastically. "Three of us? What possible hazard could we be?" He and Findlow glowered at each other.

"Findlow!" I saw little use in letting things get out of hand. "Raff's settlement has been attacked, razed to the ground. Many are dead and the survivors are now with us. We think there's an imminent threat to you also. We bring information. You may do as you wish, but you are our neighbours and for some of us, you are family."

Findlow frowned. "I've heard rumours," he said, almost to himself "We'll go to our hunting lodge, we've –"

"They'll find you, Findlow," interrupted Grenin. "They know the land. We saw a group of them north of here. They were travelling directly towards the dam on the old stone path. These men kill! Murder everyone they find. You're all at risk. Even women and children aren't safe. A move to the lodge will just delay them."

"Findlow, Headman of the Long Lakes." I stood tall and took on the voice of a formal messenger from one headman to another. "I have a message from Veld, Headman of the Land Between the Gorges. Today we will return to our land. We urge you all to come with us. This is the last time we will extend this invitation. When we go from your land, we will never return. We will not be able to."

In the silence following my message, a quiet voice came out of the gloom. "You'll destroy the bridge?"

I nodded.

A woman stepped into the firelight. "Findlow, the rumours

were right. We are in danger. Veld has now confirmed it. I'm going back. I'll take all who are mine with me and I'll help destroy that bridge. I'll do everything in my power to keep my family safe." She turned and held out her hands to me in greeting. We clicked tokens and she drew me in for a hug. "Welcome, son. How much time do we have?"

I smiled at her. "Loul sends greetings, Natia. She's looking forward to seeing you. We must move fast. They'll get to the dam settlement and find it deserted. Is the path between there and here as used as it was?"

"Not over this winter, but they'll follow it easily enough." She turned to those standing around the fire. "I'm going across the gorge. You must all come with me. Pack what you need. Quickly, we leave immediately."

There was a bellow from the corner and Findlow strode into the centre of the room. "I make the decisions here, Natia. I decide where we're going," he yelled.

She turned to him. "Decide then, and I'll go with you," she paused, "if you cross the gorge. I'm going home and everyone will come with me. The rest is up to you." She shrugged and turned away, placing items in a pack. Those around her started to do the same.

Findlow grabbed her by the arm. "You presume much, woman," he hissed.

I started towards them, but Grenin pulled me back. "They'll sort it," he murmured.

Sundas lunged forward, pushed Natia behind him and snarled at Findlow.

Natia stepped back around Sundas. "Stop it, you two. Now is not the time." She took a deep breath. "Sundas, get your things, and put them in a pack. We have to hurry."

Sundas went to do as he was bid.

Natia turned and hugged Grenin. "Welcome, my brother. How are my sisters?" They moved off, talking quietly.

"All right," Findlow yelled. "Let's get packed. We're leaving."

There was murmuring around the room, but soon they were gathered outside, ready to leave.

"Do you wish to lead us, Findlow?" asked Natia.

He grunted and stepped to the front of the group.

"Was the attack bad?" Natia asked quietly as we moved off.

"Yes, very, and we may lose more. Halse isn't doing well. She sleeps deeply and we've no answers for her future. We left over eighty buried in the hills, and we've closed the waterfall path."

Natia stopped walking. "Oh my! You meant it. You're going to destroy the bridge." She stared at me for a few moments and took a deep breath. "Well, we'd best get there. We've work to do." She strode forward and in increasing her speed encouraged everyone to move faster.

It was near dawn when we reached the gorge. Everyone was weary. It had been a slow trip, the children had tired quickly and needed to be carried.

Findlow and Sundas both did more than I had expected of them.

Sundas had walked quietly, but with one eye on Findlow and the other on Natia. When Findlow walked near Natia, Sundas snarled. Findlow snarled back, but hastily stepped away.

I looked questioningly at Natia, but she shook her head silently, a smile on her lips.

Traversing the bridge took time. It was a sturdy bridge, but it wasn't built to take a crowd and we paced them. Sundas had unlimited energy. He carried children and packs across and by mid-morning, all had crossed.

Findlow led his family towards our settlement. Grenin, Harby and I set about cutting through the thick ropes that held the bridge to the bank.

When we caught up with the family, they were no longer moving. Most of them were sitting on the ground, but Findlow and Natia were shouting at each other and Sundas hovered close by.

"You had no right to destroy the bridge," yelled Findlow as we approached.

"I told you I was going to, Findlow. What's your problem?"

"You should've asked me," he yelled. "I thought you were bluffing to get me to come with you. It should've been my decision. You had no right."

I spoke quietly. "It was Veld's right, Findlow. He built the bridge. To protect his people, he ordered its destruction. If you don't like it, take it up with him."

Natia stepped close. "We knew things were wrong, Findlow. People disappeared. Whole settlements were destroyed. Veld has just saved our lives. We should be thankful."

She picked up one of the children and started to walk. Everyone followed her.

Grenin smiled and fell into step beside me. "They weren't always like this, although you might not remember. Sundas is protective of Natia, more so when Findlow is angry."

"How does Sundas come in to it?"

"He and his mama were slaves. When he grew up, his owners felt threatened by him and tried to kill him. Natia saved him and freed them. His mama was devoted to Natia and she made Sundas promise to care for Natia. I wonder sometimes if Sundas takes it a bit literally, but he's done what was asked of him. It's a bit like sibling rivalry, I think. It won't end until Findlow stops being so angry with the world."

"Why is he?"

Grenin shrugged.

Harby joined us. "Natia's the spitting image of Cindra, Grenin. How can you tell them apart? Did you ever wonder if you'd chosen the right woman?"

Grenin laughed. "There's something about Cindra when she looks at me. That's how I know."

Everyone was exhausted and Findlow suggested we stop and rest. We found a large hollow, protected on all sides from the wind. Most of the family lay down where they were and slept. Findlow set three of his men as guards.

I slept.

Sometime later, Grenin woke me to join Findlow on guard duty. He suggested I waken Harby after the sun had moved two hand spans in the sky and get Harby to waken him two hand spans later. So we slept and guarded the family through the day and night.

I was impressed with Findlow. He was awake for part of each guard shift and for every changeover of his guards. He and Natia ensured the guards had food and drink, and that everyone was cared for.

We had a late start in the morning. Findlow and Natia snapped and sniped at each other. No one took any notice of them and I supposed they were used to it.

Food was prepared and eaten, and everything packed up again. We walked through the day with stops for meals and to allow the children to rest.

I was pleased to see the beginning of the wide path that led to our porch, but when Findlow reached the path, he stopped. I pushed forward to see what was wrong, arriving beside him at the same time as Harby.

Grenin was already there, looking exasperated. "Findlow refuses to enter the settlement because Veld isn't here to formally welcome him. He wants us to return the family to the far side of the gorge."

Natia joined us. "Veld saved your life, Findlow. What more do you want from him?"

Findlow folded his arms and took a deep breath, and looked mutinous.

"Don't you dare!" hissed Natia. "You make me so angry. Oh for goodness sake. Stay here and sulk if you wish." She turned and walked towards the settlement. The family followed.

Sundas looked from Natia to Findlow, then turned to follow Natia.

Findlow stood his ground and I thought Sundas would walk over him, but at the last moment, Findlow turned and pushed his way to the front of the group.

Harby started to snort with laughter, but Grenin elbowed him in the ribs. He turned it into a cough, composed himself with difficulty and we entered the settlement.

6

Kirym Speaks

Papa planned the new buildings quickly, although our resources were stretched. Everyone set to with enthusiasm, but Papa continued to be worried. I didn't understand why. I knew he had organised the destruction of the bridge as he had destroyed the waterfall path. Surely that would keep us safe. When I asked him, his answer stunned me.

"There's another path, Kirym, the path our people used to get into the land originally, but I don't know where it is. Slynd may know or suspect. I just hope we find it before he does."

"Shouldn't finding it be our priority, rather than building dwellings?" I asked.

He shook his head. "I've looked. For many seasons, every summer Armos and I searched the gorges and the eastern hills. We found nothing."

"The memory box says our ancestors came and went a number of times. How did they do it?" I asked.

He shrugged. "There's nothing written. That's why I searched."

"When we find the path, what will we do? Use it or destroy it?"

"I don't know, Kirym. What about the cave? If we leave here, we leave it. Can we live without new tokens?"

I frowned. "Better we live without them, than not live. You've always said we need new people here, Papa. Without them, we may die out anyway."

Just then Armos took Papa away to talk of some problem with the building materials.

A bit of friendly competition formed between the building groups to see who could complete each stage first and despite unsettled weather, the progress was exceptional. We hoped to be finished by the time Teema returned from the lakes.

Papa had figured that Findlow's family would leave their lodge during the morning, and spend the night at the bridge. They would take two days to travel from the gorge. Papa planned to go to the wide path to formally welcome Findlow and smooth his arrival in the early evening four days after Teema left.

A day before they were due, Papa and I were helping thatch the roof of one of the dwellings. I looked up and saw Teema, Grenin and Harby escorting Findlow's family into the open area below us.

"Findlow," Papa called. "Welcome. You've made excellent time. I hadn't thought you able to get here before moon up tomorrow. What perfect timing, we can stop and celebrate your arrival."

Findlow turned away, ignoring him. It was a deliberate snub, and there were angry murmurs from our family.

Papa walked towards the ladder, shaking his head. "He has the ability to see an insult in offering a starving man a meal," he mumbled. He gained the ground and patted

Findlow on the shoulder. "I'm pleased you could join us, we need your knowledge in our plan for the future."

I was the last off the roof. Everyone had followed Papa and Findlow to our porch, but Teema waited behind and when I reached the ground, he clicked his token to mine.

"I felt you with me every step of the trip," he said. "But what was that thought about another path?"

I told him what I had learned.

He laughed. "I wondered what Veld and Armos did each summer: just the two of them wandering off for days at a time. Did you know Veld drew a map of his travels? Perhaps he'd let us look at it. We may see something he overlooked."

We walked back to the gathering porch.

As the new dwellings weren't quite finished, Mama organised so everyone had somewhere to sleep. Findlow, Natia, their daughter Lyndym, and Sundas stayed with us. With fifteen in the dwelling, it was crowded, but that was temporary.

Halse still slept and Mama was really worried. While she discussed possible treatments with Natia and Cindra, I ground some harkii nuts and took them to Halse. I had not been able to spend much time with her since we came back. The healers had been trying to wake her up and I had been working on the dwellings. But now I sat, held her hand and Teema helped me feed her the harkii.

Sundas stood by himself in a corner watching us. He edged closer and closer until he was at the foot of the set she lay on.

I smiled up at him. "Hello. I'm Kirym and this is Halse."

He sat beside us on the floor and asked questions about how she was cared for.

Can I help?" he asked

I handed him the harkii and watched him carefully as he fed her and made her comfortable. He was very gentle with her.

So much had been happening — I'd had no time to think clearly about how this affected me. Now as I watched Sundas care for Halse, the implications hit me. I'd missed Halse while she was away, and now I realised she hadn't come back. Looking at her now, I understood she may never return.

Slynd intended to murder my whole family. I wouldn't let that happen.

"Teema, let's get Papa's map and see what the land looks like."

Papa was deep in conversation with Findlow, Raff, Old Harby and Armos, and he wasn't really aware of my request, nodding and waving me away. We took the map from his cupboard and opened it on the table.

Papa had put a lot of work into it, plenty of detail. Some of the information was known to me, but the area to the east on both gorges and up into the eastern mountains was new. Teema knew some of it though, and he explained what the symbols meant.

Around the edges of the map, Papa had written notes about the history of various landmarks. I was intrigued to find that when Papa's great-grandpapa opened up the waterfall path, they had cleared huge boulders away from it. So I knew it wasn't the path we were looking for. We studied the map until Mama needed the table for the evening meal.

Building the dwellings took another three days. It was hard work. Soon everyone was tired and over the excitement of doing something new. The weather deteriorated and our days were damp and uncomfortable.

As we rested on the gathering porch after finishing them, Papa reminded us that our spring festival would be celebrated the next day. We would have a formal welcome for Raff's and Findlow's families at the same time. With the promise of better weather, everyone was enthusiastic.

We gathered early in the afternoon resplendent in our festival clothes. Even Raff's family looked good in borrowed finery. Sundas carried Halse out and laid her in the shade.

Papa invited Findlow and Raff to join him on the porch.

The formal greetings took some time, everyone was welcomed.

Flasks and platters of snacks circulated. The evening meal wouldn't be eaten until quite late. Soft snatches of music whispered around the clearing.

Then Papa gave the special announcements. "We have many things to celebrate. Our family is enlarged in many ways. Findlow and Natia have agreed to stay here with their family. Their presence will enrich our settlement."

Everyone clapped and cheered.

"Twenty days ago, Cindra gave Grenin a daughter," said Papa as he stood again.

There was more cheering and gifts were passed to Cindra and Grenin.

Papa gave us time to talk and eat. Then he stood again. "Now we have another celebration. I'm delighted to announce the joining of Armos and Lantiah. Soon we'll begin our preparations to travel to the caves. There'll be new tokens to find. It'll be good for Lantiah to have a token again."

As the applause died, a voice in the crowd called out. "Why

does Lantiah plan to join with Armos? She's joined to Slynd and it seems, from what I've heard, that he's still alive."

There was a sudden silence.

Papa turned to the speaker. "Horan, do you wish to formalise that question? There are proper ways to do it. What's your concern about Lantiah joining with Armos?"

Horan stood. "Yes, I'll make it formal. Slynd isn't dead, so Lantiah is still joined to him. He has her token, so she doesn't need another. She can ask for it back."

I had never seen Papa look so angry, although he covered it well. "When did you decide that joining was so wrong for Lantiah, Horan? Would it have been before you asked her to join with you, or was it after she turned you down?"

Horan looked embarrassed. There was a buzz of speculation and a few laughs at his discomfort.

Papa waited for silence. "So that everyone understands this, let me explain this piece of our history. Slynd left our family many seasons ago. When he left, he stole Lantiah's token. When we discovered he'd gone, we followed him as far as we were able. His tracks led to the river, but none led from the river. We assumed he'd slipped or jumped and he'd have had no chance to survive that. He never returned and after much time and discussion, he was declared dead. In taking Lantiah's token, he broke their marriage bond. The joining between them dissolved at that time. If anyone had an objection, Horan, that was the time to mention it. The man we saw recently is not the man we knew. We have a great regard for life here. Slynd was declared dead and he is dead — to us. Nothing that's happened recently alters that."

When the crowd around Armos and Lantiah thinned, I went over to hug them both.

Teema joined us, hugged Lantiah and shook hands with Armos. "I hope you're very happy together."

"We will be," Armos said. "I should've asked her last autumn. Silly really, I was so afraid she'd turn me down. Now she's said 'yes' and I know I shouldn't have waited. I could've had a far more comfortable winter."

They were joined three days later.

The trip to the cave took the best part of a day. Everyone came along, Halse and Soojee travelled on stretchers.

Our first ceremony was to celebrate life. This one started before dawn and everyone dressed in their festival clothes. Grenin and Cindra entered the cave first with their baby and family. The cave was huge, big enough to hold everyone with room to spare.

Inside, the lamps were extinguished. It was inky black and everyone was quiet. Spots of light and colour lit the western wall. Even those who had seen this before were awed.

Slowly the light reduced to one area of soft light. Grenin and Cindra stepped forward as the light pinpointed a single token. Grenin picked it up and placed it in the holder he had made. The cave lit again, this time with diffused light and Cindra placed the token holder on the baby's forehead. She clicked the token with hers, and whispered a name to the wee girl. "Vandara."

The token changed to pink.

Grenin did the same thing also naming her and the pink became brighter.

We followed them to the entrance of the cave where we formally met Vandara, each touching her token and repeating her name. Back at the camp, we celebrated with Grenin's newly enlarged family.

The day was spent relaxing in a field near the cave. We played games, running, jumping and shooting. Eventually the games became more serious, teams were chosen and competitions started.

Later in the afternoon, we prepared for the joining ceremony. I looked for Teema and couldn't find him. For a while I thought he hadn't joined us for this celebration, but I could feel him close and just as the lights dimmed, I spotted him in a dark corner.

The music was hauntingly sweet, the fragrance of the flowers wonderful. Lantiah looked gorgeous wearing a new festival dress. The hem trailed on the floor and was covered with flowers so you couldn't see where it ended.

The ceremony started with Old Harby and Zelriff, our oldest family members, performing the official duties.

But I was distracted through the ceremony, my mind staying with Teema. It was only when the cave darkened and the tokens started to glow that I paid attention.

On the eastern wall, two small pinpricks of glowing gold grew. Armos and Lantiah each picked one up. Armos slipped his into Lantiah's holder where it glowed intensely. Lantiah put hers next to Armos' pink token and as she did so all other light disappeared. Armos and Lantiah clicked tokens and the colour of each changed from gold to the green of new oak leaves.

Zelriff and Harby spoke together. "They are joined," and everyone repeated the words.

Lamps were lit and Armos and Lantiah were led out of the cave. I lingered in my seat until I could move over to sit beside Teema. He seemed to be a long way away, I don't think he was even aware the ceremony had finished.

I sat beside him and took his hand. "I'm so sorry, Teema, this should have been for you and Halse. Maybe we should have asked Armos and Lantiah to wait until Halse was better."

He shook his head. "I couldn't be that selfish. Lantiah

needed the protection of a new token. Halse and I talked for so long about how it would be for us, and yet I don't think I ever really believed it would happen. I felt different through this ceremony, like I'd changed."

"You have changed, Teema, we all have. The cave has too."

"You're being fanciful today," he said, smiling.

"I'm deadly serious. These are life tokens. Our lives have changed, so they must also. That alters the cave. It's different in here now, more distant. The cave is leaving us, Teema. I realised during the ceremony this morning. We really have to leave this land. We need to find the path."

"It may not exist, Kirym," he said frowning. "Paths can be created. We created them cross each of the gorges but we destroyed them. Maybe the original path was destroyed too."

I shook my head. "When I look at Papa's map, I know there's something we're overlooking. We'll kick ourselves when we figure it out. Anyway, I'm going to start looking as soon as we get home. Mama needs to collect herbs and roots for her remedy pouch. There's almost nothing on Papa's map for one area on the south gorge. I'll get her to collect herbs there."

"Maybe there is nothing there."

"Or perhaps there's something hidden — something Papa overlooked." I paused. "Teema, do you want to go away for a few days? We could go back to the settlement or we could camp out. Papa will let me come with you, if I ask."

"Hiding won't change anything. Anyway, there's the new ceremony tomorrow, and you wouldn't want to miss it, would you? Come on, let's go and enjoy the celebrations."

Night had fallen and we needed the lamp to light our way back to the dwelling area. Food baskets had been opened and the meal was ready to eat. Lantiah had cooked honey bread full of nuts and fruit. She and Armos took it round to give everyone a piece. Eating it acknowledged acceptance of the joining so they made sure that everyone got a portion and ate it.

The celebration lasted until dawn.

7

Teema Speaks

It was late when I woke. Veld sat in one of the open shelters with pages from the memory box spread out around him. He frowned as he studied them.

I offered him a drink. "Can I help?"

He took the flask, sat back and thrust a few pages at me. "What do you think that means?"

I read the three pages through, went back and read them again.

"It's unclear isn't it?" he said. "Should I leave things as they are? If I get it wrong, could the ceremony damage Halse more?"

I thought about what I'd read. "I guess there's a risk no matter what we do. If we do nothing and she doesn't improve, we'll always wonder. The ceremony may help. Has anyone seen it before?"

Veld shook his head. "It seems we've never needed it. Zelriff knows one old story, but she's unsure of the outcome. Kirym says we should do it. She says if it works, we celebrate, but otherwise we'll know we did all we could."

"The cave has never hurt us in the past. It protects us," I said.

Loul nodded. "Kirym said that too. We must do it, Veld. I'll let everyone know and those who wish to stay can. Is there anyone we definitely need?"

Veld frowned. "There's no prescribed list, just those who want to be with us. We will need Kirym. Loul, talk to her, she'll need to understand what's required of her." He paused, frowning. "We need someone to support her during the ceremony too. Can you do it Teema? I'd thought of Loul or myself, but there's the change in your tokens. There's nothing written that explains that."

I nodded. "Of course I'll help. I'll do all I can for your family."

Loul took my hands between hers. "You have the right now to call us yours, Teema. You've done so much in helping care for us. I'll always look on you as my son." She drew me into a hug and I felt her tears on my shoulder.

During the day, groups left to return to the settlement. Soon only Veld's immediate family remained. Halse slept on a set in the shade, but even when her eyes were open, she seemed unaware of us or her surroundings. I felt she'd drifted a long way from us.

Late in the afternoon, we lifted her onto a stretcher, covered her with a rug and Veld, Tarl, Mekroe and I carried her to the cave. I was shocked at how light she was.

Kirym carried a huge bunch of flowers. She'd chosen some for their healing properties, others for their fragrance.

As we neared the cave, Sundas approached us. "I want to help," he said.

Loul smiled. "It's being taken care of, Sundas. Thank you."

He frowned. "You said if we are family or if we want to, we can help. I want to. She can be my family too."

"Maybe he's needed, Mama. We don't really know. He cares for her, so he should be here."

Loul stared thoughtfully at Kirym and nodded. "You're right," she said, turning back to Sundas. "We'd love you to join us."

Sundas walked to the stretcher and squatted beside it. He brushed Halse's hair from her forehead, picked her up and started towards the cave with her in his arms. No one moved for a few moments. Then Veld took Kirym's hand and followed.

Tarl, Mekroe and I were left holding an empty stretcher. We propped it against a tree and jogged to catch up.

In the cave, there was no indication of the ceremony we'd had the previous evening. Loul spread rugs over one of the stone benches and Sundas lay Halse on it. He covered her with another rug and sat on the floor beside her.

Kirym filled a pitcher with water and poured it into a hollow in the cave wall. She sprinkled the surface with flower petals and laid the rest of the flowers around Halse.

Loul helped Kirym remove her boots, jewellery and any fasteners from her clothing. She stood in the centre of the cave.

The lights dimmed and we waited. All I could hear was our breathing. Then there was a sound unlike anything I'd ever heard before. It was reedy, breathy and almost not there. It faded and returned thrumming and vibrating, getting steadily louder until it was almost overpowering. Just as it became unbearable, it slid off into nothing. When it returned, there was a faint light that got stronger with the sound. The light intensified further, the sound diminished.

The light narrowed to a beam that hit the hollow in the wall. The water seemed to absorb the light until it disappeared.

We waited in the dark.

Suddenly a beam of light exploded from the water, hit the token on Halse forehead and shot over to Kirym's. It lifted them both into the air. The light skimmed around the cave picking up colours and tokens. For a long long moment we were all joined and then the cave plunged into darkness again. The light formed over the water again and sparked, this time from Kirym to Halse. It flickered around the cave to some pinpoint lights on the walls, as if trying to connect to one or another. No connection was made and the light abruptly returned to the hollow. After one more flare, it disappeared.

We waited in the darkness and then Veld lit the lamp.

I raced over to Kirym and lifted her off the floor. Her body was limp and her token glowed dully. I clicked my token to hers and felt the now familiar momentary drop in energy.

Her eyes flickered open. "How is Halse? Did she get a new token?"

I hugged her, helped her stand and wrapped her cloak around her. I took her over to where Halse lay. She was surrounded and for a moment we could see nothing. Then the crowd opened. Her token seemed to glimmer slightly, although it was still mainly grey.

Sundas sat on the floor holding her hand. He looked from face to face trying to figure out if what had happened was good or not.

Loul took a deep breath. "We may not know for a few days, let's take her back to the camp."

Sundas carried Halse out of the cave. The sun had set and we walked back in darkness.

A fire had been lit for us. Findlow sat over it and as we approached, he dished up a meal.

We discussed what happened, disappointed that Halse hadn't received a new token.

Veld reread the pages from the memory box. "You know, it doesn't actually say she'd get a new one. The ceremony's described as 'a bonding of health and energy within the tokens'. Maybe hers will re-energise. As it gets stronger, she may also. We'll have to wait and see. It doesn't seem to have hurt her in any way and Kirym appears fine."

We talked until late.

In the morning we packed the final few items into storage and started back to the settlement. Sundas wanted to carry Halse all the way home by himself, but was eventually convinced to put her on a covered hauling frame. She was still sleepy, but everyone felt she was more alert than before.

It was colder this morning and the sky held a promise of rain. Just after midday, the sun disappeared behind clouds and we could hear thunder in the distance. Half way through the afternoon, the rain began.

We arrived home just before evening. Everyone was waiting and there was a rousing cheer as we rounded the elm. We were given time to change into dry clothing and eat before anyone asked questions.

There was a lot of talk amongst the women and healers and as the evening drew in, stories were told and songs sung. The fire died and the porch emptied.

Trouble had already started when we returned from the cave. Each family had different goals and there was a lot of bickering. Everyone was trying to rebuild the lives they had before, but this was a different land.

Some of the men openly rebelled when told the rules we lived by. Veld, Raff and Findlow had to work hard to contain the problems.

Sundas took over the fulltime care of Halse. He was devoted to her. She seemed to respond better to him than other part-time carers. While her health didn't really improve after we returned from the cave, she was no worse.

Raff began to record what he remembered from the stellon. At the same time, he tried to recreate the top, drawing the strange curves, swirls and holes that had crowned it. He had trouble though, because the parchment was flat, while the stellon had been cylindrical. Finally he joined the edges into a large tube so it looked like the top of the stellon. He agonised over its accuracy.

Loul's stock of healing herbs and roots had run low. She needed more with the extra people living here and it was imperative she restock them. Loul always used these expeditions to teach and invited Bildon, an orphan from Raff's family, and Findlow's daughter Lyndym to join them. Just before they left, Mekrar and Mekroe had an argument and Mekrar begged to go along.

Kirym's suggestion to go to the southern gorge to find the rare plants was accepted.

The settlement was quiet without Kirym, but we soon had excitement when Bokum returned from his guard circuit, to tell Veld that some of those new to the land were shooting at pregnant does and fawns in the top meadows.

Veld called everyone together early next morning, Loul and her group being the only ones absent.

He stood and called for silence. "There are laws we've lived with since we came to this land. We must continue to abide by them. If we don't, we'll all starve. I'll spell them out so there is no misunderstanding. We never harvest all that nature gives us in one spot. That is vital for plant life to continue. Along with that we have the unique situation here between the gorges in that there's now no way for animals to enter or leave. The herds have to be self-sustaining. If too many are killed, they'll die out leaving us with no meat. So we forbid the killing of animals with young. Nor do we kill breeding females."

Findlow and Raff nodded.

"Those are stupid rules," Salcan yelled. "You can't make us obey them. We've been forced to live in this isolated place, but if I wish to hunt, I'll hunt."

There was a shocked silence at Salcan's outburst.

"Salcan, with more people living here, we need to take more care of the land."

Salcan was on his feet before Veld had finished. "I've never been a farmer and I don't wanna be one. I'm a hunter. That's what I do. I'll not exchange my bow for a hoe."

"You were a hunter in a land where you could range widely to get meat," interjected Raff. Even there, you had rules against taking animals with young."

"If you wish to hunt unchecked," said Veld, "you can do so. But you do it outside this land."

There was silence as the import of what he'd said, sank in.

Rathay stood and was recognised. "If there are no paths, even for the animals, why are we doing guard duty? And I understand there's a plan to watch the gorges? Those paths are dangerous."

There was a roar of outrage.

Raff bellowed for silence. "Veld, I'm willing to do all you ask just because you ask. You're the reason my family survives. My people need to consider that before they refuse your requests. I think though, that it's time you told us why this is important. Men work better with knowledge, a feeling of trust."

Veld looked out at the families. "I know of no paths leading into our land, but that doesn't mean they aren't there. No land is totally isolated. If someone really wants to enter, he will find a way. We created paths, others could also. We are not as safe here as you may feel. Whatever reasons Slynd's men had for killing, they still have them. They will come. The gorges are the most obvious place for them to try first."

"Raff's settlement was an easy conquest," called Salcan. "They took what they wanted. They'll have gone back to wherever they came from. We only have your word that they even know of this land."

Veld spoke quietly. "Slynd definitely knows this land. He lived here. These men crossed the mountains five times to my knowledge. The passes aren't easy. They risk life and limb each time they use them. Why do that if they've no plan. The danger remains."

I raised my hand.

"I see you, Teema," Veld said.

"Do you think the gorge is the most obvious way for them to enter the land?"

Before Veld could answer, a voice called from the edge of the gathering area. "Yes. They'd cut a tree to bridge the gap.

8

Kirym Speaks

"Mekrar, Bildon and I heard noises near the gorge and we investigated," I said. "A tree spanned the gap, and a man was using it as a bridge. It hadn't fallen straight though and when he stepped on it, it fell. He tried to jump back, but fell onto a ledge. Bildon and I stayed to watch and Mekrar went to get Mama. Two other men argued. One turned to run away, but the other threw a knife at him. The man who was knifed was thrown over the cliff also. The rest walked towards the sea cliffs. The man who was thrown into the gorge was still moving. He's lying on the rocks about half way down. The other man is higher up. He wasn't moving. Then Mama arrived and we came home."

Mama took over the story. "When I got there it was getting dark. I couldn't see the men. One was calling out. He was hurt and sounded angry. I didn't understand his language."

Armos stood and was recognised. "The land east has no big trees near the gorge, but is there a possibility they could find one further west?"

"The trees there grow taller, but the gorge is wider," Findlow said. "They'll fail there also, but I think we have to accept your judgment here, Veld. What do you suggest we do?"

Salcan jumped to his feet. "No! I'm not accepting this. Veld thinks there's a danger and his woman backs it up. How very convenient."

There was an angry buzz from the crowd, but before anyone could do anything, Bildon rounded on Salcan.

"I'm not of Veld's family, but I saw the tree in the gorge. I heard the man calling, but I did understand what he was saying. He cursed a man called Slynd. He said he hoped the people between the gorges could hold out against him." She advanced towards Salcan, her eyes flashing. "Are you going to challenge my word also?"

Salcan backed away.

Papa asked Bildon a few questions and then turned to Bokum. "I need to know if those men still live. Take Teema and someone who knows the language. Loul can show you where they are."

"You'll need Mama's help here, Papa. I'll go," I said.

"I'll go too," Bildon said. "I know the language."

With packs of food, flasks and weapons, we left for the gorge at once with warnings from Papa ringing in our ears. It would be a faster trip than that made by us through the night. Bokum and Teema knew shortcuts and were rested. I'd keep up and I thought Bildon would also, although Teema and Bokum would help her if need be.

It was past mid-afternoon when we approached the gorge. I led them up river to where it narrowed slightly and turned south. Just over five hundred steps on, we saw the tree caught on a rocky overhang. We checked the other bank carefully, but saw no movement. One of the men had fallen to the bottom of the cliff. He lay in the water, his head at an unnatural angle. He was obviously dead.

The second rested on a small ledge to the right and above the tree trunk. He was moving slightly. He was young — about the same age as Teema, and terribly thin.

"Talk to him, Bildon, but don't show yourself. It might be a trap," Bokum said. "He may tell you more if he thinks you're alone."

She called, but there was no response. She called again and again.

As the sun lowered in the sky, he opened his eyes, but still didn't respond. She kept saying the same thing, but he didn't seem to understand.

Then it dawned on me — he didn't understand. I stepped out into the open near the cliff edge. Bokum hissed at me to keep out of sight, I could hear the anger in his voice, but I like to see who's talking to me.

"He's a boy, and he can't hurt me," I said.

"My name's Kirym," I called. "I may be able to help you get up the cliff. But you need to roll away from the edge or you'll fall off."

After a long moment, he moved back towards the wall and sat up.

My main concern was that he'd roll into the gorge, and I was relieved when he moved. He was safe for the moment, but to my knowledge, that cliff had never been climbed before.

The sun was low in the sky. The angle highlighted shadows in the cliff that I hoped were hand and foot holds, a possible path to the top.

"If you can stand, I'll help you climb. It won't be easy, but I think there are enough handholds for you to make it."

He nodded and got to his feet. He looked tired and his shoulder was obviously bothering him. I was worried he mightn't be able to reach some of the handholds and several appeared to be little more than cracks in the cliff face.

However there was no choice. If he didn't do it he would die. He might die anyway.

I directed him to the eastern end of the ledge. The first handhold was high and he'd have problems reaching it, but if he couldn't get this one, it wouldn't matter about the rest.

He did it. It was slow, but that was good because some holds became more obvious as the angle of the sun narrowed further. At one point, the crack he had his foot in broke away from the cliff and he was left hanging from a hand hold and one finger hold. But he remained calm until I guided his foot to the next toe hold.

He moved on and up slowly, one hold at a time until he reached the top and rolled over the edge. He rested there catching his breath and then sat up and looked over at us, his eyes moving from Bildon to me.

"Thank you," he called. "Why'd ya' help me?"

"Because you needed help. You were hurt, and anyway it was the right thing to do. Why do you attack people you don't know?"

His eyes widened. "I don't! I was a slave. The group — the leader of the group likes killing." He winced.

"You're hurt?"

He nodded.

"There's a tall tree with yellow leaves behind you. It has a creeper with red berries growing up it. Crush ten berries and drink the juice. It'll help. Don't eat the seeds or skin though, they'll make you die."

He went to the tree and came back with a handful of berries. "Are you sure?"

I nodded.

He pressed them into his hand and drank the juice.

I introduced Bildon. "Why didn't you answer her when she called to you earlier?"

"I couldn't see anyone and I didn't understand the words. I thought I was dreaming."

I frowned. "But that's the language we heard yesterday. We saw the tree fall. It was getting dark, but we heard you."

He shook his head. "You heard Pelak. When the moon was high he told me Slynd had knifed him and threw him over the edge. He stopped talking after that. He must have died."

I nodded. "What's your name? Where do you come from?"

"Arbreu. I'm from the south. My birth camp is a long way from here."

"Are you hungry?"

Arbreu nodded. "I feel better though, that berry juice helped. Thank you."

I told him about Teema and Bokum and introduced them. "I want to send you some food. It's the food we use when we travel so it's light. We can attach a small pack of it to an arrow. Please don't move. Teema is very good at shooting and he'll want to miss you. We'll send it now before the light goes." I wrapped some food in a large leaf and tied it to an arrow.

Teema aimed across the gorge. I saw the apprehension in Arbreu's face. Teema placed the arrow beside his left foot.

He smiled, picked up the food and started to eat.

While Teema was setting out food for us, I continued asking questions. "Is Slynd your leader?"

He nodded.

"How does he plan to cross the gorge now?"

"He's searching for a narrower place. He plans to fell more trees. It won't work though. Pelak said this is the narrowest point, and it wouldn't work anywhere else. That's one of the reasons Slynd knifed him. He doesn't like to be opposed, even indirectly. He'll keep on trying though. He'll come back and go over the passes and look at the other gorge. He's determined to get into your land. He really hates you people."

"Why?"

"I don't know. Two men asked and now they lie in the ground. But lately, he's been talking about claiming his inheritance." Arbreu shrugged. "Whatever that is."

Teema stood. "The light's fading and it'll be cold tonight. If you go to the right of the berries, there's a big mound of fush grass. It's a long wide dark green leaf. It's hairy on the underside. You need to pick two or three big armloads and bring them here."

Arbreu set off and a short time later returned with the first load. Teema encouraged him to get plenty and told him to put a deep layer of it on the ground as a base to lie on and more over him as a protection from the cold.

Arbreu built the nest in a slight hollow against a small rock bank. Bildon and Bokum did the same for us.

Fush grass is wonderful because it's resistant to water, so if it rains or there's dew, we still keep warm and dry.

I had more questions for Arbreu. "What will you do now? Will you return to Slynd?"

He shook his head. "He'd kill me as soon as he saw me, and he'd make sure this time."

"But you could tell him about us."

Arbreu came to the edge of the cliff and looked over at me. "You gave me a chance when most would've turned away. Slynd would kill me no matter what I told him, but that's not the point. I owe you my life. If it takes the rest of it, I'll pay you back. You could've asked your questions and left me on the ledge. You needn't have given me food nor told me of this grass. I owe you a life debt."

Arbreu prepared his bed and lay down to sleep. Just as we were about to do the same, I had a thought and went back to the edge of the gorge. "Arbreu, are you asleep yet?"

I saw a slight movement in the moonlight.

"Slynd and his men may be back sometime. Even if he goes right to the sea cliffs, it'll only take him a few days. You'll need to be careful. But you'll get a warning when they're close. We watched them when they left. After they'd gone from our hearing, they disturbed a large flock of birds further down the gorge. We saw them in the sky. We'll need to watch for them. When you see the birds, you'll have time to hide."

Teema came up behind me. "If you climb the rock behind you, you'll leave no tracks. Follow the rocks to where you picked the fush grass. Climb the big tree there and you'll be hidden. Does Slynd travel at night?"

"Only if he's planning an early morning attack. He won't now. He sent some of his men to the lodge by the lake. He told them to bring back food and wine. They'll celebrate for a few days."

Teema nodded. "Sleep safely, Arbreu."

Arbreu settled down to sleep. Under the fush grass, he was invisible. If he didn't move, he'd be hidden even if Slynd did return through the night. Day time would reveal him though.

"Teema, can you take me to the cave?" I asked.

He looked at me with surprise. "Why?"

"I'm not sure yet, but it's important. We must get there before the moon sets."

He nodded and woke Bokum to tell him. "We should be back by late morning. Tell Arbreu we'll be back. Talk to him, but keep an eye out for the birds. You'll not hear them, so watch carefully. You'll have a far better view of them than Arbreu will. Warn him and then keep quiet and hidden."

We took a lamp, food, a bow and arrows, but otherwise travelled light. Just after midnight we arrived at the cave. I was exhausted. I had not slept now for two nights. Teema would have lit a fire to warm us and heat some water, but I knew if I sat down, I'd have trouble getting up. So we entered the cave immediately.

"We have to think of Arbreu," I said.

We stood in the dark holding hands. Time passed. Then a streak of light hit the wall. It lit up the rock and narrowed to one large silver light.

I walked over to pick up the token but found instead a group of four. I wasn't sure of what to do. I picked one up. The light in it went out, so I put it back. It lit up again. When I picked up a different one, the same thing happened.

"Perhaps you need to take them all, Kirym."

I studied them carefully. There was a connection between them. Altogether, they stayed glowing in my hand. I held them tight.

The light disappeared and we left the cave.

The moon was low in the sky.

"Sleep until dawn," Teema said as he lit a fire.

I nodded and wrapped my cloak around me.

It was just light when I woke. Teema had a hot drink and food ready. I felt the need to get back to the gorge quickly.

We arrived there late in the morning. Everyone was pleased to see us. Arbreu looked more rested although his shoulder still pained him.

I asked Teema to make a token holder and while he did it, I went to find some dolen berries and a lemech root. Once found, I scraped the root, crushed the berries and mixed the juice into the root pulp. I spread it out near the fire to dry, and when it was ready I cut it into squares and laced them onto a thin vine. By then Teema had the token holder ready.

Bokum saw it, and was very unhappy. "It's not right, Teema. Stop her. They only go to family."

"We don't have rules like that for tokens. Anyway, Arbreu is born to the family, Bokum," I said. "When we saved his life he acknowledged it, so there's a bond between us. He'd have died if we hadn't helped him, so his life is ours. He's entitled to a token, but it's more than that. The token was there for him. It was different, but it was there."

He turned to Teema with a frown. "Could she be wrong?"

Teema shrugged. "It's part of the cave mysteries and Kirym's the only one here who could make that decision. We have to assume she's right."

Bokum looked belligerent. "Could it be for Bildon?"

I shook my head. "She's not born to us, and she has no life connection with us yet."

"And what about the other three tokens?"

I frowned. For the first time, I wasn't sure of the answer. Generally we would get a token at birth and one on joining. Sometimes a parent received one when a child was born and occasionally one was given on an extremely special occasion, but I'd never seen those occasions. I only took the four tokens because I couldn't take one by itself.

"I think they're for you, Teema and me. There's no other answer, but if I am wrong, they'll let us know."

Bokum frowned but nodded. "All right, what do we do?"

"We put the tokens into the holders. Then we each click Arbreu's token to ours and we send it over. I'll explain it to him."

Teema nodded and tied the dried berry squares to one arrow and the token holder to another. "The token's far heavier than my usual shot. I'll have to be careful."

Teema shot the berry squares first and I explained that they were to be sucked slowly for the pain in his shoulder, but not more than four a day.

I pressed Arbreu's token into his holder and we stood near the edge of the gorge, and each clicked Arbreu's token to our new tokens, me first, then Teema and Bokum. Then before Teema took the arrow to his bow, I took the token again and clicked it across both of my tokens. Teema shot the arrow over the gorge. Arbreu picked the token up and placed it on his forehead. Instantly, it blazed deep green and a beam of light curved from it to each of our new tokens.

As the light disappeared, Bildon pointed west and we saw a flock of birds rise against the setting sun and circle away to the north.

Arbreu followed her finger, picked up his possessions and ran for the trees. We also picked up everything in sight and hid in the bushes. We watched as Arbreu climbed high and was hidden in the branches.

Bokum leaned forward. "I meant to tell you. As the sun rose, the river deepened with spring melt. It washed Pelak's body away, so it'll not be strange that both have gone."

I was happy to hear that. It seemed all was going well.

9

Teema Speaks

We heard the men on the far bank long before we saw them. They were undisciplined and argumentative as they travelled. Slynd was third in line. I remembered him walking second in line when going towards Findlow's old settlement. I made a mental note to ask Arbreu about that. I counted sixty five men in the group. Twenty eight were heavily laden, about ten carried a small pack, the rest carrying only their weapons.

As they arrived opposite us an argument started, ending when one of them looked over the cliff edge and pointed to the tree now sitting partly in the water. They looked for the bodies and when they weren't found, they looked for signs along the cliff top, although they'd already placed their own over any marks that may have been there. I was pleased though that Arbreu had rolled onto an area of rock and had left no obvious marks.

A fire was lit and they settled down to eat and drink. They

got loud and quarrelsome and soon minor fights started between them. Slynd sat to one side and ate. He drank too, but less than the others and he was always watchful.

One fight got serious, with three men fighting a fourth. He was bleeding heavily, his face almost unrecognisable. When he fell to the ground, they continued kicking him violently, and stamping on his face, hands and body. When he stopped responding, the three gave up and walked back to the fire.

Slynd picked up a burning branch and walking over, thrust it into the thick bush to the east of their camp. As the wind rose, the smaller bushes caught fire, then some trees and within a short time it raged out of control. The noise was horrendous.

Kirym grabbed my arm. "Teema, we have to send a message to Papa. He'll worry over the fire."

I nodded. "Yes, it's time, but they won't see the smoke, it's too dark and the wind's blowing south."

"It's time they heard what's happening. I'll go." Bokum picked up his bow and arrows and left at a run.

Kirym and Bildon fell asleep as they watched. Kirym had had very little sleep over the past few nights. I was amazed she had been so resilient for so long.

I stayed on guard. I was shocked at the calculated damage Slynd had created.

He and his men slept with no concern for the fire that raged so close to them. The wind thankfully took the flames away from the tree Arbreu was in.

Near morning Kirym woke. "Bokum's coming back, he'll be here soon. Mama's with him; they must have met on the path." She fell asleep again.

I wondered how she knew, but when I thought about it, I knew too.

Soon after, Bokum, Loul, Tarl and Zeprah arrived.

"What made you come, Loul?"

"The flames reflected in the sky." She paused, looking at Kirym's sleeping figure. "I no longer feel her token, Teema. I haven't since the trip to Raff's. Please take care of her for me." She wrapped herself in her cloak, smoothed the fush grass beneath her and was soon asleep.

I woke soon after dawn. The fire raged south and east and the winds were rising. The flames wouldn't stop until they reached the tree line. Slynd and his men still slept and as far as I could see, they'd left no guard overnight. I could see nothing of Arbreu. I hoped it was a good sign.

The sun was well above the horizon before Slynd woke and kicked one of the other men to his feet. They walked to the trees and I noted again that he walked behind the other man. When they returned, Slynd and his companion ate. Then he kicked the other men awake. The man who had been beaten didn't waken, and eventually they left him alone. One man cursed loudly as Slynd's foot connected with his shoulder.

Slynd grabbed a spear and threw it. It pierced his chest and he fell to the ground. They put together their packs, the hunters ate and drank and then the slaves shouldered their packs. Just before he left, Slynd put an arrow into the chest of each of the injured men. This time, they went southward.

It was late morning when we finally walked to the edge of the gorge. The man who had been beaten stirred feebly. There was no movement from the other man.

Soon after, Arbreu limped out of the trees, looking stiff and tired. "I followed them," he said. "They've gone towards the lodge by the lake. They're starting more fires. It means they won't be back."

"How was your night?" I asked.

"It could've been worse. It was cold. I tied myself to the tree so I wouldn't fall out."

He checked the men on the ground and took some of the fush grass to make the man who was beaten, comfortable. I watched as he broke off the fletched end of the arrow and drove the arrowhead through the man's shoulder. He plugged the wound on both sides with a wad of material ripped from his tunic.

He saw me watching. "His name's Zelar. I think he'll die. He must have really upset Slynd, he appeared to be one of the favourites when they left here. The other one's already dead." He took a deep breath. "I'm sure you have questions, I'll answer all I can."

I nodded. "Why did Slynd come back?"

"I'm not sure, but he knew Pelak was still alive. Being thrown off a cliff makes you an enemy. Slynd's always careful about killing his enemies. Maybe he came back to check on Pelak's death and mine. He knew there was no way from the bottom of the gorge but he's thorough."

I nodded, it made sense. "He is the leader isn't he?"

Arbreu frowned and nodded.

"Well I never saw him walk in the lead position."

Arbreu laughed. "When you hunt or trap men, you aim for the person in the lead because he's generally the leader. Slynd takes second or third place and lives."

"Don't his men object to being used like that?"

"If Slynd asks you to do something and you refuse, you don't get a second chance. When asked a favour, you don't know if it's because he likes you or hates you. But you know if you refuse him, you'll die."

"Why does he let his men fight like that?"

"If they fight each other, they don't fight him. It's his

policy to divide and conquer. They don't trust each other. They get the spoil of battle, but they're expected to be generous to him. If he thinks someone's hoarding too much wealth, he'll find reason to take it. If you're asked for your treasure, you give it or you die." Arbreu shrugged. "You may die anyway."

"Why'd he start the fire?"

"To ruin land he doesn't want, or to ensure there's nothing left for anyone else. He's done it to well-protected communities and destroyed them without fighting."

"Will he come back? Zelar's still alive. Why did he get his men to beat him as they did?"

Arbreu laughed. "You have many questions, Teema. No, I don't think he'll be back. If I thought that, I'd not be here. I wonder if he thought Zelar was dead. I'm sure he would've been had I not tended him through the night. I gave him some of the berry squares Kirym gave me. Still, I'm surprised he made it. I wasn't sure if he was even breathing when I checked him. As to why he was beaten, well who knows? When they left me here, Slynd appeared to like him, but he's easy to offend. Sometimes, you offend him no matter what you do. If Zelar wakens I'll ask him, but otherwise your guess is as good as mine." Arbreu stood as Loul approached. "You have the look of Kirym. You must be her Mama."

Loul smiled. "I'm Loul. Kirym's very fond of you and she wants us to bring you over the gorge. I'm not sure how to do it though."

"I'm sure your family would argue against that. I'm happy to know I have her friendship. I owe her my life."

"It's more than that, Arbreu. You have a token and that means you're one of us. We look after our own," she paused. "First though, you may be able to help me. Did you ever see Slynd with a token?"

Arbreu shook his head. "They're very distinctive, but

they're not well known. Many people think they're part of folklore, myths."

"Did Slynd talk about them?"

"Occasionally. He was dismissive of the people who wear them. He said you were weak and hid away, afraid to face the rest of the world. I always wondered why a people he thought so insignificant took so much of his anger. He really, really hates you. He plans to kill you all. I couldn't figure out why it was so important to him, but Slynd isn't one you question."

"Well whatever his intentions, we need to get you over here somehow. Our Headman may know of a way."

Kirym joined us. "What'll you do now, Arbreu?"

"I'll care for Zelar first and then I'll follow the track Slynd made towards the sea cliffs. I'd like to know where he went. I may find something that'll be of help to you." He turned back to Loul. "What's the connection with Slynd and the tokens?"

"Slynd lived here. He has his own token, but when he left he stole someone else's. Tokens are very special, given at a birth or joining. If one is lost or stolen, it isn't necessarily replaced. It's like a part of us goes with it."

"Why doesn't Bildon wear hers?"

"She's from a different family. She lived north of the big waterfall. Slynd attacked her home a few days ago."

Arbreu went pale. "Loul, I haven't killed anyone. I couldn't. I was a slave. That's why I was chosen to cross the gorge first, Slynd wanted me dead. Everyone knew the tree wouldn't hold, but if it had and I'd made it, the next three men across would have been charged to kill me. If they hadn't, they too would've been killed. That's how Slynd kept control."

He turned away, searching through the debris of the campsite. He found a water flask, a cloak and an old bow, and returned to the cliff edge. "These things belong to

Zelar. They must've thought he was dead. They've taken everything of value. The cloak is too worn and ragged for them, but it'll keep me warm. There's some dried fruits and a flask. I can survive."

Tarl and Zeprah joined us and were introduced. Arbreu looked at them speculatively. "So Tarl is family. I'm surprised no one's taken Zeprah to get a joining token yet."

Zeprah laughed. "They're scared of me, Arbreu. What of your family?"

"I've no family, not now. I went hunting some seasons back. The weather was bad, it rained for days and the wind was very strong. I thought I'd be blown away. The rivers flooded, more than two full moons had passed before I could return home. Everything was gone. A massive landslide covered the settlement. It must have happened soon after I left. The grass was already growing on the disturbed land. No one could've survived. I walked away. I had a bad winter. I missed my family, but I joined a good group of hunters. Slynd arrived soon after I did. When we discovered him stealing, we kicked him out. He returned with his men. Most of us were killed and the rest enslaved. Few escaped. Any who tried were killed. Then he slowly worked his way through the rest of us. It was only a matter of time before it was my turn. He knew I couldn't escape and he enjoyed taking his time."

Zelar stirred and Arbreu went to tend him.

"Veld needs to know what's happening," said Loul, quietly. "Tarl can you take the news?"

Tarl left with requests and a list of suggestions.

10

Arbreu

Arbreu was surprised at Kirym's knowledge of healing. At first he thought she was passing on information given her by others, but he quickly realised she knew what she was talking about.

His concern for Zelar was echoed by everyone else. Zelar's face was battered and one eye swollen shut. He had lost some teeth and his mouth still bled. His whole body was bruised. Most worrying though, was the arrow wound. The arrow appeared to have bypassed all vital organs, but the wound kept bleeding.

Kirym sent over a kit of remedies and explained what to do with them.

Arbreu spent some time preparing and feeding them to Zelar. He wasn't sure if it made a difference, but Zelar appeared to rest easier.

While Zelar slept, Arbreu broke off some slim branches to make into spears. He wanted some form of protection.

He had no knife, although he had the arrows Teema had shot over. He sharpened the spear ends against a rock and hardened them in a fire. During the afternoon, he tried to make a quiver. The spears worked, the quiver didn't.

Late in the afternoon, Teema had finally figured out a way to send a few items over to Arbreu. He shot over an arrow with a long rope attached to it.

Arbreu was impressed with Teema's shooting, each arrow was placed so close to his foot, he just had to bend down and pick it up. He secured the rope to a tree and added the arrow to his collection.

Teema attached a pack to the end of the rope and dropped it over the gorge.

Arbreu hauled it up, surprised at the weight on the line. It took time and when he had finished, his shoulder ached again.

Kirym told him to suck one of the fruit squares she had sent over, warning that this just masked the pain. It didn't cure it. Arbreu was surprised at how quickly it worked, although it also numbed his tongue.

He opened the pack. The gifts were of huge value and he was touched at how much thought and energy had gone into getting them together. There was fresh meat wrapped in fush grass, fruit and vegetables, bread and a large pack of travel food.

Kirym sent more healing remedies and Arbreu added them to his kit along with a knife, sheath and doeskin quiver from Teema. There was a pack of bone needles with some linen and sinew threads in another small kit. Finally, there was a flint and a bark platter. Along with the rope and pack, Arbreu now had enough to keep him contented and healthy for a long time. He was lost for words.

He was stammering his thanks when Zelar groaned.

For the first time since Arbreu started to attend him, he

was fully aware. He didn't look good though. He smiled his thanks and asked where Slynd was.

"Gone, and he won't be back" Arbreu said, and Zelar seemed to relax. Arbreu gave him a warm drink.

"Why are you helping me? I forced you onto the tree."

"I helped you because someone helped me. Anyway, you did what you had to do. If you hadn't, you'd have joined me. It seems you've joined me anyway."

Zelar nodded weakly. "If we'd trusted each other more, we could have destroyed Slynd. You had more strength than I did. You refused to obey him in the worst things even though you knew he'd kill you. I'm ashamed I didn't support you." He closed his eyes.

"Zelar, why did Slynd leave you for dead? I thought he liked you."

Zelar lay with his eyes shut for a long time and Arbreu thought he'd lost consciousness again. Then he stirred and started to talk. "He. Likes. No one. We travelled all night, but he hadn't planned an attack. I asked why the routine had changed and he got annoyed. About midmorning we were ordered to make camp and sleep. In the afternoon, something woke me. Slynd leaving camp alone. I stoked the fire and heated some water and food. I was doing that when he returned a while later. He accused me of spying on him. He was so angry. I thought he'd gone to relieve himself, although normally he takes a guard. If he hadn't been so irate, I wouldn't have given it a second thought, but he went on and on. Everyone started to avoid me and when I was told to carry some packs, I knew I was doomed. I would've escaped but ..." He shrugged. "We got here and Boolan picked a fight. I knew it was the end. I'm surprised to be alive, Slynd is getting sloppy." He grasped Arbreu's arm tightly. "I thought about it. He took a full pack towards the sea. It was empty when he returned. Whatever was in that pack was important." He leaned back on the fush grass exhausted, his face was ashen.

Night had fallen and Arbreu built up the small fire to cook some of the food he'd been given. He fed Zelar some broth although he was too weak to have much. He was about to settle down to sleep when he heard Zeprah call from the far side of the gorge.

Zeprah suggested he give Zelar more crushed harkii nuts, some keeku seeds and one of the lemech squares Kirym had sent over.

Arbreu kept the fire going so he could tend Zelar, and was aware through the night of a guard on the other side of the gorge.

Just before the moon set, Zelar died.

Arbreu felt empty as he sat beside the body. They'd spent over four season cycles together and he really knew nothing about Zelar. He didn't even know where he came from.

Living with Slynd's group didn't encourage closeness. Private information could be used against you, so common sense suggested silence.

Arbreu sat by the fire feeling very sorry for himself. The longer he sat there, the worse he felt. He was alone again and frightened. It wasn't a good time of night, very dark, cold and he was exhausted. As he sat there, close to tears, he heard an arrow imbed into the ground beside him. Attached to the arrow was a small kit. Inside were a few dried berries and a small leaf.

He strained to see who had sent it.

Zeprah's voice came across. "Chew them together, you'll feel better. Then get a bit of sleep, you've been up most of the night."

"Thanks, Zeprah. What are the berries?"

Zeprah laughed. "I'm not sure. Loul gave them to me when my shift started. She said you may need them. She told me to tell you to sleep. It'll be a busy day tomorrow."

Arbreu smiled his thanks and put the berries and leaf into his mouth. As he chewed them, he felt warmth creeping down his body and he felt very tired. He took Zeprah's advice and settled in the nest of fush grass.

The sun was high when he woke. He sat up and looked around. Loul waited on the far bank.

She waved. "How are you feeling?"

Arbreu smiled back. He was feeling a lot better now and felt a little silly when he thought of the previous night.

"It's normal, you know," she said. "You've been through a tremendous amount over the last few seasons. Of late, you've put aside your feelings because you've needed all you had to just survive. In a way, everything's gone, and when one loses so much, there are bound to be emotions. Remember that although this is an end, it's also a beginning. You've a lot to look forward to."

Arbreu looked at her through a veil of tears. "I appreciate all you've done for me, Loul, you and your family." He paused. "What'll you do now? Return to your settlement?"

She smiled. "I meant what I said. You're one of us. Now we have to find a way of getting you over here. I'm sure it can be done, but it may take a while to organise."

Arbreu nodded. "Well, I'm going to bury these men. I wouldn't like their bodies to be taken by wolves. Then I want to find out why Slynd took his last trip west. Zelar told me that Slynd hid something. I think that's why Slynd had him killed."

Loul went pale.

"Anyway I want to find out what was hidden. That'll take a few days."

The ground was too rocky to dig a grave, so Arbreu collected rocks and mounded them over the bodies. It was mid-afternoon before he finished. He went to the edge of the gorge and called out.

Everyone came at his call. They were ready to leave.

Loul spoke first. "I'm going to see what we can do about bringing you over the gorge. It'll only take a few days to organise. Then we'll come and find you."

Arbreu nodded. "I have to follow Slynd's tracks, but then I'll come back here. I won't be far though. Slynd travelled at night, so I may be faster. Once I find his camp, I'll have to search for what he hid." He picked up his pack and weapons.

They walked west along the gorge but after a short distance, the track to the settlement turned north while Arbreu's route continued west. Arbreu knew this was the last he'd see of them for a while. There were waves and calls of goodbye.

Kirym came to the edge of the gorge. "Take care, Arbreu, we'll see you again soon," she called. "If you were here we'd touch tokens, but this time we can only think about it. I'll think of you every day until you're with us."

She sounded so sweet and sincere. Arbreu hoped they'd find a way to get him across, and although he doubted they'd manage, it was nice to think they'd try.

He turned to walk away, surprised when Teema kept step with him. The others disappeared into the trees that lined the gorge turning to wave goodbye just before they stepped out of sight.

"Aren't you going with them?"

Teema laughed. "You may get lost without me, and you'd get all lonely. Anyway, we may manage to get you across before they return."

Arbreu smiled. While he had hopes of finding a way across the gorge, he wondered if it would be a good idea. Any path he could use, Slynd could use. Arbreu liked this new family already and he wanted to protect them.

They walked until sundown and made camp. They each lit a small fire to heat food and water and then extinguished it. On Teema's advice, they had brought the fush grass they'd already cut. Because it would last a number of days, they would carry the leaves with them.

Arbreu slept well. He woke early, eager to get going. Teema was already up. As they ate, Teema explained how to tie and carry the fush grass so Arbreu could keep his weapons at hand. They walked through the day in companionable silence. Generally, they kept each other in sight but occasionally the tracks veered away for a distance.

Teema amazed Arbreu. Whenever they lost sight of each other, Teema would always get to the next sighting point first. On the fourth such occasion he came along the gorge to see Teema sitting calmly waiting for him.

"Let's rest and eat," Teema called. "The land gets flatter from here on and it'll be easier for you to follow the trail. Slynd chose a tough path for you. It appears he wanted his men to be tired when they arrived at their destination."

Arbreu nodded, still out of breath from the last climb. "How come you know the land here so well, Teema? I thought you lived nearer the northern gorge."

"We do, and I've not spent much time in this area. But I was taught by a man who knew this land like a second skin. He taught me with maps he'd drawn when he was younger than I am now, but he also taught me to read the land and think about what I was looking at. If you understand the animals who use the terrain and how they move with the land, you get a rough idea just by looking and thinking."

"He sounds special. Is your mentor still alive?"

"He's alive, an amazing man. Mind you, Kirym's papa has to be special."

Kirym's papa! She'd mentioned him and they were obviously very close. Arbreu hoped he could meet him sometime.

Teema lifted his pack and fush grass to his shoulder and they continued. Soon another turn in Teema's path took him away from the gorge. When the paths joined again it was close to sunset and they made camp. The gorge had widened considerably and it was harder to talk. After eating they settled in their fush grass beds. Though Arbreu was tired, he found it hard to sleep he had so much to think about. He listened to the sounds around him and watched the stars above. He realised as he rested there that his shoulder no longer ached as it had. Slowly, he relaxed and slept.

He woke next morning when an arrow embedded in the ground by his ear. He rolled free of the fush grass and was on his feet with his bow primed and ready before really awake.

Teema's laughter echoed from the other side of the gorge. "I thought you'd gone on without me," he shouted with a broad smile. "It's late. Eat something and we'll get moving. We should find Slynd's camp soon."

Arbreu decided to eat while walking, so after a quick drink he tied the fush grass together, swung his pack and quiver to his shoulder and picked up the bow and spears. They walked quickly now, the land angled down gently towards the sea although the coast was still a long way away.

Arbreu surprised a rabbit and managed a lucky shot. He skinned and gutted it quickly, while regretting not being able to share the meat with Teema. He carefully cleaned the arrow, returned it to his collection in the quiver, wrapped the meat in its skin and a piece of fush grass, and hung it from his pack.

It was mid-morning when Arbreu came to the windblown remains of a large fire. He placed his possessions under a tree and scouted the area. As with all of Slynd's campsites, debris was littered across the ground. Arbreu picked up a knife with a broken handle, a large cured skin, a long piece of woven material, a few odd arrow heads and five fletched shafts. Near the ashes of the fire he found a bone flask he'd used in the past, four wooden platters and a beautifully carved wooden flask he'd never seen before. He added these to his possessions.

On the western side of the camp Arbreu found footprints, going northwest. Slynd's, he assumed.

Arbreu followed the vague tracks for about six hundred steps and lost them in the grass. The track continued, fairly clear except for a few fallen branches. He was about to follow the path when Teema whistled and, getting Arbreu's attention, beckoned him towards the higher ground near the edge of the gorge.

When Arbreu looked back to where he'd planned to walk, he went pale with horror. The track was booby trapped. A few more steps would have taken him right into a strange looking trap.

Teema, with the advantage of height, had seen it. He'd saved Arbreu's life.

Arbreu thought of Teema's comment about thinking of the animals that used the land. "I've gotta think like Slynd," he mumbled.

The path beyond the trap was overgrown. Obviously Slynd knew about the trap, so he would have walked around it, either along the cliff edge or through the trees on the southern side of the path.

Arbreu had watched Slynd for a long time. Slynd never willingly went near a cliff edge. One man had casually mentioned that in front of others. He died during the night when someone put a spear in his chest. However Arbreu knew Slynd was devious, so he chose the path along the edge of the gorge.

It was difficult initially but he soon found a track and in one sheltered area, a footprint. The track became better defined and a wall grew up on the southern side. It was like a roofless tunnel with one wall, and was wide enough for Arbreu to feel comfortable on it despite the sheer drop into the gorge. He followed the path for five hundred steps until a rock fall covered the path.

There was an unnatural look about the way the rocks sat. It appeared to Arbreu that there was a pattern there. The rocks at the top sat higgledy-piggledy on a flat rock that sat across the fall about half way up. The rocks below had a more orderly open placement. Arbreu carefully lifted out a few of the rocks from just below the flat rock. It was easy work; none of them were very big. He worked his way in and down. He came to a bigger rock, lifted it out and dropped it in fright.

A face stared out at him.

11

Arbreu

He'd been dead a long time. The dry heat had mummified him.

Arbreu removed the rocks from around him.

The handle of a large knife still sat in his chest. Sitting on his lap was a large bag.

Arbreu placed it on the ground and continued his search. He lifted out more rocks, but they were gritty with dust and he realised these hadn't been moved in a long time. As he turned away, he saw a small edge of something behind the corpse's head. He pulled out a small bundle, tucked it into his belt and was starting to replace the stones when Teema whistled.

Teema shook his head, shouldered his pack and walked away.

Arbreu grabbed the bag and followed, realising that if Slynd had arrived to check on his pack, he would be trapped.

Arbreu walked back along cliff, surprised to see by the

sun that it was early afternoon. As he walked towards the trap, he could see how to dislodge it without being caught in it. He pulled away a branch that choked a log. It crashed through the surface of the path exposing a deep hole. In it were long sharp sticks pointing up to impale anything that fell in it. Nasty.

Arbreu picked up the bag and walked back to the camp. He'd thought to spend the night there but Teema had his pack and fush grass on his shoulder and was already walking east.

Arbreu shouldered his belongings and strode out after him.

It was harder now, the gentle incline no longer in his favour. He was carrying a lot more gear and his shoulder began to throb again. He was relieved when, very late in the afternoon, Teema directed him to a small hollow, well protected by banks and deadfall. He was very tired. He lit a small fire and spitted the rabbit over it, then set out the fush grass.

After he'd eaten, Arbreu extinguished the fire and walked to the gorge to call goodnight to Teema.

He was gone. There wasn't even a glow from a fire.

Arbreu waited for a while to see if he'd return. The wind rose. It was cold so he went back to the hollow and crawled into the fush grass. He tried to think of Kirym, but while she came to his mind, she then slowly disappeared.

He had trouble sleeping, wondering what had happened, but eventually he drifted off and slept fitfully until morning.

It was cold when he woke. The sky was grey and cloudy, it would rain before night. He felt depressed, worried about Teema's absence. He'd got used to him being there, and was scared he'd left for good.

He told himself that Teema had probably just fallen asleep

early. He'd been awake first every day and Arbreu was sure Teema didn't sleep until well after he knew Arbreu had settled.

But Arbreu knew there was nothing that looked remotely like a sleeping person on the far side of the gorge. Mainly, Arbreu was scared he'd be alone again.

When he climbed out of the hollow, he was relieved to see Teema sitting in front of a small fire. Arbreu hesitated.

Teema was no longer alone. A stranger sat with him.

Arbreu realised that Teema's headman had made a decision about bridging the gorge. He felt ill at ease. This wasn't expected. Well, not so soon anyway.

Had they decided against allowing him to join them? Arbreu knew that fast decisions were often negative decisions and he tried to put himself in the position of the headman with this sort of decision to make. Despite all he knew of himself, he wondered whether, if the roles were reversed, he'd accept a stranger into his family.

12

Kirym Speaks

It was raining when Papa and Teema reached the temporary dwelling we had erected by the gorge.

Papa set down his packs. "Right! Food and rest. We'll start work in the morning."

"We're rested," Mekroe said. "Tell us what to do and we'll have Arr … Arrb …"

"Arbreu," I prompted.

"Arr broo over here before you've finished your nap."

"We can't work in the rain, Mek. Anyway, Arbreu needs to be rested. A lot of the work must be done by him."

I nodded. "Papa's right, Mek. It'd be a shame to make a mistake because we rushed it. So let's rest and learn what to do. Then when we start, we do it right."

Mekroe rolled his eyes.

I ignored him. "I'll go tell Arbreu. He'll need shelter for tonight."

Night fell early, the clouds darkening the sky. The next

two days were wet and miserable and we were frustrated. We could do nothing and I worried that Slynd would turn up.

Despite the dangerous situation, Arbreu appeared optimistic. I suppose for the first time in a long time, he had hope.

As dawn broke on the third day, everyone was awake and watching the sky. There was heavy cloud cover and there would probably be showers later in the day, but there was no rain.

"Let's build a bridge," Papa said softly.

Everyone cheered.

Arbreu smiled broadly as he realised what the cheer meant.

Over the days of rain, we had checked and prepared every rope, every action. We knew what to do, but it was hard work.

Teema shot an arrow over to Arbreu, a long thin rope attached. Arbreu secured it and pulled it over. That held two oiled leather sleeves.

Papa told Arbreu how to wrap them around a particular rock formation that sat near the edge of the gorge. Papa watched carefully as Arbreu placed them to stop the next ropes from fraying against the rough rock.

Arbreu had to dig out loose soil that had accumulated there over the seasons, but the sleeves fitted easily.

The next rope sent across was attached to a long heavy rope and Arbreu strained to pull it over. He must have felt it would never end.

Once he'd hauled it over and coiled it up on the ground, he threaded the end of the rope through a hole in the base of the large rock and returned the arrow with the thin rope attached. Now one end had to be hauled back. It was hard work and we all had a deep respect for Arbreu doing this work by himself.

Once the foot rope was over and back, Arbreu pulled over a slightly thinner rope and guided it around the second leather protector that sat in a wide groove higher on the rock formation. This rope sat at shoulder height. Arbreu shot the arrow back to Teema and we hauled the end of the rope back. Then the ropes had to be secured and tightened.

It was mid-afternoon and we were delighted with the progress. Two harnesses were sent over, one for Arbreu and the other for his possessions. The possessions were dealt with quickly. Everything had gone smoothly, although Papa was having trouble getting the foot rope as tight as he wanted.

Then it rained again. The heavens opened and sent us running for shelter. We were dismayed. If it rained for too long, it would be night and everything would have to stop until morning. We took the opportunity to eat and discuss the work to ensure we'd done everything we needed to.

Late in the afternoon, the rain stopped and the sun appeared near the western horizon.

Arbreu picked up the harness and climbed into it. The harness was attached to the top rope on either side and another rope, held by us, was wrapped around his chest and tied to the front of the harness. This was the safety rope which, in the event of something going wrong, would hopefully mean we could pull him over, or maybe up.

Arbreu stepped into the space created by the top rope going around the rock. He grasped the hand ropes and stepped onto the foot rope.

Papa moved to the head of the rope. "The rope doesn't sag as much as it did," he said. "The rain has shrunk it slightly. That's good."

Arbreu concentrated on the ropes, where to put his feet and the best way to hold on. The beginning and the end were the most dangerous but that danger was relative compared to the rest.

"Relax, Arbreu. Don't look down. Just think of the next step."

He smiled nervously. "I can do this," he said. Slowly as the sun sank, he came closer.

Time after time, I held my breath. The tension was unbearable.

When Arbreu was just over half way, Findlow joined Papa. "Loul sent a message. You'll have difficult visitors before Arbreu arrives on this side of the gorge."

"Don't tell me — Salcan and Rathay?"

Findlow scowled. "They could be a problem. I'll keep them occupied until you're ready." He walked away and Papa concentrated on Arbreu.

This was the hardest part. The slack of the rope was at its worst. Arbreu's weight had stretched it. The sagging meant he effectively had to walk uphill towards the end, but he was still beyond our grasp. He was tired, the light was going and his boots were wet, and slipped constantly. Without the hand rope, he'd never have made it, but the hand rope hadn't stretched as much and Arbreu was having problems holding on.

As Arbreu came close, hands stretched out, grabbed him and hauled him to safety. He slipped at the lip of the gorge, falling to his knees. Papa helped him to his feet, away from the edge and out of the harness.

Everyone crowded around laughing and cheering.

Then they went quiet and the crowd around Arbreu parted. As he faced Teema, Bokum and me, Papa left his side to stand behind us.

I stepped forward. "Arbreu, welcome to our land. Welcome to our family and welcome home." I stretched up and clicked my green token to his.

They both glowed.

I took his hand and we faced Teema and Bokum. "These

are your Token Brothers. We are your family. Welcome to our family."

First Teema and then Bokum leaned in to click tokens, and again with each there was a flash of glowing green. The four tokens connected momentarily, now the same colour.

Teema and Bokum grasped Arbreu's arms and slapped him on the back. "Welcome brother." They flanked Arbreu as he and Papa faced each other.

I took his hand again. "Arbreu, this is Veld, son of Parvel, son of Vauld, headman of our land. Veld is headman of our family," I paused. "This is my papa."

Arbreu leaned forward to click tokens.

13

Arbreu

Arbreu looked into the eyes of the man who had chosen to save his life.

Kirym's papa, joined to Loul, this was the man who had taught Teema all he knew.

Arbreu felt he should have realised the position Veld held.

When Teema talked of him, he gave the impression of a man whose great knowledge went with great age. Arbreu was surprised to find him quite young.

They clicked tokens.

Arbreu found this a strange practise, but the more he did it the more natural it seemed. Sort of like kissing. He wondered if they did that also. He'd find out soon.

The quiet was shattered by voices raised in anger. At the same time the heavens opened and the torrential rain started again.

They ran for shelter. There was lots of talk and laughter,

but as Arbreu was ushered into the dwelling, he was aware of tension between three men already inside.

Two of the men were big. The third was shorter, shorter even than Arbreu. He was slim and had the darkest skin Arbreu had ever seen. He was older than the other two, but Arbreu had the impression that it was they who were on the back foot.

Arbreu stood against the wall and watched.

Everyone was alert and wary.

The two men continued shouting even as Veld and another man approached them.

Veld stood silently until they quieted. "Salcan, Rathay, why are you here?"

The smaller of them looked at him with a sneer. "We're here to cross the gorge."

"I wouldn't advise it. It's not safe, Rathay," the dark skinned man said.

Rathay turned to him. "This is none of your business, Findlow. You've never accepted me as part of your family. Now I'll do as I please. I'll be headman of my own settlement."

Salcan grabbed Rathay's shoulder. "You? Headman? Not damn likely. You're nothing. I'm in charge." He pushed Rathay so roughly, he staggered back against Bokum.

The third man who stood with Veld and Findlow moved between them. "What about Tindra?"

"She said..." Salcan suddenly had a strange look on his face. "Go away, Raff." He turned towards the door, but found his way barred by Findlow, who didn't move.

"It would be manners to ask for use of my lodge, Salcan."

"Why?" Salcan snorted. "You can't stop me. Anyway, why should I tell you my plans?" He grabbed a shoulder pack off the floor and pushed past Findlow. "We'll cross now."

Veld stepped in front of him. "Not in the rain. It's far too dangerous." Salcan tried to push past him, but Veld stood firm. "You will wait until morning."

Salcan shoved him aside, grabbed Rathay by the tunic, and dragged him outside.

The rain got heavier and there was thunder in the distance. Behind the clouds, the sun was setting. It was quite dark.

Salcan pushed towards the gorge, hindered by everyone. At the gorge, he paused as he saw the bridge. He tightened his grip on Rathay's tunic and pushed him ahead.

Flashes of lightning lit up the ropes. Rathay gasped in shock as he saw the bridge for the first time.

Veld, Raff and Findlow continued trying to talk Salcan into waiting.

The lightning got closer and struck just over the hill. The air was charged.

The storm increased in ferocity and lightning hit the outcrop of rock that held the far side of the bridge. The rock shattered and the hand rope fell into the chasm. The shockwave hit them and the rock on the far side of the gorge slowly crumbled.

Salcan roared with rage and shoved Rathay towards the remaining rope. Rathay fell to the ground screaming with terror as he slid towards the edge.

Teema darted in, grabbed him and pulled him to safety.

Veld raised his voice above the roar of the storm. "Everyone into the dwelling. NOW!"

Wet and cold, they ran for shelter. Outside, the rain continued to pour down and the wind blustered around the dwelling.

Everyone changed into dry clothing. Those with extra shared and soon all were warm and dry. Arbreu was given clothes by an assortment of people, the trousers a little short and the tunic far too big.

Salcan and Rathay stood in a corner, avoiding everyone, ignoring offers of dry clothes, food and drink.

Veld brought Arbreu a platter of stew. "I've put your packs away safely. Everything in those packs is yours, but would you mind if I looked through them? You don't have to let me, but it may give me an insight into Slynd and the threat he poses."

"Without you, Veld, I'd be dead. You can have the lot. It'll mean nothing to me."

Veld laughed. "No, no, no. It's all yours, and you'll need possessions. I just wanted to see what Slynd thought was so important and I hope you'll tell me about your life with him."

Arbreu nodded. "What do you want to know?"

Veld laughed again. "Let's let's wait until we get back to the settlement. Quieter there. We'll have some space to think."

The fire was cheery. Someone thrust a drink into Arbreu's hand followed by another platter of hot stew. The noise diminished as they ate.

"Papa, was this the original path used to enter the land?"

Veld looked stunned. "No, Kirym. No! I created this path when Teema was a baby." He smiled as he remembered. "Teema wasn't walking when I met his family. We talked across the gorge for a few days and then I figured how to make the bridge. It took a lot of doing because I wanted it so it could be taken down from this side. Tarm carried Teema across in his shoulder pack. Teema kept trying to climb out. I thought they'd both fall.

"Then Teema's mama came across, but she had problems with the distance between the hand and foot rope. Half way along she stopped and couldn't or wouldn't go on. Tarm and I cajoled and encouraged but she couldn't move. I went to help, but before I got to her she slipped and fell. I didn't have a safety rope on her. I was going to destroy the path then, but the land needed new faces and families to keep it fresh and healthy. So I kept it open until Tarm and I built a proper bridge."

"Why didn't you put it on the map or in the memory box?" Kirym asked.

"It took a life, Kirym. I resolved to never to use it again, not even pass on the design. It's intrinsically dangerous. I rebuilt it now because I had no other option, but thankfully, it will never be rebuilt again. I don't think the original path came across this gorge."

Findlow woke Arbreu in the early morning. Outside there was silence. The storm had passed. Arbreu leaned up on one elbow and accepted the warm drink Findlow offered.

"We want to finish off quickly this morning," Findlow said. "The ropes need to be removed and they won't be easy because the rain has tightened the knots. Then home. It'll be good to get back, I miss my family. It's one thing to have adventures, but the comforts of one's own porch are unequalled anywhere in this world."

As they talked, some people were being quietly woken. It was still cool, the sun wouldn't be up for a while yet. "How can I help?" Arbreu asked.

"Before we do anything, Veld wants to talk to Salcan and Rathay," Findlow said. "But he needs to let Loul know what's happening. Teema and Bokum will handle that. There are more than enough people here for the work. Which group do you want to join?"

Arbreu glanced at Kirym, still asleep on a large platform on the far side of the dwelling. "I'll stay and help with the bridge if you don't mind. I saw the beginning and I'd like to see the end."

As they talked, most of those who were up grabbed cloaks and packs and slipped outside. Teema and Bokum waved to Arbreu.

"See you at home," Teema called softly.

A meal was prepared. As the smells drifted around the dwelling, those asleep started to stir and soon the talk and banter swelled, waking the others.

When everyone was eating, Veld and Findlow took food to Salcan and Rathay.

Both men looked embarrassed. They sat up and accepted the platters of food.

Veld sat in front of them. "The bridge is unusable. I intend to dismantle what is left of it. I'm pleased you'll be staying with us."

"Do we have any choice?" mumbled Rathay. "Only an idiot would even think of using that thing." He looked up, saw Arbreu and went red. "Sorry," he muttered.

Arbreu smiled. "I wouldn't have used it if there'd been another choice. So you're right, crazy, or very frightened of the dangerous men over there."

Salcan sat with his head in his hands. Then he shrugged, rolled back on to the set and pulled the rug over his head.

They watched him for a short time and then turned away.

"Let's work," Veld said. "I want to sit at my own fire tonight."

Rathay joined the workers at the gorge. The thinner rope had already been pulled up and coiled, the frayed ends blackened and burned where they had been around the rock on the far side. One of the leather sleeves had dropped into the gorge, the other still around the rock, both were irretrievable.

They started working on the knots. They had tightened with use and rain and it was a case of worrying them apart rather than untying them. It took time but as the sun rose, they succeeded. There were plenty of hands to help pull the heavy rope over, but as they began, it parted and half fell into the gorge. The other half was pulled up. Arbreu knelt to inspect the end. It too had been burned by the lighting. Findlow hunkered down beside him. "I'm glad you were over here before the lightning hit. It would have been horrid having to wait until we'd made more ropes."

"I'm more relieved I wasn't using it when the lightning struck."

Findlow grimaced. "I don't even want to think of that."

By the time the ropes were coiled and placed into packs for travelling, the day was beginning to heat up. They returned to the dwelling to collect their packs and weapons. Arbreu found his bow and arrows but couldn't find his packs. He asked Veld where they were.

Veld smiled and thrust an unknown pack into his arms. "Oh, I meant to tell you. I sent them with Teema. Hope you don't mind, trying to be careful." He pointed to some packs strewn across the floor, their contents scattered. They all looked similar to the one given Arbreu by Teema. "It appears someone wanted to know what you brought with you," Veld said softly.

Arbreu helped him re-pack the bags.

"We'll be back at our porch tonight," said Veld. "I hope you'll like your new home."

"I'm a bit nervous, all the new faces, but I'm looking forward to it. I've missed being part of a family."

Veld raised his voice over the hum of conversation. "Come

friends, we'll be more comfortable with a roof over our heads."

He set a fast pace although no one was left behind and there were plenty of stops. As they walked, people joined Arbreu to point out various favourite places they passed: a stream where large fish were caught; an orchard where fruit would be gathered in late summer; two huge nut trees that fed the family during the autumn.

Kirym showed him some of the healing plants and roots she collected and explained how she used them. He recognised some: lavender, rosemary, marigold and comfrey, but others and their uses were exotically strange.

Mekroe pointed out a hill in the distance where he and his friends went to shoot the fat birds that flew in during autumn.

Veld took time to point out paths that led off to other parts of the land, the quickest path to the waterfall on the north gorge, a path to the lakes and a path to the cave where the tokens had come from.

Many people mentioned the cave and everyone had different memories. The men spoke of the feasts and games they had there. The women talked of the beauty of the moon and the feeling within the cave. No two people had the same memories of their visits there and it gave Arbreu some insight about them.

As the afternoon progressed, Arbreu was joined by Findlow. Arbreu was intrigued by him. His skin colour set him apart, yet he wore a token indicating he was part of Kirym's family.

He explained he'd been headman of the dwelling by the lake where Slynd had last raided. He wanted to know what was left of his lodge, and didn't seem too dismayed when told that Slynd had sacked and destroyed the interior completely when he found it empty of people.

He told Arbreu a little of his history. "When I was a young man, a friend's sibling was to join with one of Veld's people and I was invited along. The hospitality here was amazing. One evening after accepting a lot of that hospitality, I staggered towards my dwelling and fell over a tree root. I rested there for a while and then found myself being helped up by an angel. Ahhh, a vision of perfection. I was intrigued by her beauty. When I woke I was convinced I'd dreamt her, but I saw her again in the morning. She looked right through me, acted as if she'd never seen me before, so perhaps I did dream. Then in the afternoon she came and talked to me, and yes she was special. We seemed to be two parts of the same day. We had a blissful walk by a stream. We picked flowers. It was wonderful. I asked if we could sit together at the feast that night and she agreed. She kissed my cheek before we parted. I was in heaven.

I got to the feast early. When she arrived, a visual feast herself, I pulled her to me for another kiss." He laughed quietly. "She slapped my face, threw a huge bucket of cold water over me, and walked away with her nose in the air.

Everyone thought it was hilarious.

I turned away and banged into her.

She couldn't stop laughing — I'd just tried to kiss her sister. They were identical, born on the same day.

I was embarrassed. I must have looked a sight. I could still hear her laughter as I changed into dry clothes and packed my possessions.

Grenin came and watched me as I stuffed the last of my things into my pack.

I was still too embarrassed to speak.

'If you're leaving, then, you're not the man I thought you to be,' Grenin said. 'To let two little girls chase you away, especially when one would like you to stay for good.'

I was amazed Natia wanted me to stay, but I wasn't sure

what to do next. Grenin was joined to Cindra, the sister who'd tried to drown me. Apparently Natia had kept them awake for the whole night telling them how wonderful she thought I was. Well, I thought I had it made."

He took a deep breath. "She made me wait four full seasons before she'd agree to join with me. She was worth the wait, though. After we joined, we travelled a bit before moving over the gorge to start a new settlement. It's good being back though. Nice to be able to talk over the problems with an equal, not that Natia isn't an equal, but it's good to share with other men."

They walked on in companionable silence for a while before stopping to let those at the back catch up.

"Arbreu, what would have happened had my family been at the lodge when Slynd turned up?" Findlow asked tentatively.

Arbreu was reluctant to tell him. He thought of Slynd's nasty temper, his viciousness, the murders. He remembered the anguish and horror of Slynd's victims as they watched friends and family being tortured and killed. He recalled the agony, hearing them wish their children had died sooner, that they had killed them themselves. He thought of dwellings burned, sometimes with the owners inside, and all of it too horrid to narrate. Finally he told of the anguish of attempting to bury some of the victims, and being forced by Slynd to walk away before he could finish the job.

Findlow was horrified. "I was very close to keeping my family there. I had an argument with Natia and stood on my dignity. I was annoyed that Veld hadn't come to talk to me himself, not thinking of the extra work he had with Raff's family here, that he too had lost family in the raid on Raff's. You see, I hadn't learned the lesson Grenin tried to teach me. Now, I don't think I'll ever forget it, although if you ever see me making the mistake again, I give you permission to knock some sense into me."

They walked on into the evening. Arbreu was joined by Mekroe who talked non-stop. He carried a large pack of ropes that had been used for the bridge. Arbreu offered to help him carry them, but he declined.

"I got to go on this trip 'cause I told Papa I could carry them, so I want to be sure he lets me join in with the things the men do. Up until now I've always had to stay home, or if I went, Kirym went too. This time, I got to go with the men. Even though Kirym was there, I was with the men." He rambled on. He was so earnest, Arbreu found himself smiling.

The moon was high when the path widened. Cooking smells filled the air. Everyone sped up, the talk increased and Arbreu realised they were at the end of the trip. He followed Mekroe round a big tree and saw the settlement set out in front of him. Lamps lit a large covered porch and a line of lights led off into the trees. He saw the shadow of a big dwelling there.

A few people waited on the porch. There was a lot of laughter, hugging and clicking of tokens.

Arbreu hung back, just watching.

A hand slipped into his and Kirym invited him onto the porch. As he dropped his pack with the others, Loul clicked his token and welcomed him. She took him into the dwelling and gave him a robe to change into.

Veld showed him where to hang his clothes.

They sat on the porch. Loul and Kirym brought platters of meat, vegetables and warm bread. It was the most delicious food Arbreu had ever tasted.

As he finished eating, he looked up to see the biggest man he'd ever seen standing at the edge of the porch looking down at him. He glared ferociously at Arbreu.

Kirym was over getting a drink. She turned, saw the giant

and launched herself at him squealing and laughing. "Sundas, I thought you were asleep. Come and meet Arbreu." She grabbed his hand and dragged him up where Arbreu was sitting.

Arbreu stood and still had to look up at him.

Sundas bent his knees so his face was level with Arbreu's and looked intently into his face. It was very disconcerting. He wasn't wearing a token so Arbreu knew that he wasn't part of the family.

Suddenly he grabbed Arbreu in a big hug, dropped him, grunted and went into the dwelling.

Arbreu gasped for breath.

Veld laughed. "He really likes you."

"I would hate him not to," said Arbreu with a sheepish grin. "He's not part of your family, is he?"

"Well, Sundas is one of the oddities Natia adopted. Since we returned from Raff's, he's cared for my oldest girl, Halse. So yes he is. He has two claims to be family."

Arbreu looked at the door Sundas had gone through and wondered. Everything here was different. The expression family was looked at in quite a diverse way here, and he suddenly felt that maybe he wouldn't be quite the *oddity* he feared.

14

Kirym Speaks

Although celebrations organised by Mama and Papa were always outstanding, the ceremony and following festival welcoming Arbreu to the family was really memorable.

The initial ceremony focused on Arbreu, Teema, Bokum and me, but everyone was involved in one way or another. Arbreu was welcomed first with speeches from the three headmen, then Mama, Bokum and Teema. Mekrar and some of her friends recited poetry. Some of it was funny, some should not have been recited, and one Mekrar composed made me cry. The musicians played their instruments and everyone sang. Later in the evening there was music and dancing. When the ovens and food pits were opened, we feasted until we were almost too full to move.

Arbreu met and clicked tokens with every member of the family. He was hugged and kissed by every woman and girl there, and was pleased when Teema and I took pity on him and dragged him away. We sat and talked, watching Bokum dancing with Zeprah until they dropped exhausted beside us. It was late when we returned to our porches.

The next day was cool and damp. When we had finished our first meal, Papa suggested we have a quiet family day. He took a large decorated box out of the big chest that held our most valuable possessions. He opened it and, taking out an empty page, began to write.

I took a handful of pages and settled down to read them. Arbreu joined me, intrigued by the writing and patterns over the pages.

"This is our memory box," I explained. "It contains the history and laws of our family. Papa writes what happens and adds to the laws if needed. Other things are added, healing recipes, information from other families, maps, all sorts of things really."

I showed Arbreu back through the pages to where I'd been born and a few pages further back to Mekrar and Mekroe's birth. He looked through the leaves, expressing amazement at the detail placed in them.

Mama joined us. "Isn't it magnificent? There's a lot of detail there, but all of it, even the law, is only there as a guide. Everything is open to interpretation and anyone can question a decision or law."

"Your history's really old," Arbreu said. "Some of these pages were written hundreds of seasons ago." He pointed to decorations across two pages he found near the back. "What do these represent?"

Mama glanced at them. "I'm not sure they mean anything," she said. "They're interesting though, I used some of them when I made Veld's festival tunic. I put a few pages together and copied the pattern over the back and front of the tunic."

She went to the chest and took out a package which, when opened revealed the highly decorated tunic Papa had worn the evening before. She spread it out and showed Arbreu the similarities between the tunic and the pages. She'd used coloured threads, beads and fringing to create a detailed abstract scene.

"So do you all learn your history, Kirym?" Arbreu asked.

I nodded. "Most of the questions we ask today are answered from the pages of our history."

Raff arrived to work on the stellon tip, the one piece of it he couldn't really describe in words. As he sketched and cut, he explained to Arbreu what the top of the stellon meant.

In the early afternoon, Zhins suggested we join her and her twins on the porch for some fresh air while the weather held. Sundas carried Halse out and laid her on a set.

As we sat under the watery sun, I asked Arbreu about his life before joining Slynd. He told us about the storm and finding his settlement under a landslide. Soon he had quite an audience. He was surprised there was such interest. He finished his tale and sat back, inviting someone else to take over.

Mama told everyone an old family story, and Mekrar followed with one of her favourites. "Have you heard it before, Arbreu?" she asked when she'd finished.

"No," he said. "Our stories are quite different."

"Oh do tell us one," I begged.

Everyone else added their encouragement, too.

He was reluctant, but eventually agreed when he realised I wasn't about to stop asking until he did.

"I'll tell you one of our family myths." He settled one of the Zhin's twins on his lap and began.

"There was a place where the flowers lived and the four winds rested. The colourful flowers danced and sang with the moonbeams and they lived together in a land where water flowed and everyone was happy.

High in the misty hills above the land lived a solitary monster. He hated the sound of laughter and he wanted the land to be silent. He spent many thousands of moons plotting to be rid of the happy colourful little flowers. But everything he tried failed and the flowers increased in number and created even more colour and beauty.

The monster prowled around the mountains plotting and planning, but to no avail.

Then one day, he found the place in the sky where water entered the land. He formed an evil plan. He spent many moons creating a huge wodge and used it to plug the hole where the water entered.

The flowers woke to a dry barren land and slowly their colour faded. They could no longer laugh or dance and as their laughter died, the moon came down to take her moonbeams back to live in the sky once more.

But the littlest moonbeam didn't go with the others. She ignored the call of the moon because she wanted to help the flowers regain their colours, laugh, sing and dance again. During the day while the moon slept, she searched for a way to take the flowers to a new home. At night, she hid so the moon couldn't find her.

The moon missed her little moonbeam and as the sun disappeared she travelled across the night sky searching for her.

One day, the moonbeam met the wind playing in the trees. "Please wind, could you take my flowers to another land so they can find water and get their colour back?"

The wind sighed. "I'd like to, but they're too heavy for me. Anyway, a breeze told me the whole world is colourless and waterless now."

The little moonbeam wouldn't be put off. A while later she saw a bird flitting through the sand hills. "Please bird, could help you take my flowers to another land so they can get their colour back?"

The bird thought about it for a long time. "I wish I could, but I can't. Other lands are many many days away, too far for me to fly. But I'll ask my friends for help."

The little moonbeam waited by the sand dunes for many days and finally the bird came back to her.

"My friends are all dying because they need water too. Even the trees we sit in are giving up. Look," she pointed. "The pod tree can no longer hold her branches to the sky. She's so weak even her pods are weighing her down."

The little moonbeam thought about this and had an idea. If she couldn't help the flowers, maybe she could help the pod tree. She gathered her flower friends and they went to see the pod tree.

The pod tree looked terribly sad and her pods and branches dragged on the ground.

The moonbeam and the flowers climbed the tree and pulled the weighty pods off the branches. Soon the tree was able to stand up straight with her boughs to the sky.

The pods sat on the ground and the sun slowly dried them out. After many days they popped open. The white seeds lying hidden inside them drifted away in the breeze and the dry husks curled up stiff in the sun.

The little moonbeam looked at the husks and had an idea. "Pod tree, can I have your pod husks to help save the flowers?"

"Of course," the pod tree said. "I have no need for them now."

The little moonbeam was excited. She and the flowers took three of the great husks to the sea and put them on the water. They floated. The moonbeam helped the flowers into the pods and they set off on the sea currents in search of a new home.

Up in the hills, the monster saw the flowers leaving and was angry. He had liked seeing the unhappiness he created. So he worked up his rage and he roared and he spat and he blew, and he created a huge storm with massive waves to overturn the pods. But the west-wind helped the pods stay ahead of the tempest and eventually the storm gave up.

The pods drifted along with the tides and the flowers spent the nights hiding the little moonbeam as the moon criss-crossed the sky looking for her. One night, the moon turned her sight down to the land and the water and spotted the pods on the current and turned to chase them.

But the little moonbeam saw land ahead and she reached out and pulled the pods towards it.

She searched frantically along the coast for a place to hide, but the cliffs were high and sheer. The birds told her of a big cave and the wind helped push the pods into it.

The moon lost sight of them, and she travelled far along the coast searching until the sun came up and drove her away.

In the cave, the pods were washed onto a ledge and the flowers climbed out and looked around. Alas they were trapped. High above them in the roof was an opening, but there was no way to reach it. They couldn't float out of the cave because the water kept washing in.

However the moonbeam had an idea. She stretched up, grasped the hole forming a bridge and the flowers were able to climb up into a new land. Just as the moon disappeared over the horizon, the moonbeam followed the last flower out of the cave.

The sun rose, and they saw this land was also colourless and without water.

"We must search, keep looking for your colour and then we can laugh, sing and dance again," the little moonbeam said.

She encouraged the flowers to explore their new land. They saw where the trees, bushes, lakes and streams had once been, but this land was lifeless and they couldn't find a place to settle.

Evening approached and the flowers looked for somewhere to hide their friend for the night. The sun found them a little cave and they all squeezed inside.

High above was a crack in the roof and the sun peeped in to say goodnight.

The moonbeam knew that if the sun could look in, then the moon could also. So she searched for a something to fill the hole. She could find nothing. It got later and later, the sky got darker and darker and in desperation, she pulled on a rock that protruded from the wall, hoping to break it off to plug the opening.

As the rock came away, cascades of colour flowed from the crack and the flowers were bathed once again in brilliant hues.

Now when the sun was saying goodnight to them, the moon peeped over the horizon eager to again begin searching for her little moonbeam. She saw the sun looking into the opening in the hill and she wondered what she was looking at. She raced across the sky to see, and when she found the small crack in the hillside, she peeped in.

She was overcome by the splendour of the flowers now bathed in their beautiful colours, and she wept. Her shimmering tears fell onto the land and filled the lakes and streams.

The plants, who had been hiding because there was no water, came out and dug their roots into the ground and began to grow again. The flowers laughed with glee, danced out of the cave and joined the trees and bushes in the soil.

The moonbeam said goodbye to her friends and the moon took her up into the sky again.

But every morning and every evening, both the sun and the moon peep into the cave to make sure the colours are still there so the flowers are never again threatened by any monster."

"Oh that was beautiful, Arbreu," I sighed as he finished. "What happened to the pods?"

He smiled. "They're waiting in case the monster finds them and tries to take the laughter and colour away again. Then they can again go and search for another place to live, and the moon will help them find another cave."

"That's a lovely story," Mama said. "You'll have to tell it again in winter when we sit around our hearth. Others too, so we can retain your history along with our own."

As Arbreu finished his story, the sun disappeared behind the clouds and the wind rose. The rain started, light at first but getting heavier very quickly. There was a flurry of activity as people returned to their own hearths, and we moved inside.

Papa brought Arbreu a flask and sat beside him. "I'd like you to write that out for me. I felt I was being reminded of something I heard long ago."

We ate in front of the huge fireplace that took up the centre of the dwelling and divided it into two rooms.

"It's an amazing idea," Arbreu said. "If ever I build a dwelling for myself, I'll put in a fireplace just like this one."

We sat in front of the fire quietly chatting about the family. Tant and Jorlenta were joining soon, but waiting until Harnita had her baby. Then the baby could be named at the same time and we could have a whole day of celebrations. It formed a special connection between the baby's family and the newly joined couple.

Papa leaned over to Arbreu. "Arbreu, when you were over the gorge, did you get a chance to have a look at the things in the bag Slynd buried?"

Arbreu shook his head. "No, I felt it'd mean little to me. I considered it the day before you built the bridge, but —" he shrugged. "— I thought I'd wait. Perhaps now's the time."

15

Teema Speaks

The rain started again and those who'd joined us ran for their porches. Sundas carried Halse inside and made her comfortable. I carried her rugs in. I chatted to Tarl for a short time as we ate and then picked up my cloak, planning to visit the single men's porch.

Arbreu grabbed my arm. "Don't go. Veld wants to look at the pack we found at Slynd's camp. We started this journey together. It'd feel wrong to continue it without you."

"I'd love to stay. Bokum should be here also."

Kirym brought over some platters of food. "He's helping Old Harby with something. I'll get him." She slipped out into the rain.

Veld placed the first of Arbreu's packs on the big table. Arbreu was untying the first knot when Kirym, Bokum and Old Harby walked in.

Bokum put his cloak on a set by the door. "What's going on? Kirym said I was needed urgently."

Kirym laughed. "It was the easiest way to get you out of the porch without you asking questions. Arbreu's opening his packs and he wants his brothers here to clean up the mess."

She climbed onto a set so she had a good view.

Bokum came close to the table, clicked tokens with Kirym and then turned to do the same to Arbreu and myself.

Arbreu chuckled as he continued to untie the knots on the pack. "I'm still not used to that. It has a good feel though. Makes me feel like family."

This wasn't really a pack, but the large fur from Slynd's camp. There were a few smaller skins wrapped inside. I leaned in to feel them. They were beautifully soft, softer than most cured skins I'd come across. Some I recognised, others I'd never seen before.

Kirym had her hands buried in the fur of a white long haired cat. "Oh, they're wonderful. You'll have to hide them. They'll make you the most eligible bachelor around."

Arbreu went bright red.

Kirym took a smaller fur over to show Halse. She rubbed it on her arm, but there was no response.

Again Halse appeared to be sleeping. Her token was quite grey. Kirym touched her face and leaned in to click her token.

I stiffened, expecting Kirym to collapse as happened when she last did that. However, this time there was no response.

From one of the carved boxes on the bench, Kirym took out three harkii nuts, ground them to a mash and fed them to Halse. Her colour returned slightly although she was still extremely pale.

Veld, Bokum and Old Harby talked about the quality of the skins and their value, but Arbreu's eyes followed Kirym.

When Kirym returned to the table, Mekroe and Bokum took the skins to one of the sets and Arbreu opened the next pack. This one held the items he'd collected while caring for Zelar and at Slynd's camp.

Loul picked up the length of woven material and held it to her cheek. "It's very good quality, Arbreu. I don't know whether Slynd had good taste to steal it or better taste to leave it for you."

"Generally he only left broken trash at his camps. The occasions when better stuff was left, it was because he was angry. He'd insist we leave immediately. The things that weren't packed would be left. I always thought he demanded the men leave behind something they were particularly fond of, or perhaps to reduce a growing power or threat. Some sort of loyalty test. What was more important, Slynd or the item? If you chose wrong, you died. Then he seized the item as a memento. It seems he took it anyway."

Loul picked up a flask and studied it. It was made of wood and the outside was intricately carved with birds and trees. She looked around and quietly almost surreptitiously put it down, pulling the length of material over it.

Her movement caught Arbreu's eye.

He pulled the material back and picked up the flask. "You recognised it, didn't you? Who owns it?"

She looked embarrassed. "It's yours, Arbreu. It was left at the camp and everything from there is yours."

"No! It was owned! I'm not a thief. I wish I could return it all. I know most of the owners are dead. None of it should be here. Who owns it?"

"That's noble of you. If you hand it to Findlow, he'll be very pleased. It was a favourite of his."

Arbreu nodded. He tipped out an assortment of arrowheads and a few spear tips. Next to them he placed a quiver of arrows, a knife, rope and some needles and thread. He picked up a number of arrows and handed them to me. They were the ones I'd shot over the gorge to him.

I was amazed. "You must have kept every arrow I shot over."

"They were my sanity, Teema. My hope for the future. With them, I knew I could survive. I planned to return them to you some day. It gave me something to dream of, to hope for."

I looked at the items on the table. He had saved everything we'd sent over to him. I suddenly understood how desperate he must have been over there by himself. I handed the arrows back to him. "I gave them to you. They're yours to keep. I hope they give you good luck with your hunting."

He returned them to his quiver and grasped my arm. We turned our attention back to the table.

Amongst the items he had were a few I didn't recognise, a knife with a broken handle, a carved wooden flask and some wooden platters edged in green. The items were all finely made, but the knife caught my eye. It was very sharp and would be great with a new handle. It had an intricate pattern of waves and a boat, sails billowing in the wind engraved on it. There were two more boats in the background. I decided I'd carve a new handle for the blade so Arbreu could use it. I slipped it casually into my pocket.

Arbreu picked up the last bag and opened it. This was the bag he got from the lap of the mummified corpse. It was big and very heavy. I was surprised he'd been able to carry this, the skins, the pack we'd sent him and the fush grass.

The package on the top was wrapped in linen, those beneath it in thin hide. Arbreu opened the first. It contained a pile of coloured stones and exotic shells, some with chains attached. Some looked as if they'd been gouged from wood.

Veld went very quiet. "Bokum, go an' get Raff, I'll get Findlow." He pulled Bokum to the door and they were gone.

Loul took a deep breath. "Arbreu, these are from the

stellon. Look, you can see where the wood grew around some of them." She put her hand to her mouth. "Oh, Veld should have explained to you." She grabbed my arm. "Teema, this isn't his decision. He's being premature. Go stop him, quickly!"

"No, don't." Arbreu turned to Loul and took her hands. "Veld did what I'd have asked him to do had I known. They belong to Raff, I'm happy I can return them." He looked at the stones and shells. "They're very pretty aren't they? I can see why they're so important to Raff's family."

"They're more than trinkets, Arbreu. These are their memories. Look each one is different and Raff recognises every single one and he knows who they represent. If you hand Raff a blue stone, he can tell you every family member who had a blue stone as part of their memory, or any other colour. These are his family," said Loul.

"I can see the importance to Raff," Old Harby said, "but not to Slynd. Why would he take them?"

Loul nodded as she picked up a band of red stones. "Slynd knew that Raff and his family valued them. Remember he had visited them and he'd heard Raff talk of his history, and the stellon was revered. I think Slynd takes what he thinks others value. It gives him a feeling of power."

Arbreu grimaced. "I remember these green stones," he said picking them up. "Slynd gave them to Pelak, a reward for fighting well. When they went missing, Slynd suggested he'd dropped them as we travelled. He was insulted his gift had been treated so casually. Pelak was quite scared. He was insistent he couldn't have dropped them. Then Slynd asked if someone else had admired them. That caused a huge fight. No one died; Slynd stopped the fight saying they were boring him. He made some of the others share their gifts with Pelak. It caused a lot of resentment. We knew there was a thief, but no one imagined it was Slynd. I thought it was Bextan, his right hand man. Mind you, even if we'd suspected Slynd, no one would have said anything. That would invite an early death."

The door opened and Veld came in. He was alone. "Arbreu, I've been a little presump–"

"Veld," Arbreu interrupted. "Veld, I know. You were right to get Raff." He stepped onto the porch, ushered everyone inside and invited them to the table.

Raff saw the stones and sat down, gazing at them. "How can we thank you? You've returned our history, our legacy from the past for our future." There were tears in his eyes.

Arbreu leaned over the table and pushed the woven material aside. He took the carved flask from under it and handed it to Findlow. "I believe this is yours," he said.

Findlow looked bewildered, then recognised the flask and took it. He put his arms around Arbreu and hugged him.

Arbreu smiled, patted his back awkwardly. They turned back to the table.

"Well, let's see what else Slynd left us." Arbreu opened the next package. There were more stones and some gold jewellery.

Soojee picked up one of the pieces. "This belonged to an old woman from The Flatlands. She inherited it from her grandmamma and it was old then. These must have belonged to her family. If Slynd had it, I imagine they're all dead now."

"Then you take it, Soojee. You must be the nearest kin."

"No, Arbreu," she said. "There's no blood tie. In The Flatlands, families came from many places. I only recognise the brooch because it was such an attractive piece and she was so very proud of it."

"Loul," said Arbreu, desperate to find an owner. "Was she of your family?"

Loul shook her head. "You have to accept the inevitable,

Arbreu. You can't give away everything you brought over with you."

Arbreu chose another package, this one wrapped in a finely woven flax bag. As he opened it, more jewellery fell out. None of this was recognised although Arbreu thought he remembered seeing one of Slynd's men with a piece far to the south. He picked up a neck-piece of gold with green stones in it and turned to Loul and Veld. "With your permission, I'd like Kirym to have this."

Veld looked at Loul who nodded. "That's generous of you, Arbreu. She'll value it."

Kirym inspected it closely. Then she laughed and hugged Arbreu, clicking his token. "I love it. Thank you so much. Whenever I wear it, I'll think of you. It's the colour of your eyes."

There was a lot of chatter as everyone admired it.

Loul went to a smaller chest by the wall and pulled out a length of material. It was dark blue and shot with green. "I was thinking I'd use this to make you a new festival dress," she said to Kirym. "It'll pick up the colour of your tokens, but the jewels on the neck piece will fit in also."

While the women talked about styles, Veld, Mekroe and Bokum set a meal on the table.

After we'd eaten, Arbreu and I walked to the door and stood there breathing the early evening air. Part of the sky was clear and the stars shone brightly.

Kirym joined us, taking Arbreu's hand as she looked up. "I love looking at the stars. They're so friendly and they tell so many stories." As she spoke, a star shot across the heavens.

"I wonder where it's going."

Both Arbreu and I laughed.

We all returned to the table. The next package was lighter in weight, but bulky. As Arbreu opened it, the items started to fall out. There was a sharp sob from Natia and everyone looked at her. She had her hand across her mouth and tears ran down her face as she stared at the table.

In front of her was a carved wooden plaque. The deep relief carving was of a wood scene with a woman in the centre. Fruits and birds were carved around the top of the frame, animals and flowers across the bottom. The detail was exquisite.

Natia was still crying and Loul put her arm around her.

"Oh, I'm being silly, but I didn't think to pack it and once I was here I thought I'd never see it again. I so regretted leaving it behind."

"It's magnificent," Loul said. "Where did you get it?"

Natia smiled through her tears. "Findlow carved it. All those seasons I made him wait for me and most of the time I wouldn't let him visit me in the evening, or I'd send him off early. So he made this for me. He gave it to me on the night we joined, and I've kept it safe ever since. When we left the settlement, I didn't completely understand the danger and I thought we'd return at some stage, so I left it. Slynd must have taken the dwelling apart piece by piece. It was so well hidden."

I looked at Findlow with a new appreciation for this hidden talent. He smiled bashfully and gave Natia a hug. "Silly, now you've told them the last of my secrets."

Arbreu turned back to the package and emptied the rest of the items onto the table. There were bits of jewellery set aside for various family members and a few pieces were put by to query ownership.

Another package was opened. This contained more jewellery and a set of small creamy white carved bowls which, according to Sundas, came from the massive horns of a huge animal that lived in the northeast. He told us it had huge ears and the horns grew near its mouth. He said the animal was very old to get horns that big, older even than Harby. Silence followed this revelation. I wondered more about Sundas' life before he met Findlow and Natia.

The bowls were put aside and the next package opened. This was a number of smaller packages wrapped together. Sitting on the top was a yellowish grey token. I had the impression the owner was distant.

Kirym picked it up. "It's Lantiah's."

Veld looked at her, his eyebrow raised. He turned to Mekroe. "Son, can you go and get her and Armos, please."

No one spoke while we waited for him to return.

Veld invited them to sit, explained what we'd found and handed Lantiah her token. The colour deepened when she reached out and touched it.

She pulled her hand back and looked up at Armos. "Oh my goodness, I'm not sure what to do with it." She turned to Arbreu. "It's not that I don't appreciate you returning it, I really do, but I don't, I — I have another — I don't really want the memories this one brings with it. The connection scares me." She turned to Loul. "Is it possible to destroy it? Would that affect me in any way?"

"I'm not sure. It connects with Slynd's token and we've long said he was dead. But this is beyond my knowledge. Zelriff may know."

Tarl was already putting on his cloak. "I'll go and get her," but as he reached the door it was flung open and Peet rushed in. "Papa, Harnita's in labour. It started very quickly and the pains are coming fast. I think she's having problems."

Loul grabbed her birthing kit and cloak and left immediately with Peet, Armos and Lantiah.

Everyone else returned to the table and Arbreu opened the next package. Another token and holder fell out, this one more grey than yellow and streaked with black.

Veld looked nonplussed, but Kirym laughed. "It's a shame Lantiah left. This is the answer to her safety, Papa. It's

Slynd's token."

"You can't know that. You were a baby when he left."

Kirym shrugged. "When I look at it, I see Slynd. It's the only answer. He took it when he left here, but he didn't wear it after that. Even so, he'd want to keep it safe. Anyway it looks similar to Lantiah's, and who else could own it?"

Veld shook his head. "You may be right, Kirym, but even if you are, what do we do with them?"

"Take them to the cave. That's where they came from. Harnita's baby will be named and Tant and Jorlenta will join. We can return the tokens the following day."

She turned back to the table as Arbreu opened the next package. Hundreds of tokens cascaded out, all of them dark grey.

Dead! Dead tokens. Everyone was speechless.

Veld rubbed his face. "What are these? Where'd he get them? Why would he want them?"

There was a long silence as everyone stared at the tokens.

"Mama says he takes what others value," Kirym said. "He doesn't appreciate things until he sees how important they are to their owners. Remember the gifts he gave his men? He didn't have to give them away, and yet he did. Then he stole them back. Natia's plaque is here, but not her woven rugs, which are exquisite. If the plaque had been sitting on a table, he'd probably have left it. Because it was hidden, he took it."

"But Lantiah's token wasn't hidden. He took that," I said.

"It's perceived value, Teema. Lantiah had nothing when she came to us, she'd been a slave. Her token was the first thing that belonged only to her, and she loved it. It suited her. I remember someone saying that Slynd felt he did her a favour in joining with her. He implied she'd be nothing without him, unwanted by everyone else. But the token was hers. It gave her an identity she grew with. And above all she treasured it."

Veld nodded. "It makes sense." He pointed to the tokens on the table. "But what about these? Where'd he get them from?"

"The burial sites," Kirym said softly. "He robbed our dead."

Veld turned to Harby. "You're keeping quiet, Harbs, what do you think?"

The old man sat looking at the tokens. "You know as Kirym said it, I knew she was right. Her instinct for tokens is unlike any I've seen before." He picked up a token. "Even in death, tokens retain the characteristics they had while alive. You see this one has an inclusion in it. It looks like a fault. When the owner lived it was mid blue and the inclusion glowed much lighter." He looked up at Veld. "It belonged to my mama. She wore it in death. Kirym is right. Slynd robbed our dead."

There was silence at this revelation.

The door opened and Peet and Armos entered, beaming.

"I'm a grandpapa again," Armos said. "It's a good feeling. He's the image of Peet as a baby."

"Oh dear, I must pass my sympathy on to Harnita," I joked.

Everyone laughed.

Armos handed a flask to Harby. "Your first great-grandson, Papa."

Almost everyone fell asleep waiting for Loul to return with the real news of Harnita's baby. Arbreu and I sat on the porch talking and watching the stars until she joined us soon after the moon began to fall towards the horizon.

I told her about the tokens and Kirym's conclusions.

She thought for a while. "We can only be guided by what's in front of us and Harby recognised his Mama's token. Kirym is almost definitely right. She has good instincts. Her idea of taking them to the cave is sensible. What happens there may mean something or nothing. What else was in the package?"

Arbreu laughed. "We didn't go any further than that. More important things happened. I wonder how Slynd would feel if he knew these things have less value than he thought. The people are important, and tonight they got in the way of his treasures. It's sad really, he already had the people."

16

Teema Speaks

We woke early as is the way with large families; when the early birds waken, everyone does. We ate on the porch in the sunshine. Veld, Arbreu and Peet had been up earlier and the outside oven was already lit. Many people brought their early meal to eat around the gathering porch, and by the time we had finished, everyone was there.

Veld passed on the news of Peet and Harnita's baby and the planned trip to the cave.

As he sat down, Raff stood. "Veld, Salcan disappeared overnight. All of the large earthenware storage flasks have been opened and the water in them is a strange colour."

Veld frowned. "Don't use the water or the flasks. We can replace the flasks, there are plenty in storage. You'll need to check if anything else in your dwelling has been interfered with."

Almost everyone accepted the news with level-headed calm, Rathay the only one to raise his hand.

Veld acknowledged him.

"Why have you let that crazy man loose?" he asked. "Why wasn't he watched? He could do all sorts of irrational things. How could you let this happen?"

Raff stood to answer, but I grabbed his arm and pulled him back. "That's a question you should answer, Rathay," I said. "How could you let it happen? You were friends with Salcan, closest to him. You obviously knew he was unbalanced and yet you supported him. If you'd approached us with any concerns, we might have been able to help him." I turned to Veld. "Veld, I'd like to make a formal complaint to the Judicial Summit about Rathay's behaviour. He may have put us all in danger."

Comments buzzed around the clearing.

Behind me, Loul quietly explained to Arbreu what this meant. "This is almost unprecedented and requires Veld take immediate action. It's going to be interesting."

Rathay looked around, suddenly unsure now he no longer had the advantage.

Veld stood. "Very well, we'll appoint the Summit members now."

Rathay opened his mouth and closed it again.

Veld waited.

"I'm not part of your family, Veld. Your Summit can't judge me."

"Yes we can, Rathay. You're in our land."

"But I'm part of a different family."

Veld shrugged. "Yes, but when you came to live here, your headman agreed on your behalf that you'd live by our rules. This is an important aspect of old law."

Rathay swallowed. "Findlow, you can't let him do this."

Findlow thought for a moment before shaking his head. "The old law takes precedence, Rathay. I have no power to change it. I'll humbly ask though, that I be allowed to sit on the Summit to watch over your interests. Also I insist you be allowed to have someone to talk for you, of course."

Rathay looked relieved.

Loul raised her hand. "I'll speak for Rathay, if he'd like. Unless someone else would champion him, in which case I'd withdraw my offer."

Rathay looked around hopefully, but most people had a sudden interest in their feet. "Could you talk for me, Natia?"

Natia smiled at him, but shook her head. "I'd like to, Rathay, but Findlow's on the Summit and it'd be a conflict of interest."

"But Veld is on the Summit, so how can Loul speak?"

Findlow didn't even bother to stand to answer him. "They have different rules here for Judicial Summits. Here, she's allowed."

Rathay looked sick.

Then a voice called from the back of the gathering porch. "I'll speak for Rathay." Kirym stepped through the crowd and stood beside him.

Rathay was speechless and then turned to Findlow. "She's a child. And she's Veld's daughter."

This time Kirym answered him. "I may be a child, but I want to help you. Do you want help? I have no worries if you don't, but you do need it."

There was a long silence. Then Rathay looked down. "I don't suppose I have any choice," he said in a small voice.

Kirym beamed.

"I'll help her." There was a gasp from the crowd as I spoke. I stepped off the covered porch and joined Kirym. Rathay looked totally demoralized.

Kirym raised her hand.

"I see you, Kirym."

"Papa, could the Summit be delayed until Raff's dwelling

has been checked and cleaned?"

Findlow moved over to Raff and Veld and they talked quietly together.

"Harby, is there a precedent for this?" asked Veld.

Harby shrugged. "It's never come up before. It would be up to the Summit to decide on the correct protocol."

Kirym spoke again. "As long as there isn't a precedent, I think delaying the summit would be best for everyone."

"That's up to the Summit, Kirym," Harby said. "But why?"

Kirym smiled brightly. "It's going to rain tomorrow and Raff's family will have no home until their dwelling is thoroughly checked. If we do it today, they'll be more comfortable and everyone will be less crowded."

Harby talked to Veld and Findlow, then stood and addressed the porch. "We'll accept Kirym's suggestion. The Summit is adjourned until Raff's dwelling is checked."

Rathay moved away from everyone and sat down by himself. He didn't look happy.

Groups around the porch made their plans for the day, most to do with cleaning and sorting Raff's dwelling and possessions.

Veld asked me to destroy the flasks. I suggested Arbreu, Mekroe and Bokum help. I was surprised when Rathay asked if he could join us.

"Why?" I asked bluntly.

He hesitated. "Well, maybe you were right. Perhaps I should've watched Salcan closer or talked to someone. I didn't know he'd put stuff in the water. I just thought about it and, well that was nasty."

I was collecting food for the trip when Kirym joined me

carrying a pack, a bow and quiver of arrows. "I'm coming too. I heard Rathay ask. We can get to know him."

"Why did you offer to help him?" Bokum asked.

"He's scared and needs a friend. I don't think he's bad. He just needs to think before he speaks. He has tried to be Salcan's friend and Salcan manipulated him. He could become a great asset to us."

I looked fondly at Kirym. She had an amazing ability to see the best in everyone.

We took food, scrubbing brushes and cleaning powders, although I intended that we mainly use sand to scrub the flasks. We piled the flasks onto two of the oldest stretchers, secured them with fishing net and carried them to a small stream.

Everyone started scouring the flasks. It was fun. Though it was still early in the season, it was warm and sheltered there. While they scrubbed, I walked away from the stream and dug a hole. I returned and we sat with our feet in the warm water eating and talking.

We finished cleaning the flasks, loaded them back on the stretchers and carried them to the hole.

"Well, this'll soon be the end of the job." I took a rock and started to pound the first flask to powder. There was silence around me. I looked up.

Everyone stared at me as if I was crazy.

Bokum spoke first. "Why are you smashing them?"

"They may have contained poison."

"But we scrubbed them," Mekroe spluttered. "We scrubbed the poison out of them."

"Alright," I said. "Fill one and have a drink."

Mekroe looked at me with his mouth open.

"No? Anyone?"

No one moved.

I smiled. "Well, I wouldn't drink out of them either. Look

the thing is, the flasks may have contained poison. We scrubbed them, but what if we missed something? We could bury them, but things resurface. This way, they're as clean as we can make them, but they're also totally destroyed. It's safer and we don't ever have to worry about them again. If you've a better suggestion, let's have it."

No one answered, but Rathay picked up a rock and started to pound away at a flask. Everyone joined in. As the pieces were ground to powder, I shovelled it into the hole.

Rathay laughed. "You know that felt really good."

There were murmurs and smiles of agreement.

Mekroe looked at the hole. "There's a fair bit of filling in to do, why'd you dig it so deep?"

For an answer, I handed him a stretcher. "The poison may have spilt onto those, and I've seen children suck them. So they go in also. Why do you think I got the oldest two I could find?"

The stretchers were ripped to shreds and put into the hole. I started to shovel the soil over the remains, but Kirym knelt by the pile and pushed the soil in with her hands and arms. She was helped by Mekroe and soon they were both covered with dirt. We all had a fine covering of dust over us so we walked back to wash at the stream.

I lit a small fire to heat some water.

It was still warm in the shallows but cooler than it had been. We quickly washed and dressed.

"Teema, why didn't we throw the flasks into the stream? They'd've been battered to pieces by the rapids and that would've saved us all this work."

"What if they sank before the rapids, and in a place where they could be retrieved?"

Mekroe reddened. "Oh, I didn't think of that." He looked sideward at Rathay who was sitting apart from us. "Can you really help him, Kirym?" he asked softly.

She nodded. "Remember what Harby says. 'Nothing is usual'. I've as much chance as anyone, maybe even more. They may give me leeway because I'm young. Mind you, Papa knows I'm aware of the workings of our law, so he'll be hardest on me."

I hugged her. "You'll make a great headwoman one day, Kirym."

"Not likely with four older brothers and sisters," she said laughing.

I took a platter of food and sat beside Rathay.

"Hot, isn't it." he said, ignoring the food.

I nodded. "You're planning to run, aren't you. Before the summit meets."

He nodded. "Thinking about it. I've no chance in front of them."

"Kirym can't defend you if you're not there. Anyway, there's nowhere for you to go."

"You made the complaint about me, Teema. Why did you then offer to help me?" Rathay's eyes were filled with distrust.

"I complained because someone needed to. Findlow and Veld would've talked to you about Salcan once everyone was settled. When you challenged them on their handling of him, I decided to bring it to a head. It's nothing personal. I've no dispute with you, just your actions. Now we've a chance to sort it out. My goal — no! Our goal! Our goal is to have harmony. Now you'll make friends and we'll get that. I'm helping because it's partly my fault. I didn't offer you friendship earlier. I didn't suggest a way to help sort out the problems. My mistake, I'm correcting it." I smiled at him. "You can have good friends here, and we'll sort it."

Rathay took a deep breath blinking back tears.

I handed him the platter. "If I was in your position, I'd want Kirym talking for me. She'll do you proud. There's a case to answer, but you'll live through it and we'll support you."

He smiled tentatively. "I hope you're right."

It was late afternoon when we returned to the settlement. The children were playing games and the younger men had set up a target for their bows and arrows.

We joined Sundas on the gathering porch. Halse was asleep again and looking far too thin. Sundas kept checking her, adding and removing rugs.

Kirym went into the dwelling and brought back a mortar, pestle and a handful of harkii nuts. I helped her to grind a few of them, and she and Sundas fed them to Halse. There was absolutely no improvement in her.

Kirym ground the rest of the harkii and made Sundas eat them.

I raised my eyebrow when she returned to sit by me.

"Sundas needs support too," she said softly. "He puts a lot of energy into caring for Halse. He has hardly slept over the last few nights. It takes its toll."

Rathay sat by himself watching the bow practise. Kirym went over and asked him to join us. They argued but eventually he came with her.

As they sat down, Kirym turned to me. "How do we convince Rathay we want to be his friends?"

At Kirym's words, he blushed.

"You're as much a part of this family as I am, Rathay," Arbreu said. "You know my story and if anyone wasn't welcome here, it'd be me. I know it's hard with the Summit coming up, but for goodness sake, what's the worst they'll do to you? They want to sort this out too. If you isolate yourself, you'll be very lonely. No one wants that."

Rathay nodded thoughtfully.

Mekrar plonked herself down between Rathay and Arbreu. "What's your defence for the summit? It's better to have one."

"I'm not really sure. I guess they'll want to know what I knew of Salcan's plans, which wasn't much. He avoided me after we returned from the gorge, and I didn't know much before then either."

Mekrar shrugged. "Why do you keep challenging the head men?"

"I guess it was the way I was brought up. My folks didn't get on and whatever Papa did, Mama would criticise. She challenged and ridiculed every decision he made. My brother and I copied. Eventually Papa left. A while later, Mama died, my brother walked away and I was alone. I realised I had no friends. Those I thought were helped me get into trouble and left me to take the blame. The community kicked me out, but I didn't ever fit in there anyway. I had no one, and they were all one family. I heard that Findlow's family took in others and asked if I could join. Once there, I guess I criticised to get attention. It worked, although, well it was the wrong sort of attention."

Kirym nodded and smiled. "That's helpful. Why did you want to go to Findlow's settlement when Papa built the bridge?"

"It was Salcan's idea. He suggested we start a new family. He said someone was trying to kill him and would get me too. He told me some things about Kamdra's death."

Kirym went very still. "What did he say about it?" she asked.

"He said Kamdra had been poisoned. Said that was why he lost all the blood, the poison affected his lungs. He was scared he'd die the same way. It seems a bit implausible now I look back, but at the time," he shrugged. "Well, I was eager to believe what he said about the headmen, that they were evil." He laughed. "That's the word he kept using, evil. He said he could feel the evil here and we had to get away from it. Tindra wanted to come too, well that's what he said, anyway. Then just before we went there he said you'd all turned her against him and she wouldn't come after all. Initially he said it was my settlement and I should be headman, but when we got to the bridge, he changed. That was the first time I saw that rage. It left me feeling — well — frightened. But that bridge. It was terrifying. I was so glad when even he realised we couldn't use it. When we got back here, Salcan didn't want me as a friend any more. He said I'd let him down and now he had no one. But that was stupid really, he had Tindra. It'll be harder for her and the baby now. She's still getting over Kamdra's death. Now she has no one."

"She has all of us, Rathay," Kirym said quietly. "We're her family. She'll never be alone."

"If I'd talked to Findlow, Salcan may not have left. Maybe I can help Tindra too. Everything Salcan said was a lie. I realise that now."

"Not everything," Kirym said. "Anyway I'll talk to Papa and Old Harby,"

Rathay looked up sharply.

Kirym laughed. "Some things shouldn't be said in an open forum. They need to be mulled over in advance. Papa will ask some questions and the Summit will talk together. Then when they meet tomorrow, they can move quickly to resolve any problems.

"Who'll be on the summit?" Arbreu asked.

"I'm not completely sure, but Papa obviously because he's headman. Old Harby, he has the ancient knowledge of the land, and Findlow because he's your headman, Rathay. Raff too. He's Salcan's headman and even though Salcan's gone, he still needs to be cared for. It'd be far too easy to blame him completely because he's not here. They'll add another to give an uneven number, probably Armos or Grenin. If you wish, you can request someone else, but it's a good group."

"How did you learn the law, Kirym?" asked Arbreu.

"My first memories are of listening to the stories from the memory box. Then Mama taught me to read. It's my favourite thing to do when it's raining. I realized there was a rhythm to the stories, a pattern. They tell of the past, but also the future. There are principles there, the values everything is based on. I understood why and that was the most important thing — why!"

The food pits were opened and Zeprah brought over a platter of meat. Mekrar and Arbreu got an assortment of other dishes for us to share. It was pleasant sitting with my friends.

"Sundas, tell us more about the monster with horns in its mouth? The horns that Arbreu's carved mugs came from. Have you seen one?" Mekrar was being mischievous, her eyes twinkled, although she sounded serious.

"I saw a family of them when I was very little," Sundas said gravely. "Even the babies were big. The horns are beside the mouth, not in it, Mekrar. It's the old full grown male that has the huge horns. By themselves the horns stand taller than me. Mama called them imantas. They had big ears and could hear well, and long noses too. Mama said that it could smell things from a long way off. We stayed upwind and watched them. It was fun, they were a big family. They found a pool and let the babies play in the water. They squirted water at each other. Mama said that they were mamas and their daughters and babies. A big male came close to them. His horns were long. His ears were all ragged around the edge. The biggest mama chased him away. They make a huge noise at each other. A bigger male came and she let him stay close, but not too close. Then Mama said the wind was going to change and we had to leave."

Mekrar picked up a stick and drew a picture in the dust of a person's head with oversized ears, a long nose, and horns sticking out from its cheeks. She was nearly purple trying not to laugh.

Arbreu glanced at the picture and rubbed his foot through it. "I haven't seen them, but I've heard of them. Sundas must have travelled many seasons to get to their territory. By all accounts they are massive."

Mekrar went bright red. "I'm sorry, Sundas, I didn't believe you. I was rude."

Sundas patted her on the head. "If I hadn't seen them, Mekrar, I wouldn't have believed me either. It was a funny picture, but they don't really look like that."

Kirym leaned against him. "Sundas if I write about your imantas, will you draw a picture of one and we'll put it in the memory box. It should be there because it's your memory."

He beamed at her. "I'll try, Kirym, but I've never drawn stuff before."

She smiled up at him. "I'll help you draw it and you can help me write about it."

The sun set and lamps were lit. The musicians brought out their instruments and everyone joined in the singing. Mekroe's pipe soared above the general noise and everyone stopped to listen. He played a quick bright tune and then slowed the pace. The mournful refrain made one want to cry.

His next melody was brighter and Armos sang. It was a funny song about how the sun and moon argued. The sun stamped away in anger. He tried to return to apologise, but the moon also wanted to express regret and she followed him. So they chased each other, but stayed on opposite sides of the world, and only occasionally did the moon catch a glimpse of her lover, but he was always looking in the other direction.

As Armos finished, I asked Arbreu to sing something from his home settlement. He was reluctant, but we all insisted.

He asked Mekroe to accompany him and started singing. His voice was soft and powerful. The chorus was simple and fun and soon we were all able to join in. The last note drifted away and everyone clapped and cheered.

The cheering died and I heard a strange sound. I turned to see Halse, her body wracked with convulsions.

Sundas knelt by the set trying to stop her from falling off.

Loul and Veld rushed to help, Loul pulling at the pouch at her waist. She took a packet out, opened it and placed a pinch of the powder from it onto Halse's tongue. Moments later the seizure stopped and Halse lay on the set with her eyes open, staring up at the sky.

Soojee, and Natia helped Loul work on Halse's unresponsive body, even trying to breathe life back into her.

Loul was crying as eventually they stopped and sat back.

Natia straightened Halse's arms, closed her eyes and pulled the rug over her.

Sundas looked at Loul and then at Halse. He put his head down on the set and cried.

I looked round, stood up and walked out of the settlement.

<h1 style="text-align:center">17</h1>

Kirym Speaks

I found Teema soon after dawn. He was asleep in a hollow under a large fallen tree. I suspected he'd be here. Last summer, just before Halse went to visit Raff and Soojee for the winter, they had brought me here for a picnic. It was a special place for them. This was where Teema asked Halse to join with him.

He looked exhausted. I think he'd just fallen asleep when I found him, so I waited. The rain started soon after I arrived. I spread his cloak and some fush grass over him to keep him dry.

Although we all knew it would happen sooner or later, everyone was upset when Halse died. She hadn't been eating and had spent less and less time awake. Over the last few days, she had hardly woken at all and if it hadn't been for the care given her by Sundas, Mama and Natia, she'd have died much sooner.

Sundas was devastated. He'd cried late into the night until

Mama and Findlow concocted an infusion of tea, herbs and skafarhn, a powerful spirit Findlow made from grains, to make him sleep.

It was only just light when I woke Mama and told her I knew where Teema was.

The sun would have been reaching the top of its journey when Teema woke and sat up. At first he didn't see me, but then he felt his cloak over him. I crawled in next to him under the tree trunk and held his hand. We sat quietly for a long time.

"I should never have asked her to join with me. I was so selfish. I had big dreams. Illusions of grandeur," he said bitterly. "Joined to her, I had far more chance of being headman either here or at a new settlement. But to do what I wanted, she'd have to accept more responsibility. She needed more knowledge. She wouldn't have gone to Raff's if it hadn't been for that."

"She'd wanted to go for a long time, Teema. She had her own dreams."

He talked on as if I hadn't spoken. "I thought it would help me belong. I always felt different, apart, like I didn't fit in here," he paused. "But I did. Loul and Veld made sure of that. I was their son even before Papa died. Look how I thanked them. I endangered their daughter, and she died." He frowned. "It's not that I didn't love her, I didn't love her enough. Even when she was hurt, I went on with my life as if it didn't matter. Look at Sundas. Now that is love. Not even related and he did everything I should have. It was so easy to leave it to him." He sounded very bitter.

I squeezed his hand. "Had you tried to take over, Sundas would have fought you. It was his gift to her, to you and to us. You couldn't have taken that away from him. It would have been unkind." I thought for a moment. "He is related, though. He adopted Halse, all of us really. We're his family and he'd have done it for any of us. That was his way of belonging, although Halse was special to him. He'd have felt guilty if he'd allowed anyone else to care for her, even you. He blames himself that she died."

Teema stared at me, his mouth open. "But — but it's because of him she survived so long. How can he blame himself?"

Sometimes Teema was thick.

"He feels he let you down, that's why you left."

"What! That's ridiculous. Of course he didn't!"

"He knows you stepped aside to let him to care for her."

He shook his head. "You make me sound noble. I didn't step aside. I almost knocked him over in the rush to get away."

"You did other things that only you could do. You cared for me on the way back from Raff's. Halse needed the healers then. When Sundas arrived he needed to feel he belonged. Findlow and Natia were settling down, and he wasn't really needed there. You allowed him to do what was necessary for him to belong, and you did what you were best at. Sundas thinks you left because he didn't do enough."

Teema looked at me and slowly smiled. "All right, I'm being selfish. Let's go and put his mind at rest."

"Eat first, you must be hungry." I handed him a food pouch and a flask.

He took a mouthful of drink, coughed and laughed. "I didn't know Findlow brought skafarhn with him. Does he know you took a flask of it?"

I nodded. "He gave it to me, but actually, this belongs to Papa. Did you know he and Armos have a store of it up on the plateau? They all hoped it would help you realize you are part of us too."

We walked slowly back to the settlement. The rain was soft, gentle and refreshing to walk in.

Half way home, Teema suddenly stopped. "Rathay!" he cried. "What's happening with the Summit?"

"It's been deferred. He'll have more time to prove himself and we'll carry on with other things in the meantime."

"Is there precedent for that?"

"There is now. That's how precedents are created."

"Will it help him?"

I nodded. "I think so. We'll have the burial and in a few days, the baby will be named and Jorlenta and Tant will join. Then the tokens will be returned."

"So the Summit may be put off for quite a while. Life goes on, doesn't it?"

Sundas was waiting on the porch with Findlow. He rushed up to Teema and lifted him off his feet in a big hug. "I thought you'd never come back," he sobbed.

Teema extracted himself and regained his footing. "I'm home, Sundas. It'll be fine now."

Sundas shook his head. "I didn't do enough for Halse. I'm so sorry, Teema. I understand if you're angry with me." Tears streamed down his face.

Teema patted him on the back and led him to the porch. "I wanted to tell you how sorry I am, Sundas."

Sundas stopped sobbing and stared at him. "Why are you sorry? I'm the one who left Halse occasionally to do other things. I should have stayed." He started to sob again.

"Sundas," Teema said gently. "You've done more for Halse than anyone. When you went to help others, you told Loul you'd be away and she looked after Halse." He frowned. "Loul did look after her properly, didn't she?"

Sundas looked up in shock. "Of course she did, of course she did. But I should have done it," he wailed.

Teema patted him on the shoulder and smiled over at Findlow and me. "Sundas, we're in your debt. I'm in your debt. You looked after Halse as if she were your own. I can't thank you enough for that. You've done all a brother should, and I owe you a great debt."

The sobs subsided and Sundas rubbed his eyes on his tunic sleeve. "You want me to be your brother?" he asked incredulously. "I've never had a brother before." He pulled Teema into another big hug. Then he realised I was there. He hauled me onto his lap and burst into tears again, wailing that I'd be so lonely now I'd lost my sister.

We calmed him down and reminded him of Mekrar, Zhins and Lyndym.

Eventually we were able to take him inside.

It was chaotic. Everyone was there to support our family and there was little room to move. Findlow sat Sundas in a corner and pushed his way over to Papa. They spoke briefly and he climbed onto a chair trying in vain to get everyone's attention.

Sundas watched for a few moments and then stood. "QUIET," he bellowed. In the sudden shocked silence, everyone turned to him. "Listen to Findlow," he said, and sat down.

"It's too crowded in here. It makes more sense to move to our dwelling. I'd like some volunteers to help carry Halse. Her set is too heavy for Veld, Tarl, Mekroe and Teema."

He pushed his way to the doors, opened them and everyone started to move out. Once there was room to move, eight men picked up the set and carried it onto the porch.

It had stopped raining, but the sky was grey and the clouds were low and heavy.

Halse's death affected everyone. She was extremely popular and there were tears in everyone's eyes at some time through the day. Food was prepared for those who wanted it and we sang and shared memories of our lives with Halse through the last day and night we'd spend with her.

I slept towards morning and when I woke, I felt depressed. Soon after dawn, Halse was carried out and we followed her to our burial area.

The hole had been dug in the lea of a large rock which was covered with a rug. A long wooden box lined with soft material sat on the ground beside it. Papa, Tarl, Mekroe and Teema picked up Halse's body and laid it in the box. We surrounded her with flowers and herbs until only her face was visible.

Papa stood and looked at her for a long time. Mama moved up beside him and Harby spoke the words that would be the last we'd share with her.

"Our darling daughter Halse, beloved by all who knew her. Daughter of Veld and Loul, sister to Tarl, Mekrar, Mekroe, Kirym and Zhins. Beloved of Teema and Sundas. Little daughter of Natia and Cindra, Grenin and Findlow. Big sister to Lyndym, Seeta, Findee, Nysia and Vandara. Child of The Land between The Gorges and loved by everyone. My sweet sweet daughter. We'll remember you with the love and care you showed your family and all those you met. We'll remember your fun, your laughter, your kindness and generosity. You'll be talked of as the seasons pass and we'll continue to love you. We leave you here but the memory of you goes with us. You are part of us, our memories, our past and our future."

Just before the container was covered, Papa removed Halse's token. He handed it to Mama who slipped it into a small embroidered bag she carried.

There was a murmur of speculation as they did this. Tokens

had always stayed with the dead.

The container was lowered into the ground. Harby picked up a spade and gently placed the first load of dirt on top of the body. Everyone joined in and soon there was just a mound of dirt. We planted Halse's favourite herbs and flowers over and around the mound.

Papa and Findlow removed the rug from the rock at the head of the burial mound. Leaning securely against the rock was a plaque carved with Halse name and lineage. In the centre of the plaque, Findlow had carved a figure that looked surprisingly like Halse. The wood was covered with bees wax to preserve it.

Mama was sobbing, and Papa took her in his arms. Mekroe and Mekrar had their arms around each other and Zhins comforted Tarl.

I felt empty. I'd known for a while that she would die, but suddenly the reality hit me. Slynd had stolen her from me. As tears streamed down my face, I resolved that somehow I'd make him pay for this.

I felt an arm around my shoulder and Teema hugged me. Arbreu, Bokum and Sundas crowded around us both.

The rain started again as we returned to Findlow's dwelling. Once inside there was a general buzz of conversation as everyone discussed the events of the morning.

Papa stood and called for silence. "There have been questions because today's burial was different from those we normally have. The container holding her body isn't something we've done before. This was a final gift from Sundas. It's a custom where he was born. We're thankful for his devotion to Halse." He allowed time for the comments to die. "You saw that we removed and kept Halse's token. Times are changing and this will now be our custom." Peet leapt to his feet.

"I see you, Peet."

"Why change tradition? It shows a lack of respect for Halse

and our traditions."

"Our lives have changed, and our traditions must follow that," Papa said. "Recently, we discovered that all the tokens we previously left with our dead have been stolen from the graves."

The room erupted.

Eventually, Papa called for quiet. "We have recovered the tokens, and we have Arbreu to thank for that. He brought them with him when he came across the gorge. By removing the tokens before burial, it can't happen again. Halse's token will be returned to the cave after the naming and joining ceremonies. Now the others are back, the cave can care for them." He acknowledged Tarl.

"Surely it'd be easier to take them from the cave."

There was another buzz of comments and Papa allowed time for everyone to talk and settle down again.

"I don't relish digging into the graves to try to find the owners and I wouldn't ask anyone else to do it. We'll see what happens when we return them to the cave. If we find it isn't an option, then we'll make new decisions."

We spent the night with Findlow's family and returned home in the morning.

18

Arbreu

"What say we do a bit of hunting? It'll show you the lie of the land between here and the cave and we can meet everyone up there in a few days' time."

Teema's invitation sounded inviting, but as Arbreu turned to accept, he spied Kirym sitting partially hidden in undergrowth beside the stream. He had never seen her look so distraught. He motioned to Teema and they crawled in beside her.

"Come on Kirym, Halse wouldn't want this. We rely on you to keep us cheerful," Teema said.

"Slynd is winning," she said. "He's still affecting us. Even now he has control. We're locked in here with no way out, and yet we must escape, get away from this land. We may not be able to destroy Slynd, but I want to thwart him. If we stay locked in here, he's won. Sooner or later he'll get in. Then more people will die. That path is vital. The sooner we find it the better. It must become our priority."

Teema nodded. "You're right. If there is a path, best we find it before he does. Let's talk to Veld and see if we can start searching."

Veld listened to them and was silent for a while as he thought over Kirym's arguments for the search. "Because I can't guarantee the path is no longer there, I will allow this. It's important to have continuity in the family, but within that, I'll give you as much leeway as I can. I'll bring the trip to the cave forward. We'll go tomorrow." He turned to Arbreu. "Before we go to the cave, we need to see what else Slynd had in the pack, Arbreu. There may be something else significant."

Arbreu nodded.

Veld stood. "Good. Let's get everyone together."

Mekroe took the furs off the chest that now held Arbreu's belongings and brought the pack to the table. Teema helped him set aside the packages they had already opened.

"I was thinking about that knife blade you found, Arbreu," Teema said.

"Oh, have you found the owner?" he asked hopefully.

Teema nodded and pulled it out of his old sheath. "Yes, it's you!" he said as he clicked Arbreu's token.

The new handle was a work of art. The wood glowed, fitting Arbreu's hand as if it had grown there. It was beautifully balanced.

Arbreu looked at the sea of beaming faces and realized everyone knew about it.

Bokum handed him a leather sheath for it, engraved with the boats and his name. Findlow handed him a belt to go with it which he proudly put on. There was a pause as the knife was brought out again and everyone compared the engraving to that on the sheath.

Teema told him about the wood used for the handle. "Once Findlow was involved, we had to fight to do any of it," he laughed.

Arbreu was overwhelmed.

Eventually the knife was put aside and they turned to the pack on the table. Arbreu opened the package they had been looking at when the arrival of Harnita's baby interrupted them.

Slynd's token had changed. It had a red tinge to it.

Veld picked it up. "Harby, what's happening to this token?"

Harby shook his head. "The women know about these things better than I do. Any ideas, Loul?"

"I've never heard of this happening. Tokens don't change like that." There was real concern in her voice. "What do you think, Kirym?"

Kirym stared at the token, frowning. "Our tokens reflect how we feel. If you're sick, your token reveals that and it's the same if you're unhappy or excited. That looks angry."

"What would he be so angry about?" asked Raff.

Everyone looked to Veld but it was Teema who answered. "We know Slynd gave gifts to his men, some of which he'd steal back. He didn't ask for them, he stole them or manipulated things so the items were left when they broke camp. He returned for them later. He left things at the last camp. Really nice things. They'd be gone when he returned and it's reasonable to assume he'd check his hoard."

The horrified silence was broken by Soojee. "He couldn't know we have them, could he? Wouldn't he accuse his own men?" She looked around hopefully.

"He would initially." Arbreu said. "But even if he accused them, he'd know they didn't have the opportunity. If he retraced his steps, he'd find Zelar's burial mound. Only the living bury the dead. He'll look across the gorge and he'll blame you, because he blames you for everything anyway. He'll redouble his efforts to get here."

Veld looked grim. "Once we've been to the cave, we must find some way to leave here. Arbreu, tell me about Slynd. You're the only one who's spent time with him lately."

"I don't know much," said Arbreu. "No one got close. He didn't let them. He was a chameleon. We saw what he wanted us to see."

"What do you mean?" Veld asked.

Arbreu frowned as he tried to think of something. Then his face lightened. "Well, he acted like he was scared of heights. He'd never go near a cliff edge. But he walked over the mountain passes with no problem at all. That's why I looked towards the cliff edge to find these." Arbreu paused, thinking. "He boasted of being the only one who knew of the waterfall path. When we found bandages with fresh blood on them, we knew Raff's family had been there and Slynd knew we knew. He told us he built the bridge across the river. When we got there and it was gone, he didn't have the knowledge to rebuild it. We watched three men walking away, they'd obviously destroyed it. Slynd was livid. He gave us reasons for the first time, Veld. He told us you'd stolen his land and enslaved his people. He said killing you would free them. He implied it was an honourable action, to save people's lives. His sacking and murdering Raff's family and the other settlements he's come across wasn't mentioned, and no one dared bring it up. We knew when he got here, it would be no different."

Veld nodded. "You've confirmed some of what I'd already guessed. I cut it so close in ensuring everyone's safety."

Findlow snorted. "I took more time than you. Thank goodness we'd crossed the bridge. What if he'd arrived earlier?"

"We'd have fought," said Teema, shrugging. "Given you time to get over and cut the ropes."

"And become his slaves," said Findlow with a grimace.

Veld smiled. "But it didn't happen that way. Teema had to make sure he got you here, Findlow, even if he had to get Sundas to carry you."

Everyone roared with laughter and Findlow slapped Veld on the back. "I don't know if my pride would've survived it, but I'm touched you cared so much." He became serious. "What else is in the pack, Arbreu?"

The next package revealed five pieces of rolled parchment. Arbreu opened the first, a page from the memory box. There was a pattern around the edge and some writing. It was faded and water damaged across the top and bottom. Kirym brought over a lamp and they tried to read the words. Most of it was indecipherable, but the bit in the middle said:

... rived at our new home.

A true sanctuary!

One day we will return. The cr ...

Arbreu smoothed out the next page. There was a pattern along one edge. Lines with arrows going in both directions went diagonally across the centre. The third page, badly damaged, was just a swirl of blues and greens, although it too had arrows across the centre.

Kirym studied them. "Of all of the pages he could have taken, he took these. He thought they were important. Why? Does he know something we don't?"

Loul picked up the memory box. "Let's see where they came from, that may help."

"Perhaps it's something to do with the dead tokens?" said Mekrar. "I mean, he took every one he could find."

Veld placed the pages to one side as Arbreu grabbed the next package.

What looked like a giant token fell out. A large blue stone

that, like the tokens they wore, seemed to glow from the centre.

Everyone was silent, awed.

Loul looked up and gasped. She reached out and tentatively touched it. "Oh Veld, I wondered what happened to it. It belonged to Veld's mama," she explained. "It disappeared when she died. We searched and searched for it. It's belonged to the Headwoman of the family since our memories began. It's one of the first things mentioned in our writings. I was devastated when it vanished."

Kirym leaned over to touch it. It seemed to pulse as she stroked it. "I always wondered what it looked like. It's magnificent." She paused, frowning. "Papa, this went missing before I was born. Did Slynd plan all of this back then?"

"He's been stealing for a long time, but the killing? Such a waste."

Arbreu jumped up and rushed over to his chest, digging deep into it. He emerged holding another small package wrapped in fush grass. Back at the table, he opened it revealing a page from the memory box wrapped around a second large token, the partner to Loul's. This one appeared dead.

Kirym picked it up. The moment she touched it, it began to glow, pale at first, but soon it was a deep green. She clicked it to the large blue token. A vibration between them resonated around the room.

On impulse, Arbreu took it off her and clicked it across her two tokens. There was a flash of light and the two large tokens both glowed intensely and connected with every token in the room.

Everyone stood, mesmerised.

Kirym broke the spell. She reached forward to pick up the parchment the token had been wrapped in and smoothed it out. Scrawled across the centre were four words.

They fit.

BUT WHY!!!

She read it out loud. "Three exclamation marks. Whoever wrote this thought it was important."

Teema picked up the page. "What fits? Hold on," he paused. "Is this connected with the rest of the writing? It's different. Different writing tool, I think the writing is newer. So who wrote it? Slynd?"

There were suddenly lots of questions as Loul picked up the two glowing stones.

"Why did they do that?"

"What made them come alive?"

"Did they do that for Slynd? Is that what he meant by them fitting?"

Arbreu picked up the next piece of parchment and smoothed it out. "A lot of this page is smudged and parts seem to have been eaten away, but there is more of that swirling pattern and a few lines. Umm, the beginning of the first words is gone. I'll spell what I can see."

"I'll write it down," said Mekrar.

Arbreu nodded. "Umm it could be *frightening*, but the first three letters are missing. Then it says, *but I've been there and*. Then there is a hole in the page and *c k again*. The next line is smudged, can't read it. Next line, first few letters are missing — um *rough storm* I think, the '*h*' is gone. Then, *One more trip*, another hole *and returned*. The next line says, *Travel not in winter*. I'll spell this bit — *r o u d e d* and another smudge. Then it says *delivered them*. Another smudge, *n e* there's a hole *ttlements*. Then a line that's too faded and the next three lines are in the centre of the page. *Go west and north ~~ The path is obvious ~~ It will take you ...*" He paused. "I'm sorry the next three lines are too smudged to read. Below them are more swirls."

"A lot doesn't make sense, but that could be 'new settlements', couldn't it?" asked Mekrar. "It's more than one. Does that mean the Flatlanders and even Arbreu's family came over with our ancestors?"

Veld shook his head. "We can't speculate, Mekrar. It could mean that, or any of many other things. It certainly expands the ideas. Old Sheen always said there were connections between the families we had no idea of."

Loul looked up from the memory box. "As far as I can see, these pages come from the beginning of the book. Everything else fits together. These seem to be an inclusive set. I don't recognise the writing. It's interesting, Veld. I used some of these patterns on your festival tunic, but those I used aren't here anymore."

Veld stared open mouthed. "You mean pages are missing? But that may be where the clue is. We may never know what it means."

Loul shook her head. "There's only about seven missing and I'm sure they had no words on them, just patterns and shapes. So why would Slynd take them? There'd be other things he could have used to wrap the things he stole."

"If he could have used anything, then there had to be a reason why he chanced getting caught taking these." Kirym picked up the last piece of parchment and smoothed it out. It also was water damaged and the ink had faded. The bottom of the page was disintegrating and a few lines were missing. She read it out loud.

'out where it's wild and windy
the clouds black and low
we stand upon the highest cliff
and watch the waters flow
far off in the darkest sky
the clouds begin to glow
while into the deepness of the land

the winds begin to blow
to work against the wind blast
come here in the early morn
climb into the shaded earth
to miss the glowing dawn
then walk across the water
bring the token o'er to me
to a valley deep and wide
your future there to see
my path across the water
you'll find it bold and straight
you'll sit and watch it pass you by
'twill bring you to my gate
I sit upon the map you have
for you must come to me'

"And that's all," she said. "So what does it mean?"

Loul pulled it towards her. As she did so, the word map fell from the bottom. "Oh my goodness, we must preserve it." She pulled three blank sheets towards her and slipped the page onto one of them. She took the second and copied out the words. When she had finished writing, she carefully covered the original page and placed it in the bottom of the memory box.

"I wish we had the last lines," said Kirym. "I wonder how much is missing. The pages are all different sizes, so it's difficult to say if it's one line, three, five or more. This sheet has no patterns on it. Could that mean It's not related to the others?"

Teema lifted the cover from the original page and looked at it closely. "It's the same writing as the first bit we found. We have to assume they go together. I wish I knew why Slynd took these pieces. Did he know something?"

"I've got it." Kirym jumped up from the table and ran over to the big family chest. She brought a linen wrapped package to the table and opened it to reveal Veld's festival tunic. "We do have some of the missing pages, look!" She spread it out on the table and placed the pages around it. "It's a map. The swirling pattern is the sea and the tunic is land. The writing is extra." They crowded around as Kirym leaned forward and placed the large blue token on a shape on the tunic.

Veld nodded. "You're right, but it could be a map of anywhere, Kirym. There's nothing to identify it. We need a known starting point, and we still need the rest of the map. I don't think we ever had it. Only a few pages are missing now and that's not enough to fill in the empty area. There's nowhere for the other token, so it remains a puzzle."

They looked at it for a while longer and then most lost interest.

Kirym stayed at the table studying the map. She moved the green token closer to the blue. At one point, the glow intensified. She moved it in a semicircle and suddenly, a ray of light arced between the two tokens. She frowned in concentration as she traced a line at the bottom of Veld's tunic.

"Arbreu," she hissed. "I need your help."

She took him to the shelf where Raff kept the reproduction of the stellon. They lifted it down and carried it to the table.

Raff had joined the edges of the parchment pieces to give it the cylindrical shape of a tree. The top edge had been cut in strange curves and holes copying the carved top of the stellon.

Kirym placed it so the curved edge sat on the table. She turned it around slowly. It fitted into the pattern at the bottom of Veld's tunic.

Arbreu used his new knife to slit the back of the parchment.

Kirym laid it out on the table, and everyone crowded around again. Now they could see it as a full map. She placed the green token into a space that seemed to be made for it. It pulsed brightly and the tokens they wore picked up the beat.

Kirym sighed happily. "That's what Slynd meant by it fitting. This is the last piece, Papa. It's the journey of our ancestors. Raff's, Arbreu's and ours. We needed to do it together."

"Well, you have done it," Veld hugged her, "but it's still meaningless. We don't know what it's a map of."

"Oh, but I know that," Kirym said. She pointed to some raised square stitches near the blue token. "That's the settlement and the token sits on our token-cave." She pointed to a line on Veld's tunic that ran from his left hip to his neck. "That's the northern gorge." She placed her finger on a swirl of white and grey. "That's the top waterfall. The green token must represent another cave in another land."

Veld sat down, frowning. "All right, but how does this help us?"

"This must somehow show us where the path to safety is, Papa," said Kirym.

Then Arbreu understood. "Veld, we need to leave here. This tells us where to go. We go to a place where there's a cave."

"Well, that makes sense, but how do we get there?" said Raff.

Arbreu pointed to the verse. "The poem. They're instructions. They tell us how."

Loul read the words again. "The first instruction seems to be the second line — we stand upon the highest cliff and watch the waters flow. That has to be the sea cliffs. So we go there and find the highest point. Next it says, far off in the darkest sky the clouds begin to glow. What does that mean?" She looked around to blank stares.

Kirym put her finger on the map. "The cliffs face west. When the clouds to the west glow it's because the sun is setting. So we'd need to be there in the late afternoon."

"It's dangerous along the sea cliffs. That's why we don't go there. If we do decide to, we'd have to be very careful," said Veld. "But all right, we go there. What next?"

Bokum laughed. "It seems that we wait until the wind blows into the land, and that doesn't make sense."

"It could be poetic licence, Bok." Veld turned to Harby. "Harbs, you know more about the sea cliffs than anyone else. Where's the highest point?"

Harby pointed to an area near the northern gorge. His finger sat on a small shaded area.

Veld and studied the map. "What's that?" he asked.

Harby leaned over and looked. "I don't know. I can't remember anything being there. Perhaps we need to go and find out. See, next it says we can work against the wind blast. So the wind must be important, maybe not poetic licence. But why?"

"It says climb into the shaded earth. Is it a valley? " asked Teema.

"Not there, lad. There isn't even a dip in the land. It's all rock," said Harby.

"Well what about a cave? If there's a cave, the entrance must be on the cliff face."

"I don't know, Teema. The shaded area is back from the cliff edge, so probably not." Harby shook his head. "I mean, next it says to walk across the water, so how do we do that?"

Raff looked up. "What if the instructions are for them to come here, not for us to leave?"

"Oh, but they can't be," said Kirym. "It says go north and west. They must have come east and south. Oh, Papa, let's go to the cliffs and see."

"Such enthusiasm," said Veld, laughing. "All right, we'll go and have a look, but not until after the cave ceremonies. I still don't understand how we can walk over the water, but there's a lot I don't understand."

Teema took a deep breath. "What if it's a path under water? Under the gorge. We walked under the water up at the waterfall, so maybe there's something similar there. Maybe it should have said, go west and north. West takes us to the cliffs and then north, that would be towards the gorge. That may be why we haven't found the path. We tend not to go there because of the danger from the cliffs."

"Hold on, the green token sits out in the ocean," said Bokum.

"It's northwest of The Flatlands, and we don't know the land, Bok," said Kirym. "The coast beyond there could go in any direction."

"Maybe it's an island just off the coast," said Findlow. "A traveller told us about one further south, although he said it was small and rocky. But islands come on all sizes and shapes."

They broke up into groups, chatting excitedly about the map.

19

Kirym Speaks

The next day we travelled to the cave.

Sundas had been very quiet since Halse died. He seemed to feel he was no longer needed, so Papa asked him to join Armos and Teema to ensure that no one fell behind or got lost.

We took all we needed, extra rugs because it was still cool at night, our food, festival clothes and musical instruments. I carried the tokens. Bokum, Rathay, Mekroe and Arbreu pulled triangular frames with extra gear on them.

When we arrived at the dwellings we used when visiting the cave, the young men went off to collect wood for the fires. When I realised Sundas wasn't with them, I searched for him. Eventually I found him sitting under the trees at the edge of the meadow.

"I miss Halse. I wish she was still with us," I said when I was sitting beside him.

He took my hand in his. "She was very sick and it was

good we had her as long as we did. If she'd died when Slynd attacked, I wouldn't have known her at all. We just have to remember her. Remember her forever."

He was quiet for a while then turned to me. "Kirym, instead of writing about the imantas for the memory box, will you write about Halse instead?"

"I can do both, because they're both important," I said, smiling. "Papa has already written about her life and death. When we get home, I'll read it to you. Then you can add your memories of her, and your other recollections too. I'll help and when we're old, we can sit and read it together and think back to now."

Sundas sat silently for a long time. "I'd like that, but let's make it yours and mine, because some of my memories aren't so good. Maybe we can add some of Arbreu's too." He smiled happily and we went to collect wood.

Everyone was pleased when Sundas helped because he carried twice as much as anyone else, and his logs were much thicker.

As darkness fell, we stoked the fire carefully and walked out of the camp to watch the moon rising over the horizon. Then we settled for the night knowing we'd rise before dawn.

It seemed I'd just fallen asleep when Mama woke me. We dressed warmly and put on my cloak. Lamps were lit and we walked to the cave entrance.

Again, our first ceremony was for birth, celebrated at the beginning of the day. Peet and Harnita entered the cave with their son, followed by Old Harby, his children, grandchildren and great-grandchildren. Everyone else followed.

We filed around the walls ensuring that everyone was able

to see and there were plenty of seats for those who wished to use them. I was always amazed that even little children were aware of the occasion and behaved themselves while in the cave.

Peet and Harnita stepped to the centre of the cave with Harnita holding their son. The lights dimmed and we waited in the dark.

Two things happened at once. We heard a single, long, plaintive note, and a flash of light lit up the cave. The light raced round and round the cavern until it settled on a small recessed area on the far western wall. Peet and Harnita moved towards it, but it danced away. Again the light sped around the cave, pausing to light up one area after another. Finally it stopped, and highlighted a gold token. Peet picked it up, pressed it into the holder he'd made for the baby and placed it on his forehead. Harnita whispered the baby's name to him as she clicked her token to his. The tokens changed to a pale green, the colour of new oak leaves.

Peet leaned forward and clicked his token to the baby's, saying the name so we could all hear it. "Parlansho. This is Parlansho." The colour in both of their tokens intensified, now more like Harnita's. The light around them faded and lamps were lit.

We followed Peet and Harnita out of the cave. At the entrance we were each introduced to Parlansho. We repeated his name and clicked tokens. He slept through it all.

Papa had decided not to let the family know of the coming search. If there was a path, we would have to find it before telling them. So after a meal, we relaxed and played games in the meadow. It was a warm drowsy day and no one was very energetic. In the afternoon I helped pick flowers to decorate the cave. There were always masses of them growing nearby — they seemed to like the climate there. I could hear the men moving over to the stream to wash off the sweat from their games and change into their festival clothes. I'd asked Teema to make sure Sundas didn't slip away by himself.

In the cave, I sat with Sundas, Teema and Arbreu. Arbreu looked around, carefully taking everything in. This was his first joining.

Tant stood in a large circle of flowers. The candles occasionally flared, then faded again. A soft windy sound built up from the far side of the room. It became more rounded and stopped abruptly. It built up again and slowly faded. The women sang as a group of our littlest girls danced around the circle scattering flower petals. As they danced, the light faded and just before it disappeared completely, Jorlenta appeared at the tunnel entrance.

She looked stunning. Her dress was covered with embroidery and beads. Her dark hair was done up with lots of curls and plaits. She wore a circle of flowers around her head.

The light went out and after a moment of darkness, the areas Tant and Jorlenta were standing in lit up. Jorlenta walked slowly into the flower circle. There was soft music as Zelriff and Harby stepped forward and talked to them about the important step they were taking.

Harby turned towards the men. "Tant has requested a joining. He chose Jorlenta. Is everyone happy with his request?"

As he finished his question, Parlansho started to cry.

Harby roared with laughter. He picked up his great-grandson and took him over to Tant.

"It seems you have a challenger, Tant. How do you wish to resolve this?"

Tant looked uncomfortable, unsure what to do.

Harby laughed again and addressed Parlansho. "You are too young for us to consider your objection. You are also too close in relationship to Jorlenta to challenge Tant to the joining, with your papa being her sibling. Now let's return this precocious lad to his mama," he handed Parlansho to Harnita, "and continue with the joining. Is there any other challenge to Tant's request?"

With no response, the music swelled until a prolonged drum beat drowned it out. The drumming slowly got softer and softer until it was more a feeling than a sound.

Zelriff addressed the women: "Jorlenta has requested a joining and she has chosen Tant. Does anyone object to her request?" There was no answer.

The candles flickered, went out and in the darkness, small pinpoints of light grew. Two pulsed brighter than the others and Jorlenta and Tant walked forward to pick them up and press them into each other's token holder. They clicked tokens and the lights in the cave came on.

Zelriff and Harby spoke together. "They are joined."

Everyone repeated the words.

Jorlenta and Tant were led out of the cave, stopping at the entrance to wait for Harnita to bring Parlansho out. They clicked tokens with him, then Harnita and Peet, followed by everyone else.

Back at the dwellings, food was brought out of the ovens and food pits. Jorlenta and Tant took their loaf of sweet bread around for everyone to share, and we sang and danced in celebration.

The moon was high in the sky before we slept.

But I couldn't sleep.

Wrapped in my cloak, I walked out to watch the full moon. The camp was silent. I was about to build up the fire when I saw a shape dart between the dark of two trees.

I slipped into the shadows and followed.

The figure walked around the camp, keeping to the darkest places and moving towards the cave.

He was tall, with broad shoulders and wore a hood.

I followed carefully, trying to identify him. As we approached the cave entrance, he disappeared into the deeper shadows of the rocks.

I'd lost him in the darkness. I waited silently to see if he would move again.

Suddenly a hand clamped over my mouth and I was lifted from the ground.

I struggled, trying to see who had me. Then I heard a low voice in my ear.

"Quiet."

I was lowered to the ground.

Teema beckoned me to follow him and we slipped through the trees to the far side of the cave entrance. He made the sound of an owl.

The figure I'd followed walked out of the shadows.

It was Bokum.

"Great guard you make, Bok. It's a good thing you have me to watch your back."

"Why!"

"Kirym just followed you from the camp without you even noticing."

"Well, she is very small," Bokum said.

"So, you're only looking for giants?" Teema shook his head in mock disgust.

"You should have let me know you'd seen me, Kirym. We could have checked the perimeter together."

"I needed to identify you, find out where you were going before showing myself," I said. "Your new hood threw me."

"Come on," Teema said snorting with near silent laughter. "Let's get a hot drink."

We walked around the rock to where there was a wide low

overhang. The ground underneath was covered with layers of fush grass and scattered rugs. We joined Papa and Sundas beside a small fire.

Arbreu slipped in from the other side of the rock. "It's clear up to the far stream, Veld, but there's a small valley there. It looks overgrown at the top, but I wonder if it is further down. We should check it, but it looks steep and I couldn't see how to get down safely. I'm unhappy climbing down into the unknown without a rope."

Papa smiled. "You're good, Arbreu. I'm happy with your ability to read the land. I know the valley. I've already checked it out. There's a path in, but it is difficult to see, especially at night."

Arbreu frowned. "Is it the same valley? I checked the ground for footprints."

"It's the only valley there," said Papa. "Over the far side where the rock goes down?" Arbreu nodded. "That's the way in. It looks impenetrable there and it's the one area that leaves no prints."

Arbreu nodded and accepted a flask.

"Papa, do you always set a guard?"

"Yes, always, here and back at the settlement. Guards keep an eye on what's happening within the settlement. At Raff's, houses were fired and that can happen accidently. By setting guards, we get an earlier warning if there's an accident. Moments can save lives."

Findlow and Zeprah walked in from the shadows. "You're well hidden but we heard you from the oak grove. Fortunately, there's no one else around to notice." Findlow's gruff tone was belied by his smile. He sat down beside me. "Well, sweetie, why are you here? Learning to be a guard?"

20

Teema Speaks

Veld looked at Kirym. "Yes, why are you here?"

"I couldn't sleep. Then I saw someone in the shadows and followed." She sighed theatrically. "It was only Bokum."

"Why were you awake?" Veld asked.

"I was thinking about the cave. There was something different both times we were there yesterday. I was trying to figure out what it meant."

"Something different? What do you mean?" Veld asked.

This was serious. Kirym had an understanding and affinity with the cave we had never seen before, never heard of. I'd never known her to be wrong about the tokens and she was rarely unsure about them.

"The tokens normally light up easily," she said. "But Parlansho's didn't. It was almost as if the cave wasn't sure whose token should be glowing. I've never seen that happen before and it isn't mentioned in the memory box. Then when we were there for Jorlenta and Tant, a number of tokens shone but two shone brighter. Once Jorlenta and Tant accepted their tokens, the lamps came on but the other tokens continued to shine."

"It may not mean anything, Kirym," I said. "Maybe it's to do with the moon."

She shook her head. "We've been here during full moon before, and it didn't happen then. So it must mean something. Other changes have been written about. When Harby's Sheen had her babies, there was only one token in the cave. The token only glowed when put into the holder that belonged to Armos. Ambro and Sharmond were so sick and they died before the family left the cave area. The details are in the memory book for us." She paused, frowning. "These are life tokens and the cave knew there was no life for those babies. If tokens are glowing, there are people for them."

"You may be right, Kirym, but we can do nothing until morning. We'll call the Council of Women together and talk to them. It should be sorted before we take the tokens of the dead in." Veld paused, frowning. "Maybe it's to do with them. There's probably never been dead tokens near the cave before. Possibly the ceremony for Halse is still affecting it. Still whatever the answer, it's time we checked the settlement again. We'll walk you back."

We piled ashes over the fire to reduce its speed of burning and picked up our bows and quivers.

"Papa, when you write for the memory box," Kirym said, taking his hand, "do you write about the differences in the cave ceremonies?"

"I write about them when I notice them. You see, Kirym, I write my memories. When others tell me about things I didn't see, I write that also. This may have happened before and no one noticed. You have so I'll write of it, but this is the problem with the memory box. History is biased by those who write it, by what they know and how they feel.

Remember, we've no memory of coming to this land, so our memory isn't intact. That's why we use the book as a guide only and that's why Harby always says, 'nothing is usual'. It's possible this hasn't happened before, but it's also possible it's just never been noticed."

"The trip here will have been written about, Papa. We just haven't found the pages yet," she said seriously. "Think about how long we've been reading the book, yet recently we've learned all sorts of things because we finally looked at it properly."

"What do you mean?" Veld asked.

"Well, like the map of the land. It's been there all along. You've actually worn it in front of everyone. But we just saw a pattern, because we didn't know what we were looking at. Now we know and recognise it for what it really is, we can put that knowledge with everything else we learn to find a way to escape. These changes in the cave must be important, but I don't think it has happened before."

"You may be right, darling. The Council may have some ideas. Let's wait and see."

The moon had set and it was very dark, the dark that comes just before dawn. As we approached the cave, we saw the reflection of lights moving in the cave tunnel. We stopped, staring, but Kirym broke away and raced towards the entrance.

I was momentarily rooted to the spot.

Sundas was the first to react, followed closely by Arbreu. There was a mad scramble as the rest of us followed.

Kirym stood in the centre of the cave, Sundas next to her holding her hand. Tokens lit up the wall. As we entered the cave, all except two of the lights went out. Still holding

Sundas' hand, Kirym moved towards one of them. It got brighter as she got closer.

"We have new family members here, Papa, and these are their tokens. Teema, can you get two token holders?"

I rummaged in small storage basket we kept in the cave.

Kirym took the token and pressed it into a holder. "Sundas, this is for you."

He looked surprised. "But, I'm not a member of your family. I don't belong."

"Yes, you do, Sundas," she said gently. "The token proves it. Put it on. If it isn't for you it'll go out. Just try it."

He looked at it and placed it on his forehead. It glowed brightly. He leaned down to click it to Kirym's. The token settled to a green blue glow that was almost dimmed by his huge smile. "I've not had a family since I was little," he said happily. Then a look of consternation crossed his face. He looked at Findlow. "No, that's not true," he said. "I'm part of your family, Findlow. Can I be part of two families?"

Findlow patted his arm. "Yes Sundas, and you're a very special part of both. It's really great, because I am too." Findlow stretched up to click his token. Both tokens changed colour slightly. Sundas' took on a slightly bluer glow and Findlow's light blue token darkened a little. Sundas clicked tokens with the rest of us.

"Welcome to the family, Sundas." Veld grasped his arm.

The cave darkened again and Kirym took Zeprah's hand. A token lit up. Kirym pressed it into a holder and handed it to her.

Zeprah slipped it onto her forehead and clicked it to Kirym's. Her token was dark pink.

She smiled and then burst into tears. "Oh, I'm being silly, but I've felt so isolated since Ranot was killed."

She smiled through her tears as Bokum clicked his tokens to hers. Her token took on a bluer tinge, his light blue token now the same colour as hers but paler.

We crowded around to touch our tokens to hers. The light in the cave dimmed and Arbreu lit his lamp.

Veld started towards the cave entrance, but Kirym stopped him. "Papa, this has to be explained. People will need to be prepared. There'll have to be an understanding from the Council of Women."

"Can they refuse to accept it?" I asked.

Kirym shook her head. "No. The cave gave the tokens and there'll be no argument there. But there may be resistance." She looked anxious. "I don't want anyone to upset Sundas. He's been through enough. It's a shame it happened with so few witnesses, but the timing was right and it may not have happened later."

Everyone looked worried except Sundas who was happily unaware of everything except really belonging.

"Times are changing," Veld said with a nod. "I wonder why the cave has changed the way things are done."

Findlow smiled wryly. "Veld, you saw it happen. They can scarcely challenge you as headman. If you tell them, they have to accept it. I can back you up and you have Teema and Bokum. Both are respected. It's only a group of women."

Veld laughed. "Only? Oh, right," he said, wryly. "Kirym, Sundas, Zeprah and Arbreu, go back to the guard camp. Stay there until I send for you. Teema, Bokum, Findlow, let's go and sort this out."

The camp was stirring as we arrived and, Loul who was about to start looking for Kirym, was relieved to know where she was. Veld and I told her what happened through the night.

She leaned back on the set. "How will you tell everyone, Veld?"

"I'll tell the Council of Women. This is their territory. But what's the best way to explain it all?"

"Don't ask their opinion. The cave made the decision. Give them the facts and keep it simple."

"What about Kirym?" I asked.

She frowned. "What do you mean, Teema?"

"Where tokens are concerned, there's generally a woman there to guide the handling of them. Ours was Kirym. Can they object to her involvement? She's very young for this."

Loul thought for a while. "No, they can't. She noticed the change in the cave. They should have — grief I should have." She paused. "You know, I did on a subliminal level, but it didn't register deep enough to make me question it. Kirym saw and questioned. She's far more in tune with the cave and tokens than anyone else. They can't challenge that. Above all, Veld, you are headman. That's your strength. Use it."

The Council of Women made the decisions about the cave and how the ceremonies were organised. There were thirteen members, although technically every woman who wore a token was a member and could have a say.

The current head of the Council was Yanda, Zelriff's younger sister. She was a sour woman who always found fault with others. I suspected she became head of the Council by nagging her fellow members into submission, but perhaps I was being uncharitable.

Decisions could be made casually, but Yanda had always preferred formal meetings.

The members sat on one side of the big table with Yanda in the centre. They listened as Veld told them what had happened through the night.

Yanda was not happy. "You entered the cave without our permission, to hand out tokens to those who are not members of our family?" She sounded shocked.

"No one needs permission, Yanda. The cave made the decision. I happened to be there at the time."

She looked at Veld with dislike, obviously annoyed she could find no argument with his explanation. "What gave you the right to organise a ceremony without coming to me — ahh, or to one of the Council members to administer it?"

The other women leaned forward. Many looked annoyed, others frustrated, and I realised there was a division within the group.

"Nothing requires that you be present when the cave gives tokens, Yanda. We didn't have a ceremony. The cave gave two tokens," Veld paused. "Are you suggesting the cave shouldn't have given the tokens?"

"These people aren't family," she snapped. "There have been too many tokens given to those not entitled. There should be more control. I've long thought that people with no full blood alliance shouldn't be offered them."

Zelriff leaned forward. "Would you give yours up, sister? Our grandmamma wasn't from this land. If the requirement for wearing a token is one of pure blood then you should be the first to remove yours. That would, of course, remove you from the Council."

Yanda looked at her sister with even more dislike than she had for Veld. She turned back to him. "Get the child. We'll hear from her."

Veld motioned to Bokum, who headed out of camp.

Yanda looked at Veld coldly. "I told you to get her."

There were raised eyebrows and a few smiles. Yanda had exceeded her position.

Veld leaned across the table and spoke quietly. "I am

headman, Yanda. You do not tell me what to do. I allow you to sit and give advice, but you have no entitlement to do so, and I have no obligation to listen to you. Take great care." He sat back and waited for Kirym to arrive.

She had somehow contrived to have her best clothes delivered to her and her hair was done up in looped plaits. She looked pale, the two tokens on her forehead glowing brightly. She stood respectfully before the Council.

Yanda leaned forward, her pale token dimming in the sunlight. "Who gave you permission to use the cave for a ceremony?"

"We didn't have a ceremony," Kirym said simply.

"So without permission, you organised an unlawful gathering and gave tokens to people who have no right to them?"

Zelriff looked annoyed, but Loul grasped her arm restraining her.

"The cave gave the tokens," said Kirym. "Permission isn't needed. Nothing was organised. The tokens had been attempting to find their owners all day yesterday. They found them early this morning."

Yanda looked triumphant. "You claim to read the cave?"

"What did you think the cave was trying to say, Yanda?" said Loul, as Yanda took a breath. "How did you read the extra lights?"

Yanda stared at her. "What lights? What are you talking about?"

"You mean you didn't see the lights in the cave when we were there yesterday? A child sees them but the head of the Council doesn't?" Zelriff turned to Kirym. "Child, tell us what you saw at the two gatherings yesterday."

Kirym repeated what she'd told us earlier.

When she'd finished, Zelriff nodded quietly. "We should have seen it, and questioned it if we didn't understand. I understand why the cave chose Kirym to talk to rather than us. We put on impressive ceremonies, and take the forefront in them every chance we get. It's become about us. We no longer allow the cave to be the focus."

Yanda glared at her sister. "You have no right to challenge my decisions. I'm the head of this Council. You'll do as I say or you'll leave."

"You are the guide for these meetings, Yanda," Loul said gently. "If you don't see what's happening in the cave, perhaps you should step aside."

"Never! My position lasts another two season cycles." Her voice rose to a screech. "I am the Council. You will leave and no one will use the cave for anything I've not organised."

Loul stood. "You can't do that, Yanda. We will now choose another guide for the Council."

"Personally I'd be happy to have Kirym," said Lantiah. "She seems to be most intuitive where the cave is concerned." She looked at Yanda who bristled with annoyance. "However, I'm aware her age is against her. So would you be our guide, Loul."

Loul shook her head. "I'll not stand for this position. I'm happy to be a member, but I have other responsibilities. Perhaps Zelriff would accept it."

"She has to be elected," screeched Yanda. "I shall stand too. It's my right. This is totally underhanded."

Parchment was sent around for the members to vote.

Lantiah collected and opened them. She read the names, placing them on one pile or another. Yanda got the second vote and the fourth. The fifth vote went to Zelriff as did the next four. At that stage Lantiah showed the seven votes to the other members and when they all agreed with the result, placed them on the fire.

Zelriff turned to Kirym. "We'll inform the family we have two more members."

"I'd like to tell Soojee and Raff first," said Loul.

We invited Raff and Soojee to join us for a hot drink. Once they were sitting in the sun, Veld and I explained what had happened overnight.

Soojee was thoughtful for a time and then smiled. "It's good for Zeprah to have somewhere to belong. I love her dearly and she was good to my son, but she has felt distant since he died."

Loul took her hand. "She's still your daughter, Soojee. The token means we get to share her. I wonder what it'll mean for the future though. Life here is changing and everything is so uncertain."

Raff and Veld nodded.

The Council of Women led Sundas and Zeprah into the gathering area. They were welcomed amid much discussion about the changes in the cave.

We returned the dead tokens to the cave during the afternoon. Everyone dressed again in their festival clothes and Kirym nestled the tokens on fragrant flowers in a wide basket. They were a heavy load and she accepted Arbreu's offer of help to carry them.

When we arrived at the cave, the members of the Council walked in first, followed by Kirym and Arbreu and everyone else.

Once everyone was inside, the cave lit up. There were disjointed noises whispering through the air above us.

Kirym placed the basket in the centre of the floor and the light concentrated on it. A spot on the wall glowed and one of the tokens lit up. This was the token that had belonged to Harby's mama. He picked it up, touched it to his and placed it on the bright spot. The token glowed brightly and then dimmed.

One by one the tokens blazed and were returned to the cave, generally by someone who had or felt they had a connection with the dead person. Other times, a member of the Council chose someone to take it to the final resting place.

The final token was the one Veld had removed from Halse's forehead just a few days earlier. Loul began to stand to pick it up, but it faded and she settled back in her seat.

Kirym leaned against her. "Perhaps Teema and Sundas should return it."

Loul took her hand and nodded. "Yes, it may be the answer," she said gently.

"No," I said. "Just Sundas."

Sundas looked at me, started to object, but then nodded and picked up the token. It flashed to his token and faded slightly. A point on the wall lit up, he placed it there, and again, a faint glow stretched between them. The light then flashed around the cave and all of the tokens glowed momentarily. Then the light and the tokens vanished.

We waited in the dark silence for a short time, Zelriff lit a lamp and we filed out.

Night had fallen while we were in the cave. More lamps were lit for our return to the settlement. Once there, the fire was built up and the oven and food pits opened.

Kirym came and gave me a big hug. "Thank you, Teema. That was the loveliest thing to do. It meant such a lot to Sundas."

It was a quiet evening. We all had a lot to think about.

In the morning almost everyone returned home leaving only a few who wanted to help with the final ceremony.

Lantiah had been asked what she wanted to do with her token. She had no idea and was reluctant to even touch it. She refused to have anything to do with Slynd's.

"Why don't you nominate someone to carry them into the cave for you?" Loul suggested.

"Can we let Kirym and Bildon carry them?" asked Lantiah. "They're innocent and have little knowledge of what life can do. Then my thoughts won't get in the way. Given the choice, I wouldn't even be here. I was all for going home this morning. I only stayed because Armos felt I should."

Zelriff nodded. "And he's right, Lantiah. You'll find afterwards you'll feel more at ease with the situation."

Bildon and Kirym and agreed happily to help with the ceremony.

A small group walked with them to the caves. Yanda walked ahead and entered the cave first. Once we were all inside, the lamps were dimmed and placed in niches in the wall. Kirym and Bildon had each brought a bunch of flowers and they spread them in a circle in the centre of the floor around the platter holding the two tokens.

Yanda walked around the cave peering into various crevices and hollows and mumbling to herself. She turned to see Bildon helping Kirym. "How dare you contaminate our sacred ceremony, you evil child!" she screeched, pointing a scrawny finger at her. "You're an outsider. You've no right to even be here."

Bildon shrank away from her.

We stared at Yanda with horror.

Zelriff stepped between them. "These ceremonies aren't sacred, Yanda. The child has done no wrong. Lantiah asked her to help. She can do that. It's her right."

The two old women stood nose to nose, glowering at each

other. Yanda stepped away first.

"It's a mistake," she mumbled. "A big mistake."

Zelriff shushed her and spoke quietly to Kirym and Bildon for a few moments.

They finished arranging the flowers, and stepped back to sit with Zelriff, Loul and Lantiah.

Yanda walked around a little more and then as the light faded, she sat on a rock on the far side of the cave. The rest of us sat together on one of the stone forms and waited.

The ceiling of the cave rustled as if the wind were rushing through. A beam of light focused on a single token on the eastern wall. Yanda walked towards it, but as she got close it went out. She stood for a moment in the dim light then turned and stamped back to her seat. There was another rustle and the token shone again.

Zelriff stood and stepped towards the token, but again it dimmed.

Yanda cackled with laughter.

Zelriff looked around. "Kirym, can you find its owner?"

The token was high in the wall, way above her head. Sundas lumbered forward and lifted her up to reach it.

"It's not right. It's not right," mumbled Yanda. "Bad things will happen."

However, the token continued to glow brightly. As Kirym walked back to her seat, the token started to pulse. "It's for you, Bildon," she said.

Lantiah reached for her old token holder, removed the stone and handed the holder to Kirym. She pressed the new token into it and placed it on Bildon's forehead.

Bildon clicked Kirym's token then turned to Lantiah. Bildon's token took on a golden green hue to match Lantiah's, with a jagged inclusion of blue, similar to Kirym's. She was so delighted.

Everyone gathered around welcoming her to the family.

Lantiah's token sat where she'd left it. The platter containing Slynd's sat nearby.

Suddenly, the cave plunged into darkness. A shaft of light slowly crept towards the tokens. The light touched Slynd's token and paused.

We watched and waited.

The rumble started deep in the earth. It continued for a long moment before I realised what it was.

"Earthquake! Everyone out!"

There were screams from those near me. Veld grabbed people at random pushing them towards the tunnel. Sundas grabbed Mekrar, Zhins, and Bildon and rushed them out, followed by Bokum with Loul, Zeprah and Zelriff.

I looked for Kirym. She was running towards Yanda who was still sitting at the back of the cave, frozen with fear.

As I started after her, she reached Yanda.

Yanda twisted and screamed, pulling away from her, but Kirym grabbed her arm, kept hold and hauled her towards the exit.

I grasped Yanda's shoulder and pushed her ahead of me into the tunnel, relieved when she stopping fighting Kirym and stumbled forward. Kirym pulled her steadily onward.

I reached the beginning of the tunnel and glanced back.

The area where Yanda had been sitting collapsed in a heap of rubble. The debris flowed around me. I turned back to follow Kirym, and was suddenly engulfed and disoriented by the billowing dust. I reached to steady myself against the tunnel, but the wall collapsed. I was left holding a piece of loose rock with no real idea which direction to go.

A hand came out of the dust, grabbed my tunic and I was hauled through a dark jumble of rocks, debris falling around my feet.

I clung to my rescuer's hand, fearing I would lose contact. It seemed like forever before we were free of the tunnel, out into the night and away from the mouth of the cave.

Veld shouted for quiet, calling names; Loul, Mekrar, Mekroe, Kirym, Findlow, Bildon, Zhins, and down through the list.

Slowly the dust settled and I was able to see the dirt streaked faces of my family. I was so relieved they were all safe.

The hand I still grasped belonged to Arbreu. He had saved my life.

He slipped to the ground coughing the dust out of his lungs. I squatted beside him to pat his back, dropping the rock I had brought from the cave.

Kirym dabbed some water from a flask onto a piece ripped from her petticoat, washed the dust from Arbreu's eyes and offered him a drink.

He looked up. "Is everyone out of the cave? Where's Findlow? What about the old lady?"

"Everyone's safe, Arbreu. You saved my life. Thank you so much," I said gratefully. I helped him to stand.

I heard an exclamation and looked down. Kirym picked up the rock I'd dropped, wiped it on her dress, and held it out to me. It was a large token similar to the blue one that had been in the family for so long. This one glowed with all the colours of the rainbow.

There was an awed silence as those closest to her saw what she held, followed by a rush of comments.

"Where did you get it?"

"Why have we been given it?"

"Are there more buried in there?"

Veld raised his voice above everyone else's. "Is anyone hurt?"

Yanda complained loudly again, but was uninjured.

Loul squeezed Veld's hand. "We're just shaken. Zelriff isn't breathing too well but she's coming right. What do we do now? We need to get back to the settlement, they'll be worried."

Veld nodded. "Sundas, Bokum, check the path down the hill please?" The two men disappeared.

"Are you all right, Zelriff?" Kirym knelt beside the old lady.

She nodded. "Yes, yes, yes. Just being a silly old woman." She spied the token and her thoughts turned from her breathing. "Child, where did you find it?"

"I didn't. It was given to Teema, the last gift from the cave. Perhaps it's telling us we need to move on, find another home."

Zelriff nodded, but there were tears in her eyes. "Why would the cave give it to a man?"

I chuckled awkwardly. "I didn't even look at it, Zelriff. To me it was just a rock I happened to grab, and I could just as easily have dropped it in the cave as out here. Kirym saw it for what it was."

Before any more comments could be made, Sundas and Bokum returned.

"There's a rock fall across the path, Veld. It's unstable, so even when it's light it probably won't be the safest path," said Bokum. "Perhaps we can go around the hill and into the valley past your cave."

Yanda's head came up. "There's another cave? What cave?" She stalked over to stand in front of Veld. "How dare you hide a cave from the Council? I'll deal with you later."

"It's nothing to do with the Council, Yanda," snapped Cindra, pushing her aside. "Veld, can we get back that way? I left Vandara with Harnita. She needs a meal. I didn't think we'd be long."

"It's a tough climb, Cindra, but it'll be quicker than going up to the lake and back. Those who don't feel they're up to it can stay here and I'll send assistance in the morning."

I knew no one would stay.

Veld organised us into groups to help each other.

As we prepared to leave, Kirym paused. The moon, emerging from behind a cloud, shone on the blocked entrance of the cave. On the ground in front of it was a token holder, complete with its token. She leaned forward to pick it up. As she grasped it, the ground rumbled briefly. She held the token up in the moonlight.

It was Slynd's, but now appeared almost dead, mid grey streaked with black.

Lantiah gasped in shock.

Neither Loul nor Zelriff had an explanation.

"What do we do with it? Do we take it or leave it here?" Zelriff was deathly pale.

Kirym slipped it into her bodice. "If it was meant to stay, it'd be buried in the cave. We have to take it. We can decide what to do with it later."

Yanda complained loudly about everything. The guard camp she'd known nothing about, the speed we travelled at, the lack of food and the stale taste of the water. When she started to complain about the distance she had to walk, Sundas enthusiastically offered to carry her.

She stopped complaining loudly, but continued to mumble under her breath.

The small valley was difficult to negotiate in the dark. It was particularly frightening when another strong earthquake struck. Although this wasn't as bad as the first, we could hear trees and rocks falling. The path had been obliterated.

"Test every tree and bush before you trust it," said Veld. After shaking a trunk to see it was still safely lodged in the ground, Veld tied a rope to it as a guide and to give us something to hold on to.

Arbreu went down first. He helped Loul and Zelriff and in ones and twos we followed.

Sundas volunteered to help Yanda, but I saw the look on the old lady's face and suggested he go ahead and get lamps from Veld's cave while I assisted her down the slope. She wasn't easy to help.

Eventually we all reached the floor of the valley. Climbing up the other side was much harder. Again Arbreu went first with a rope, but there was no path and we pushed our way through thick undergrowth to get to the top.

Halfway up, Yanda sat down and refused to move. Veld and I helped everyone around her. We managed to shield her from Sundas' view as he climbed past, however, Kirym saw her and said she'd sit with her for a while.

She sat down. "Would you like my cloak around you, Yanda? It's still cold this early in spring."

Yanda ignored her.

Kirym leaned in close. "I can ask Papa and Bokum to help us. I'm sure they wouldn't mind."

Yanda bristled. "I don't need help. I'm not weak. I'm older than them. I should be leading. I always used to lead. Even when I was little I used to skip ahead and everyone followed me." She got to her feet and pushed past Veld and on up the hill mumbling under her breath.

I was surprised by the compassion in Kirym's face as she followed the irritating old woman.

21

Arbreu

The moon had almost set when they spied the fires they had left late the previous afternoon. Cindra pushed past everyone and ran towards those grouped in the centre of the open area. Someone shouted when she was recognised.

Daylight showed the full extent of the damage to the site. The land across the northwest corner looked as if it had been gashed open with a huge axe. Water flowed down it, getting deeper with each aftershock.

The land the dwellings were built on had sunk and was still moving. The buildings were buried. Fortunately, those in the dwellings had been rescued quickly. Had they stayed with them, they'd not have survived.

After a hasty meal everyone set off towards the hoped-for safety of the settlement. They carried everything they could find, not knowing what would be usable when they arrived. The heavy load was piled onto a triangular hauling frame. However it was impossible to pull it over the damaged land.

Much of the path had disappeared and the frame snagged on rocks and fallen debris.

Veld asked Arbreu, Teema and Mekroe to carry it on their shoulders instead.

Many landmarks had altered or disappeared and much of the path was obliterated by fallen trees and debris. Cracks had opened and while most could be stepped across, they had to detour around the biggest. Eventually they walked across country, feeling it was easier and possibly safer.

Safer was questionable though. The ground continued to shake as they travelled, and just after midday a tree fell across their path moments after they had passed it.

"It's like travelling in a different land," said Teema.

It took most of the day to do the trip, and they were pleased as they neared the path that marked the beginning of the gathering area.

The elm had gone.

The massive tree had fallen into the settlement, demolishing Grenin's dwelling, a number of store sheds and an oven.

They climbed over it and walked into the wreckage of Veld's porch. The roof of the porch had collapsed and five mature trees had fallen into the open area. Raff and Soojee were tying packs on to a stretcher.

Soojee ran to Loul. "Oh Loul, I'm so pleased to see you, we've been so worried. We didn't know what to do. It's chaotic here. The stream has disappeared and the dwellings have collapsed. What happened up there? Is everyone all right? Oh my, my, my, oh," and she broke down sobbing on Loul's shoulder.

They cleaned up the gathering area as much as they could before dark. Only five dwellings were useable. Oven bricks were strewn over a large area and there was no running water, but most importantly, there had been few injuries — a broken arm, a twisted foot, and some bumps, bruises and a few cuts. Sojaff had been hit on the head and was still groggy, but she had improved and Loul felt a good sleep would make a great deal of difference to everyone.

They slept cheek by jowl, but everyone had somewhere warm and sheltered to sleep.

Arbreu slept well despite the crowding. He enjoyed waking to the chatter of children.

The early morning was busy as everyone fitted washing and eating around the general tidy up. The clothes worn by those in the cave were in need of cleaning and repair and Arbreu was back in borrowed clothing, his only clothes dusty, ripped and ragged.

The sun had just bathed the gathering area when everyone arrived to hear Veld's plans for the day.

He got straight to the point. "We'll eventually need to sort out the dwellings but at the moment everyone has a place to sleep. I want the water restored and I want to know what has happened to the land. The perimeter must be checked, the gorges, the lake, the eastern hills and the sea cliffs."

Those most able went furthest. Teema and Arbreu were asked to check the western end of the southern gorge and work their way along the sea cliffs to meet Veld and Findlow. They took little — a cloak each, food, weapons and rope — for this was to be a quick trip to get an idea of the changes in the land.

As they were preparing to leave, Mekroe approached Veld. "Papa, who do I go with?"

"I want you to help Old Harby redirect the stream, lad," said Veld as he turned to leave.

Mekroe looked rebellious and began to argue.

Veld frowned and turned back.

Teema grabbed Arbreu by the arm as he drew a breath to comment. "Come brother. The sooner we leave the sooner we return."

They hitched their packs to their shoulders and waved in the general direction of the family.

Kirym waited at the head of the path. As Teema and Arbreu approached she stretched up to click their tokens. "Take care and travel quickly. There's another adventure waiting for us. Her eyes sparkled with a knowledge they did not have.

Arbreu hunkered down and looked into her eyes. "I'm sure we have many adventures ahead of us, Kirym."

They walked away and Arbreu turned to wave just before he lost sight of her.

Bokum and Tarl had travelled with them until they reached the middle path to the eastern hills. They would check the lower lake, and return by way of the eastern end of the gorge.

Teema and Arbreu travelled straight to the bridge that Teema, Grenin and Young Harby had destroyed to thwart Slynd's entry into the land.

Teema set a fast pace and by the time they stopped for a drink it was mid-afternoon and they were at the gorge.

As they rested, Arbreu had his first chance to question Teema. "Why couldn't Mekroe join us? He's old enough and quite capable. Tarjin got to go and he's the same age."

Teema smiled. "Tarjin is almost three seasons older than Mek and he needs the experience. His parents are overprotective. Mekroe's problem is obedience. He's not so good at that. An earthquake doesn't mean lessons can be forgotten."

Arbreu thought for a few moments. "It seems a little unfair though. He was a great help on the trip from the cave and in repairing things at the settlement. Surely he could be a help now."

"He will be," said Teema. "Involving him in checking the

land would add nothing to our understanding. He has less prior knowledge, so he couldn't tell what had changed. He'll learn a better lesson at the settlement. Once he gets over his disappointment, if he gets over it, he'll realize he has responsibility. Old Harby has to find the stream and get it flowing again. I'd be happier playing with water in this weather, than running all the way to the sea cliffs and back. Mek can learn a lot. He's the oldest of the young men so he'll have to take the lead. It's only a punishment if he sees it as such."

Arbreu nodded; amazed that Teema had seen all of this while he'd just seen unfairness. He started to envy Mekroe.

"Still," Teema added. "Harby can be a hard task master and Mek'll still have to do as his mama says. Imagine having to cope with all those women." He laughed at Arbreu's expression, packed their flasks and doused the fire. "Tarl may be the eldest, and destined to be headman, but Mekroe is next in line. He needs many lessons. Second sons often go on to lead new groups. So he needs to learn all aspects of being a headman."

They set off towards the sea.

The water in the gorge was muddy and much higher than Arbreu remembered. There was a lot of floating debris. Trees had fallen on both banks and there'd been rock falls from the steep sides of the gorge. There was evidence here of the massive land upheaval they'd witnessed near the caves.

As the sun set, they made camp and ate the dried travelling food they'd brought with them.

Arbreu slept as soon as he lay down. Just as he closed his eyes he had a picture of Kirym smiling and waving.

He woke to the smell of hot food and opened his eyes to see Teema sitting beside him with a platter of roasted rabbit. Combined with a hot drink, he felt it was the best meal he'd ever eaten.

Taking the fush grass they'd used with them, they returned to the gorge. They soon found the reason for the higher water flow. A rock fall had created a dam across the river. Already the water had reached the top and was cascading down the other side. The dam was becoming unstable but it was also being added to as debris washed against it. Arbreu wondered if the debris would shore it up, or create enough weight to push it over. Only time would tell.

The walls of the gorge were still too steep to climb and the raised river level did not endanger them, or make it any easier to cross.

They stopped opposite Slynd's camp. Trees had fallen across the middle, and the remains of the fire had been blown away by wind, rain and time. They searched for the ledge where Slynd had hidden his treasure. It was gone. The quake had detached it. The remains lay by the water, the mummified corpse barely visible amongst the rocks.

"Had that happened before Slynd returned, he'd never have known I'd been there."

"You said it yourself, Arb. It wouldn't have made any difference. Nothing would change Slynd's plan. Anyway, you can't look back. Cope with what is. Now, you see that hill over there?" Arbreu nodded. "I'm going to climb it and check the surrounding area. You follow the gorge, make sure no trees have fallen across it and see if any rock falls make it easy to scale the cliffs. I'll catch up with you nearer the coast." Without waiting, he shouldered his pack and strode off.

Arbreu watched him go and continued along the gorge. By early afternoon, he was way past the hill. He'd tried to keep an eye on the summit but the trail became rough and he had to concentrate on his own progress.

In time the trees changed, growing further apart and he was able to move faster. It was pleasant walking through the cool shade. Arbreu could now smell the salt in the air and knew he was closer to the sea than he'd ever been.

The trees stopped abruptly and as Arbreu stood looking at the sparsely covered land that led to the cliffs, he heard a voice behind him.

"At this rate we'll never catch the men who are over near the cliffs."

He turned to see Teema leaning against a tree.

Arbreu felt a moment of panic. "There are men on the sea cliffs?"

Teema nodded. "If we move we'll intercept them before they get to the gorge."

He started to jog and Arbreu needed all his breath to keep up. They reached the cliffs and they both stood and stared.

The sea was amazing. The many colours of blue and white were unbelievable. The water heaved and crashed and where it met the cliffs, the spray flew high in the air. Where the river ran into the sea there was a wide line of brown that flowed towards the horizon getting wider and more diluted the further it got from land. Birds swooped above the cliffs, screaming at each other and the two young men.

Arbreu was awed. He could have stayed watching for the rest of the day, there was so much to see. However Teema pulled him away and they walked along the cliff. They moved slowly now, the potholed path was treacherous and some of the holes seemed quite deep. When it improved, they ran northward along a rutted path.

The sun was close to setting when Teema ducked behind a rock formation and put his finger to his lips.

They waited.

Arbreu caught his breath and listened carefully. He couldn't see the path, but eventually heard footsteps on the rocks. They'd walked past before Arbreu recognised the figures of Armos and Tarjin.

He and Teema quietly stepped in behind them.

Arbreu had taken only two steps when Armos rolled sideward, his knife poised to throw. He recognised them and laughed. "You're good, Arbreu, but not good enough. Teema can do it though. Followed me once, for half a day without me knowing. I learned from that to check behind me — frequently."

Teema helped him to his feet. "This way," he said, as he led the way to where they would camp for the night.

In a small hollow was the framework of a dwelling, roughly covered with fush grass. To one side a ground oven was just beginning to steam. With relief, Arbreu dumped his pack and fush grass next to the dwelling.

Armos sniffed the air in appreciation. "Thank goodness it's not travelling food again," he said. "Ahhh, this is the life!"

He sank down and looked around while Tarjin smiled contentedly.

"All right boy, you can speak, but remember you learn much more by listening." He turned to Teema and Arbreu. "Talked me into senility before we'd gone a stone's throw from the settlement." He playfully punched Tarjin in the shoulder.

Arbreu watched Teema sorting out his pack with some wonder. "Did you get to the top of the hill?"

"Teema nodded. "Old Urbrill's new forest has pretty much fallen. It'll be good for firewood in the future. There's a landslide on the west face of Curpitt's Hill. Lingles path is a bit boggy. That'll have to be watched, but it could be a new water source in the future. Lots of minor stuff too, but that's the worst of it."

Armos nodded. "Papa always said there was water near Lingles."

Arbreu stared openmouthed at Teema. "You mean you

went up the hill, hunted, came here and set up camp, found Armos, and then came and found me, in the time I walked along the river?"

Teema laughed. "Not quite. I knew Armos would be around here by now, and I saw signs of him from the hill. I knew where you'd be. It wasn't difficult. I just read the land. "

Arbreu shook his head in wonder. He picked up the fush grass he'd brought with him and slit the vine holding it together.

Tarjin rushed over to help and together they finished roofing the dwelling. The remaining fush was laid on the ground for them to sleep on.

Armos settled back and watched Tarjin with a half-smile.

Teema opened the oven, brought out a steaming grass-wrapped bundle and slit it open. Steam enveloped him and when it cleared he pulled out three plump birds and split them apart.

They risked burnt fingers to eat the tender meat immediately.

Arbreu was famished and the food was wonderful, almost as good as the rabbit from that morning.

After eating, they leaned back contentedly with a drink each. Tarjin fell asleep where he sat and Armos told Arbreu and Teema about his trip.

"The lad was so excited about coming along. I had to make him walk behind me to stop him running out of steam before we lost sight of the settlement. He has a good eye if he's allowed to learn how to use it." He looked serious. "This land is damaged. That rolling thing has unearthed much that's been hidden for generations. It's a different landscape from the one I grew up with. I know nature is forgiving, but the force that came through here is frightening. How do we settle again with the peace we knew before the land became so angry?"

Their talk turned to the changes in the gorge and as the moon rose they roused Tarjin and settled under the protection of the fush grass dwelling.

Teema woke them at first light, as they still had a long way to go. It was cooler this close to the sea and Arbreu was hungry again.

Teema had set out the remains of the meat from last night, and water was boiling to give them each a hot drink. Dousing the fire, Armos led them onward through the grey dawn.

Early in the afternoon they met Danth and Tant, so they stopped to exchange notes over a hot drink. Danth and Tant were returning to the settlement and words were exchanged between Danth and Armos when Danth ordered a reluctant Tarjin to return with him.

Armos shook his head in disgust as they left. "How will that boy ever learn?"

Arbreu, Teema and Armos continued along the land edging the cliffs, far enough back to be away from the sharp edged rocks and potholes, but occasionally having to detour as the cliff edge claimed the land.

Armos had a wealth of knowledge about the land. He was inspiring to travel with.

Arbreu learned a huge amount. By evening, he was exhausted.

Late the following afternoon, Arbreu smelled food cooking. At the same time, an arrow embedded in the ground in front of him. He dived for cover, disconcerted when Armos and Teema just laughed. Teema pointed towards a rock formation ahead, but even then it wasn't until Kirym moved towards them that he saw her.

"I told you there was another adventure waiting for us,"

she said. "It's so beautiful here, but there's no valley."

"Another dead end," said Teema. "I wonder why it was on the map. Mind you, whatever it was could have disappeared. I mean these rocks erode over the seasons, so possibly that section of the cliff has long fallen into the sea."

"That's possible. The cliffs here are unstable at the edge. We've not been able to look over. But all I said was that there was no valley, and Old Harby said that anyway. There is something really strange here, and that may have far more to do with why we're here than a shadow on a map."

With that, she would tell them no more.

They followed her to where Veld waited with a small group who knew about the search. This was the area they had pinpointed on the map. Veld had kept this in mind when organising the checking the land.

The view was magnificent. The sea stretched out in front of them, merging into the horizon far ahead. North of where they were standing was a brown smudge far out near the horizon. Otherwise there was nothing seaward of note.

Landward the trees closed in around the rocky area. Across the open area were a lot of boulders, and areas of scrubby bush. All in all, there was nothing unusual to make them look twice.

"Well, we've waited for you to get here before we investigated anything. The verse says we stand on the highest cliff," said Veld. "But I can't see why. There's nothing here."

"Perhaps because this isn't the highest point." Klrym pointed to a small hill behind them. "That is."

Veld shrugged and picked up his pack. "Very well, let's see if it makes a difference."

At the top, they looked around. They were on a plateau with rock formations around them. To the north, the cliffs curved around and they could see the gorge opening up to the sea. As with the southern gorge a brown line curved northwest towards the horizon widening and getting more diluted as it went.

"Well, Kirym. What's different here?"

Kirym pointed to the gorge. "We can see where the water from the gorge goes. Down there it was just a smudge. Here it seems to go to the horizon and beyond. Maybe that's what we needed to see. We might see more in the morning too."

Sundas and Findlow built a curved wall in front of one of the rock formations. The area between was sheltered on all sides from the wind and soon they had a fire roaring and food cooking. The half-light lingered long after the sun disappeared but it was good to be in the rock shelter. The wind was sharp and it was a shock when they left their refuge.

Veld insisted they not wander after dark. "There are a lot of crevices in the rocks around here and it'd be easy to fall into one. At best you'd break a leg." He set guards at the entrance to make sure no one did.

They settled around the fire wrapped in cloaks and rugs.

Then the noise started. At first it was a low throaty whistle but within a short time, it rose to a roar. The sound seemed to thunder and rumble around them, making Arbreu shiver. After an extended bellow it settled to a husky moan, increasing to a howl on occasion.

In the safety of their rock enclosure, they stared at each other. The fire added its own roar to the night sounds as the wind gusted around them.

"We heard it last night, and I think that's why we're here," said Veld. "I want to know what it is. Maybe it has a bearing on the verse Arbreu found."

They settled in the shelter and listened. After a while it became quite friendly and they slept.

Findlow and Arbreu were on guard duty when the sound died. "What do you make of that, Arbreu? I've never heard anything like it."

"Nor I," Arbreu said. "It sounded like a trapped animal. It didn't appear to get closer, just louder on occasion."

"It's caused by the wind," said Kirym sleepily.

"How'd you figure that out?" Findlow tucked her rugs around her shoulders.

"Every time the noise roared, so did our fire, although the fire wasn't as loud."

"But the wind doesn't make that sort of noise normally, why here?"

"With the fire there's a rock sitting at an angle in the wall behind it. The wind came through the hole it created. To make the huge noise, it must be blowing through something big. We have to find out what."

"The wind's blowing now but there's no noise. There was no noise yesterday either. You may be wrong, sweetie." Findlow smiled gently.

She sat up and shook her head. "The wind has died. The noise reduced as the wind did. Anyway, it's directional. Last night, it blew west, away from the land. Yesterday it was blowing towards land. It's the difference between day and night."

Findlow looked at Arbreu and shrugged. "Sounds plausible, I'll be interested in what Veld has to say when he wakens."

"He'll agree with her," said Veld from beneath his rug. "We talked about it while you two were sleeping. It must be to do with one of the fissures. Kirym pointed out the line of verse that said 'into the deepness of the land the wind begins to blow'. We have to find out where it goes in. It seems to be northwest of here. We'll move today and try to isolate it. Then we'll decide why we need to find it."

Findlow laughed. "It's a bit like a puzzle, isn't it? We find one piece, it leads to the next and each new piece alters our perception of the last."

There were a lot of fissures on the lower plateau, but they were able to dismiss most of them as being too shallow or unable to be affected by the wind. By early afternoon they had reduced it to three possibilities.

They set up a new shelter between them and Teema and Arbreu went hunting for their evening meal. Sundas, Findlow and Armos collected more firewood. It was easier there, the land side of the cliff angled down gently and much of it was wooded.

As the sun set they watched the sea. A long way out Arbreu saw five or six large fish. They surfaced occasionally and then disappeared for a while. He pointed them out to Kirym and they watched until it was too dark on the water to see them.

As they were eating the noise started again.

"It's different here," said Teema. "You could imagine a caged animal out there."

"Kirym's right. It rises and falls with the wind," Arbreu said.

As with the previous night, it settled to a low roar that increased and decreased through the evening.

Once the noise was steady, they lit lamps and ventured out to inspect the crevices. The first two were silent. The third was on the far side of a thick clump of scrubby bushes. The crevice was silent, but the bushes vibrated with the wind.

"I'm sure the noise comes from there, but we can do nothing more now. Back to the shelter, we'll check in the morning." Veld was adamant and insisted no one leave the protection of the rock walls.

Before light the noise deepened and faded, and as the sun

rose it stopped.

The plants looked unremarkable in the daylight. They had grown in the lea of a waist high rock outcrop. The plants were small and stunted. They looked old, and seemed to crawl along the ground.

Arbreu pulled at the first bush. It was stringy and resisted movement.

The roots had dug into the rock cracks, but came away with some firm encouragement. He attacked a second and third. Sundas helped him, and as they worked their way in and around, they realised the bushes had grown to cover a large hole in the ground. The surface of the rock around the hole was sound so they attacked the growth on the northern side.

The hole was a lot bigger than Arbreu thought it would be, wider than his height. "I'm amazed we missed it as we searched over the cliff top."

"It was well camouflaged, and the bushes are thick. There's nothing obvious to encourage us to come anywhere near it," said Veld.

He lay on his belly and looked into the hole, but could see nothing.

Armos tied a lamp to a rope and lowered it into the hole. When he came to the end of the line, they still saw nothing. "It's too light out here. First, we need to measure the hole. Then after dark, we need to see what's down there." He pulled the rope up, added another four to it and lowered it again. When he could no longer feel the weight of the lamp, he assumed it had reached the bottom. He tied a knot in the rope, pulled it up and measured it.

"I'd say it goes almost to sea level," he said as he looped and tied the rope. "That creates a problem. We want to go down and explore, but we can't just slide down the rope. We'd get too tired, burn our hands and we'd never be able to climb out again. So we must find a different way down."

They spent the morning trying to think of ways to reach the bottom.

Teema sighed. "Well, let's wait until we know if this is the hole making the noise. We may not have to climb down."

"We have to," said Kirym. "The next part of the verse says, climb into the shaded earth."

Veld shook his head. "I just wish I knew how. It's a long way down."

Sundas solved the problem of descent. "If we make a body harness like you used at the waterfall and tie the ropes to it, and then we put the lightest person in it, but not Kirym. We can lower them into the hole, and bring them back up if we all work together. We shouldn't let Zeprah go either, 'cause it could be dangerous and we should protect her too." There was an uncomfortable silence, but Zeprah roared with laughter.

Sundas looked mystified amid a general chuckle.

"It'll work, Sundas, 'if you anchor the rope." Veld looked around. "Now, who's the lightest? I think it's between Findlow and Arbreu."

Arbreu hung over the hole, his heart in his mouth. It seemed a long way down. The wind whistled past him, chilling him somewhat. At first the rope swung round in circles, and he worried it would unravel.

Armos suggested he put his feet on the wall to steady himself.

It helped.

Findlow, Raff and Sundas were on the rope and Arbreu knew they wouldn't drop him, but he worried about it fraying as it rubbed against the edge of the hole. Veld had placed a cloak over the edge, but Arbreu wondered if it was enough. He peered down, trying to make out something, anything, but it was too dark to see anything around him. The lamp on the ground below him seemed so far away, and it only lit up a small area.

At first things went smoothly and he went down steadily, but then the rope started to catch and there were a couple of sickening drops. Then suddenly, he was being pulled up rapidly for a distance before jolting to a stop.

Veld called out that all was well and Arbreu hung there for a while before continuing down.

He thought about the knots Armos had used to tie the ropes together and hoped they would hold. Armos seemed sure of them and everyone else was happy, but they weren't the one hanging in mid-air and relying on them.

Arbreu was relieved to see a ledge just below and to one side. He called up to Veld, and swung on the rope to reach it.

Just as his toe touched it Veld called out, but his voice echoed too much to be understood. Again the rope jolted and Arbreu thumped down onto the ledge. He sat there for a short time getting his breath back. Veld's voice again echoed from above, unclear in the cavernous space. He called back, but the answer evaded him.

Arbreu sat on the edge of the ledge, readjusted the extra rope attached to his belt and pushed himself off. He dropped straight down for a distance and jolted to a sudden stop again, the harness biting into his arms and legs. As he waited he looked up. The ledge was silhouetted against the hole above him and Arbreu had the impression of worked stone. He wanted to explore it more, but needed to see what was at the bottom first.

Eventually he reached the ground and climbed out of the harness. He was cold and stiff. The cave around him seemed vast. He could hear strange noises all around, but couldn't identify them and wondered if the cave was home to wild animals. Something was roaring, but he realised it was too regular to be an animal.

Arbreu loosened his knife in its sheath, squatted down and checked the ground around him. The rock below the hole was weatherworn and littered with twig and leaf debris from the shrubs above.

Rock pillars dotted around the cave, and he tied a rope around one.

Taking a guide from the hole above him, he walked north, but found his way barred by a swiftly flowing stream. It was too wide to jump over, so he returned to the hole and went south to the cave wall.

There was no sign of animals even in the dirt build-up near the walls. He followed the wall towards the sea, letting the rope out as he walked.

A broken branch lay on the ground half way along. The bark had been stripped off it and another shorter branch had been expertly notched into it about a quarter of the way along. People had been there before.

The wall ended with a rock-fall. A little exploration showed there had been a tunnel here in the past. Arbreu could hear rhythmic noises coming through the hole; waves crashing in the distance, he thought.

He removed enough rocks from near the top where there was a small space, and after he checked to ensure no more rocks would fall, he climbed through. The rock fall wasn't very big, and would be easy to clear if necessary.

At first Arbreu wasn't sure what he was looking at. It was still night, but way ahead was a big opening, the sky lighter than the darkness of the cave.

He stared in amazement.

Silhouetted against the cave entrance was a boat. It looked

similar to those carved on the blade of his knife. He took the knife out and tried to compare the two in the lamp light. It was impossible and he returned the knife to its sheath. He walked along the length of the boat staring in awe at the massive vessel. It sat on a wooden path with large blocks of wood chocking it along the bottom. A second boat sat in front of the first. Arbreu could see no easy way to get on board so he climbed back through the tunnel and returned to the lamp sitting beneath the hole. He climbed into the harness, attached the safety line and tugged it to let Veld know he was ready.

Surer of the rope now, and more aware of his surroundings, he saw what appeared to be more ledges as he rose, although many were quite distant from the hole. He rested at the same ledge he'd stopped at on the way down. This time he walked around it finding more wood similar to the piece on the cave floor, although this was very weathered and crumbled at his touch. At the far end of the ledge, was what seemed to be a step down. He was about to search further when he was suddenly jerked upward again. This was frightening. Because the back of the ledge was far to the right of the hole. He swung left as soon as his feet left the stone. It was a while before he got them on the wall to steady himself.

They sat around the fire as Arbreu talked of his trip. He thought about his impressions of the ledges.

"Veld, I think they're man-made or maybe partly man-made. There could be a path between them and if I'm right, then except for the drop to the first ledge we may be able to climb down. Even if there isn't a path, it may be easier to get from one ledge to the next, rather than using the ropes and going right to the bottom each time."

22

Teema Speaks

As we discussed Arbreu's impressions, the sun rose in a cloudy sky.

"What do we do next?" Findlow asked.

"We clear the tunnel and check the boats. We need to see if they're usable before we raise any hopes. And we need to find the easiest way down." Veld turned to Arbreu. "Tell me about the ledges. Are you sure they connect?"

He shook his head. "I really don't know, but even if they don't, we could make ladders or something to connect them. If they do, we'll still need to organise handrails to make them safe, and we'll need to have safety ropes on all levels."

Veld smiled. "Are you ready to go down again, Arbreu?"

He nodded.

"Let's find out what's on the first ledge. Teema, you come too. We'll stay down for the morning. I want us back up before the sun begins to travel to the western horizon. I think the wind that blows across and down the hole during the night may very well blow up the hole once the land heats up. I may be wrong, but today we find out. Armos watch the sun, please."

Arbreu went first because he knew where the ledge was. Sundas insisted on being the anchor on the rope. He'd been the same when Arbreu first went down, staying on the rope all of the time.

The back half of the ledge was in darkness and it was bigger than I'd imagined from Arbreu's description. The far end was chipped from the rock, and had steps leading up and down. There were more ledges than Arbreu had seen, some of them well away from the light and difficult to see. Some of the ledges had areas chipped deep into the walls. We were down three levels when Armos shouted. His voice echoed around the cave, and we couldn't understand him. So we climbed back to the first ledge again.

"Now, Veld. Now!" Armos called.

"The day passed by so fast," I said as we helped Arbreu into the harness. "I didn't imagine it was this late."

I went next, surprised at the force of wind buffeting me. At the top I was grabbed, the harness striped off me and sent back for Veld. Sundas, Harby, Arbreu and Armos all grabbed the rope to pull him up as quickly as possible.

We sat in the sun and discussed our exploration.

"We have far less time to work down there than I thought," said Armos. "The wind came up so quickly. Had we waited, I doubt you'd be here now. Probably stuck down there until evening. If you're not up before the wind rises, you're down there until it dies. It's quite freaky." He was visibly shaken.

Veld nodded. "Best we find these things out now. We need to ensure that anyone caught on the ledges is safe and warm.

We know there's a path down for three levels. Hopefully they go right to sea level. It'll be safer when we add handrails. Even then, safety harnesses must be used. It'll take longer, but if you slip, well, you wouldn't survive."

There were various noises of agreement.

"I don't think we can work on the ledges as the wind gets stronger," I said. "We'll have to be careful where we put things and I'm wondering if the areas cut into the walls are there for that reason. And if you're stuck on a ledge, that'd be the place to stay until the wind dies. We should store protective gear there.

"It'd be better to ensure no one's caught down there at all," said Kirym. "Papa, the writings talked about the early dawn. If we want time to work on the boats we'll have to spend the whole day down there."

Kirym was right.

We needed Armos with us this time. He was the boat builder and the only one who knew enough to say whether the boats were useable and, if not, how to fix them — if they were fixable.

Armos talked to Arbreu to get an idea of what to expect. He studied the engraving on the knife and asked more questions. We took food, water and rugs, tools, jackets, lamps, extra fuel and ropes.

Veld asked Arbreu and me to join him. That left enough men to let us down and pull us up. Kirym begged to go, but Veld refused until we knew what the dangers were.

We slept early knowing we'd again be up before light. We ate well. For those of us going into the cave, there'd be no hot food until we returned. We dressed warmly and strapped on our knives.

Everyone came out to help or watch.

Arbreu went first, I followed, then Veld, Armos and the basket of gear. It was cold and dark in the cave. We searched for the steps leading to the bottom ledge, but couldn't find them until I walked further into the hill.

They were narrow and steep, but with the addition of handrails they'd be quite useable. We climbed to the first ledge and inspected that, then to the second, third and fourth. Most had storage places chipped into the cliff and out of the weather.

Veld found some tools at the back of one of the ledges and on the third from the bottom, I found a large package wrapped in waterproof material and tied with a strange type of rope. Dawn light filtered into the cave and with a wave to those above us we walked towards the tunnel.

Clearing a narrow path through the tunnel was simple, it wasn't a bad fall and the roof seemed strong. It looked recent; I wondered if it had happened during the earthquake.

We stood open-mouthed.

Silhouetted against the cave mouth were the two boats. They were wide bottomed, bigger versions of our small boats.

I was amazed that for the age they must have been, they appeared intact, although I wasn't an expert on aged things nor boats.

While Armos inspected the keels, Veld gave me a leg up to get aboard. It wasn't easy, the boat had high sides, and I'd not have managed except for two small ledges that ran around the boat, about one and a half arm's length apart.

In the middle of the deck was a small dwelling, the door hanging drunkenly on one leather hinge. The mast stood in front of the dwelling. About the height of six tall men, it sat just below the roof of the cave. The bottom of the mast was engraved, almost identical to the carving on the top of the stellon. A beam sat across the deck at the base of the mast.

I tied a rope to the mast and threw it down to Veld. While everyone climbed aboard, I studied some rope strands I'd found sitting against the cabin wall. They had fallen from the mast, perished with passing time. The strands would give us an idea of the thickness we'd need to replace them.

Armos was last on to the deck. "She's very similar to those we use on the lake," he said. "Quite wide, there'll be plenty of room inside. I'm impressed with the condition, I'm not sure what they've coated it with, but it's aided the preservation. If the other boat's as good, there'll be little to do before we use them."

As the light strengthened I dragged the dwelling door open. It was light enough now for us to not need lamps. There were bench seats along each side and we could see through the top half of the front although there were shutters on both sides to give protection from the weather. On the far side, a trapdoor led into the body of the boat.

Lamps lit, we descended the steps to a door at the bottom. It opened onto a huge open area, almost the width and length of the boat. Near the centre, the mast came through from the deck above, and disappeared through the floor. At the far end was a wall with two wide doors in it. Cupboards lined the bottom of the walls with shelves above. Piles of folded material with coils of rope attached, sat on the shelf.

I lifted one down and shook it out.

Armos laughed. "It's a hammock. It's the easiest way to sleep aboard a boat." He counted the number in one pile and the number of piles, glanced around the boat and whistled. "About one hundred and twenty and there's room for more. It caters for a lot of people." He showed us how they hooked up. "I wonder where the stores were kept." He opened the doors in the front wall. Inside were huge barrels.

"These are for water, I think," called Armos, "and there's a trapdoor down so I can check the mast stepping."

Veld opened the cupboards. Most were empty, but a few had large chests in them. One was particularly handsome with metal edges and a solid handle at the front.

Veld tried to pull it out, but it wouldn't budge. Close inspection showed it was bolted into place. The bolts slipped aside smoothly and it rolled out.

Veld stared at the crest carved into the top of the chest. He gave a whoop of delight and grabbed me in a huge bear-hug, dancing around the room. "This is it, this is it," he crowed.

Under the crest was a list of names. Arbreu read them out.

"Tarj son of Varl

Arbros son of Tarj

Arabos son of Arbros

Vald son of Arabos

Vauld son of Vald."

Vauld was Veld's great-grandpapa.

I looked at him. "It's your lineage?"

Veld nodded happily. "This is it, the final piece of the puzzle. We've found the hidden path. Without the names I wouldn't have been sure, but this has to be it." He lifted the lid of the chest.

A thick journal sat on a pile of maps.

The writing in the journal was small and interspersed with drawings. The first map showed a section of land with an enlargement of an area. The second showed our land and the land to each side although not enough to tell us much more than we already knew of the coast to the north and south.

Veld piled them together, and placed them aside to put in his pack. "I'll study them in better light."

Under the top tray, there were bolts of material, containers of jewels and delicate chains. A pack of journals sat to one side of the containers.

Veld added them to the pile to take with him. He closed the chest, pushed it back into the cupboard, fastening it into place.

The next cupboard held three huge piles of coarse brown material.

Armos leaned forward and touched them. "I wondered where these'd be," he said. "These are the sails. If they've perished, we'll be able to get a pattern and I'd like to have spare sets on both boats anyway. These look good though, well preserved."

The next cupboard revealed sacks of rope, and containers, which when unsealed revealed a thick black liquid.

Armos grunted his approval. "I think that's the stuff they've put on the outside." He pulled a wad of parchment out from behind one container, studied it for a few moments and nodded. "Yes, and this tells me how to make more. We should paint it over the outsides of both before we leave." He flicked through the leaves of parchment and nodded. "As long as it's dry before entering the water, it works. We'll need to do it after the trip when we pull them out of the water too." He pointed to a sealed flask. "That holds something for the sails."

We found platters and flasks, large and small, wall hangings similar to those in Veld's dwelling and more material, more fine and everyday cloth. It was a treasure trove of goods.

At midday, we sat on the deck to eat. Armos looked around happily. "There were tales of big boats, but I never thought I'd see them, let alone sail one. Six men can easily sail it, even in bad weather. Everyone should learn though, Veld. It seems to be a larger version of the small boat, so we can use the small ones to teach everyone the principles we'll need on the journey. Papa, Grenin and Young Harby can help teach those who don't know."

Veld nodded. "We'll need more ropes, although I think we've enough in storage. These seem to be well preserved but I want extra. Let's look at the other boat."

Arbreu grabbed the rope ready to climb down, but Armos pointed to a ladder sitting on the deck. Veld checked it was sound while Armos showed us how the boat was steered.

"What's that?" I asked, pointing to a huge stone with a large hole through the centre sitting on a large metal plate at the back of the boat.

Armos looked at the ropes lying on the deck near it. "It's the anchor. We'll definitely get new ropes for this and ensure we have more of the same weight. The ropes have to be good. I'd hate to lose it at sea. It's not something you can replace." He grinned as the others laughed.

The second boat was also in a good state, although an area of the boards at the top of the deck were a little more weathered than Armos was happy with.

"The board will be easy to replace," he said. "Both are well provisioned. If need be, we could bring rugs, food, water and leave, although personal possessions would make for a more comfortable voyage."

Armos showed us how the boats were chocked and how they'd been brought ashore. It was ingenious.

We walked to the cave entrance and looked out at the sea. Armos explained how the water had come into the cave and pointed out the line of the highest tide. We looked back at the boats and saw that both were named. Dream Seeker and Dragon Quest.

Our arrival at the settlement at sun high coincided with Harby getting the water running. He and his boys were celebrating. All were covered with mud and Harby was as happy about it as the boys.

Mekroe, no longer upset, was having fun.

Veld set a large sheet of parchment on one of the big tables. He sketched a rough map of the area and was noting the changes in the land. As each group reported to him, he sketched in their observations.

Arbreu and I studied it.

Raff had reported the devastation of a large area of forest on the northern side of the gorge. The gorge was stable although a big rock fall had extended the rapids below the lower waterfall. An area of land on the south side of the north gorge between the rapids and the waterfall had sunk and was much closer to the water. However the cliff was still sheer and the water churned along its edge. Some of the big waterfall had fallen away. The rock fall that had closed the path was partially visible, and there was no access from the far side. The small cliff to the east of the graves had collapsed and covered the burial site.

Arbreu and I added our notes to the map, with a few extra comments in the journal placed next to it.

As the afternoon wore on, I realised there were only a few people in the settlement and I wandered off to find the rest of them.

The stream was muddy and sluggish, the flow more reduced than before. I couldn't see it being any use to us. I followed it east to see what had happened to it. Soon I heard screams and laughter and I turned through the trees towards the sound.

When the earthquake diverted the stream, it created a large pool and this was being used to play and swim in. The far side where clean water flowed into the pool had become an area to wash clothes. The clean washing festooned the nearby bushes.

Sundas sat in the middle of the pool and the children climbed over him, using his shoulders as a platform to jump into the water. They splashed him and each other, laughed, screamed and squealed.

Sundas' booming laughter echoed around the clearing.

I leaned against a tree and drank in the wonderful scene.

"Yoohoo-hoo" Mekroe's war-cry echoed around the clearing as he broke the edge of the pool away and rode the wave of water as it streamed towards the settlement. That was accompanied by a corresponding groan from the children who realized their pool was fast disappearing. Reluctantly, they climbed out, wrapped up in rugs and towels and headed back to the settlement.

I joined Loul as she folded washing.

"Will the water run clear?" I asked.

"Probably by sun high tomorrow, but we've plenty of stored water. We've enough of everything to ensure there's no particular shortage. It's been a generous land and in some way I'll be sorry to leave it."

Checking the land had been a good exercise, but everyone was still unsettled, jumping at the occasional aftershocks and loud sounds. Veld suggested a feast and we spent the day getting ready.

Everyone worked hard with the preparation and it was almost like old times. The fire burned bright and the food was excellent. Once we'd eaten and the food put aside to snack on, the music began.

I joined Arbreu under one of the remaining standing trees. "Not dancing?" I asked.

He shook his head. "Wouldn't trust the seat of my trousers to any excessive movement, they're pretty threadbare. Slynd's men stole clothes from their victims, but I refused. It'd be better if my tunic was longer, but I tore it again during the earthquake." He paused. "There's so much happening, but I'll have to get something together, these won't last much longer. I'll ask Loul for some advice tomorrow."

Kirym danced up to us, her festival dress well above her knees. An extensive tear had exasperated Loul so much she'd ripped the hem off rather than mend it. "Isn't it nice to be with the whole family again?" She sat between us and lowered her voice. "Tomorrow, we start preparing for the trip. I'm going to help get the small boats out of storage. Everyone has to learn to sail them." She stood and danced away.

"You'd best come with me," I said to Arbreu.

Perplexed he followed me as I entered our dwelling and opened the chest that held my possessions. I rummaged in the bottom and brought out a pair of trousers. "You'll need these if you're to dance tonight and travel tomorrow." I added a tunic and a cloak to the pile and walked towards the door.

He joined me a short time later looking the best dressed I'd ever seen him.

I shrugged off his thanks. "It reflects badly on me if my brother shows his behind to the family," I said, with a laugh that he shared.

23

Kirym Speaks

Papa revealed our plans. We would leave in late summer. That would give us time to prepare the boats, learn to sail and gather what extra food we could. He sent Teema and Sundas with a group of men back to the cliffs to start work.

Bokum, Arbreu and I joined a group sent to get the small boats out of winter storage. Danth took charge, planning lessons for those with us who hadn't used the boats before.

Our usual paths were a jumble of uprooted trees and dislodged rocks, so we walked across country. We had an overnight stop and it was still early when we climbed the hill that led to the lake and shelters Armos had built to house the boats over winter.

I didn't recognise the view. No one did. The lake was flooded, the water a great deal higher than at the beginning of spring. The clearing we had rested in on our trip to Raff's was under water, with just the tops of the trees we rested beneath showing above the surface. The slipway Armos and his boys had built two summers ago was completely submerged and the shelters holding the boats were mere shadows below the water.

"Bokum, you were supposed to report this sort of thing," Danth said accusingly. "That's why you were sent here after the quake. You waste our time. Why didn't you tell us?"

Bokum shook his head. "It wasn't like this then. The water was marginally higher than usual, but that just looked like spring thaw."

"So why's it so high now?" Danth looked around.

Northwards the lake with its new banks was hidden by trees. "Go and check the top lake. See if it's flooded too. I'll check the gorge. You can catch up with us. And if you can't get it right this time, boy, don't bother coming back."

Bokum, Rathay and Mekroe shouldered their packs and weapons and jogged southeast.

Danth flicked his pack over his shoulder and we followed the edge of the lake. The track was rough and difficult, so he led us down the hill to an easier path.

We walked until late morning and stopped for a meal.

While waiting for water to heat, I walked through the small trees to the top of the hill.

The view was even more disturbing here than when we first saw the lake. Most of the trees had fallen and the water lapped near the top of the hill. Ahead where the river left the lake on its journey to the gorge, a section of the hill had slipped. The massive scar on the land indicated just how much soil and rock had fallen. The river was completely blocked. With no outlet, the water had backed up.

Even so, there was more water in the lake than I thought there'd be from one blocked stream.

I couldn't understand what was happening here.

Suddenly a rainbow erupted from the hill a little north of me.

I'd never seen that before, the sun was in the wrong place for a rainbow. The hill looked warped and it seemed to be the wrong colour.

I walked down to talk to Danth.

He dismissed my concerns, but when I insisted, he followed me back up the hill.

Arbreu and Mekrar came too.

I pointed along the hill. "It seems to bulge there. It shouldn't do that. There's something wrong."

Danth shook his head. "It's an illusion. Worry about the water, not the hill."

"It is the water," said Arbreu.

Danth snorted. "Most unlikely."

"I saw something similar many seasons ago. The hill is saturated. The water will break through soon and wash down towards the sea. This part of the hill was never meant to contain water. And it won't hold out for much longer," Arbreu said.

Danth looked across the lake. "Nah! The landslide will wash out first. It won't be a problem."

Arbreu shook his head. "I don't think so. The landslide comes from the far side. It's made up of clay and rocks. It's solid. Even if it does wash out, the water won't drop quickly enough to allow the hill to dry. The soil here is too friable. The water soaks through easily and the hill will begin to seep. But the hill will breach as much from the weight of water as anything else."

Danth looked uncertain. "I'll talk to Veld when we get back. He can decide what to do."

"If the hill breaches," I said. "The water will swamp the settlement. Papa needs to evacuate everyone immediately. We have to go back straight away, Danth, but we need to warn Bokum too. He can't return this way. It would be safer for them to go on the south side of the cave, and take the central path."

Danth wasn't listening to me. He seemed distracted.

Arbreu squatted down and pressed the ground firmly. As he lifted his hand, I could see a film of moisture coating it. Water pooled in the depression he made. He grabbed Danth's arm. "Danth, we must get off this hill and get back to the settlement. NOW!"

Danth nodded shortly. "All right, boy! We'll go." He strode down the hill, mumbling under his breath.

At the camp, he kicked the fire, scattering it over the hill. "Get your packs. We're leaving. Going back to the settlement. Now!" He grabbed a pack and hurled it towards Mekrar, then snatched his up and walked back along the path.

Arbreu grabbed his arm. "We should get to the bottom of the hill. It'll be safer."

Danth changed his direction.

I caught up with him. "What about Bokum?"

He kept on walking.

I began to panic, he wasn't listening. "Danth!" I screamed.

He stopped and looked around. "What now? You said go back, and we're going back. That is what you want, isn't it?"

"Yes, but we need to let Bokum know."

"So tell him," he said angrily, and turned away.

"I'll go with her," Arbreu called, but Danth had already continued on, the others trailing behind him.

Mekrar also turned back.

I handed her one of my packs and stretched up to click her token. "Go with Danth, Mekrar. Make sure Papa understands how dangerous this is. You tell him if Danth doesn't."

She nodded and ran to catch up with the others.

I hitched my pack onto my shoulder and started to run.

"Kirym! Stop!" Arbreu sounded nervous. I turned back to see what was wrong.

"Until we're off this wet area, we need to step cautiously. I don't know what would cause the hill to breach and let the water through, but a heavy footstep could do it. We must tread softly, and possibly the bottom of the slope would be safer for now."

I saw the sense in his argument.

It was mid-afternoon before he felt the ground was dry enough to move faster. We ran until the light was almost gone.

"What if Bokum returns on a different path, Kirym? What if we miss him?"

"We have to hope he doesn't. But I intend to light a fire when it's dark. If he sees it, he'll investigate."

We collected wood and fush grass. The sky was clear and there was a chill in the air. It wouldn't rain, but there would be a frost before morning. We created a nest of the fush grass to keep us warm and dry. In the darkness, we lit the fire and heated food and water.

Once it was really dark, I walked away from the fire and climbed a tall tree to see if there was any sign of Bokum. The whole area was in darkness. I watched until Arbreu called me down and suggested we eat and rest. When he was sleeping soundly, I again climbed the tree. There was still no sign of Bokum.

I climbed down to find Arbreu waiting for me. "Kirym, you must tell me if you leave camp. I was worried."

"I'm not a baby, Arbreu, and in case there's any question of who's in charge here, it's me. I'm aware there are things you know that I don't, it goes both ways."

He thought about it and nodded, with a wry smile. "All right, you're in charge, but you still need to let me know."

I took a deep breath. "I'm sorry. I will in future. But now we have to contact Bokum. We have a special connection to him. He's our token brother. So we click tokens and think about him and what we want him to do."

Arbreu pulled back. "That's fine, but what do we want him to do?"

"It has to be simple. Um — light a fire and stay with it. Then we can find him. That's simpler than having him find us."

Arbreu nodded and leaned forward to click his token to mine.

I thought of Bokum and of him lighting a fire overnight. I could almost see him sitting up and looking at me. Then a picture of Teema came into my head.

I opened my eyes and looked at Arbreu's shocked expression. "What was Teema doing there, Kirym?"

I shook my head. "I don't know. He's aligned to us too and maybe he read the message we sent Bokum."

"Should we send one to reassure him?"

"No. Bokum could read that and get it wrong. We'll contact Teema later." We sat together and waited. Images of Bokum and Teema flashed through my mind. Then I felt the flare of a fire.

Arbreu smiled. "Wow, it got through. I didn't think it would. But where is he?"

I laughed. "I'll climb the tree and see."

I wasn't half way up before I saw the distant glow of a fire. I noted the direction and was about to climb down when another fire flared to the west of the first. I watched, wondering which had been lit by Bokum. My eyes kept returning to the first fire. I climbed down and drew an arrow on the ground.

"Shall we eat before we go?" he asked.

I laughed. "Sleep, then eat, Arbreu. We don't travel in the dark. Too dangerous in a land we don't know. We'll leave at dawn."

Before light I climbed the tree again to recheck the fire. It still burned brightly. The other fire had died. We started walking.

Arbreu was good to travel with. He didn't complain or hold me up. As the sky lightened, I again climbed a tree and checked. The fire still glowed.

When I gained the ground, Arbreu had a meal set out. We ate and again clicked tokens, sending a message to Bokum to stay with the fire. Once more I saw Teema.

We walked on as the sun rose. It was hot and soon I was carrying my cloak. As we breasted a small rise, I saw a pall of smoke ahead.

Bokum was adding green wood and leaves to the fire to make smoke. Better than the flames during the daytime.

The sun was two hand spans above the horizon when we finally arrived at his camp. We sank thankfully beside the fire as Mekroe scraped away the greenery, built it up and heated water.

"Well, I wasn't sure who was coming, you or Teema. What's going on?" said Bokum.

We explained about the hill and the threat to the settlement.

Bokum listened in silence. "Are you sure about this, Arbreu?"

"It'll breach within three days, Bok. I personally wouldn't step on it again."

Bokum nodded thoughtfully. "Where does Teema come into this? We thought he was at the sea cliffs."

"He is," I said. "This must affect him somehow. If the water goes through the settlement, it'll wash out the path to the cliffs. He needs to go south before returning home."

Bokum nodded.

"Did you get to the top lake?" I asked.

Mekroe's eyes shone. "It's gone, Kirym," he said. "Now it's a massive mountain."

"Don't exaggerate, Mek." Bokum turned us. "The lake bed rose in the earthquake. The water must have emptied into the lower lake. That's why it's so high. It would have been spectacular. The rivers draining the lakes are blocked and more water is flowing in than ever before. It'll keep getting higher and even if the hill holds out, the lake will overflow anyway.

We need to get back quickly."

"First we need to let Teema know he can't use the usual path." I clicked tokens with Arbreu first and then Bokum and felt Teema's nod of understanding.

"Right," said Bokum. "Let's go. Danth should be there soon, but will he explain the danger?"

"Mekrar will make sure Papa understands," I said. "There's something else we need to do first." I told them about the second fire I'd seen.

Bokum was concerned. "You should have told me sooner, Kirym."

"You should have told me last night." Arbreu looked really annoyed.

I was furious with them both. I felt my tokens pulsing on my forehead. "And what would you have done had you known sooner? Nothing! The most important thing was to find you, Bokum. The other fire is pretty much on our way home." I took a deep breath. "Perhaps you two can stop treating me like a child."

They both looked chastened. Mekroe laughed quietly to himself. Rathay just looked embarrassed.

I picked up my pack and walked away. After a few steps, they fell in behind me.

"Sorry Kirym, I keep forgetting how competent you are.

Anyway, we like protecting you."

"That's fine, Bokum, but I don't need protecting. If ever I do, I'll ask someone who respects me. Someone like Zeprah or Sundas."

He had the decency to go red.

We made good time although the land was rough. By midday we were in the area where the fire had been. Again I climbed a tree. I could see the area where Bokum had spent the night although not where Arbreu and I had been.

There was a small ridge to the west of us, and as nothing else was obvious, I suggested we climb it.

On the far side of the hill, nipped in behind a large rock was a small dwelling. Some distance away, face down on the ground lay a man, his foot caught in a narrow gap between two large rocks. It looked like he'd been jumping across the top of the rocks and slipped.

"Hey!" Bokum called.

He looked up.

Salcan!

"Oh, thank goodness. I thought I'd die. Can you get me out? I'm stuck!"

We checked the rocks on both sides.

The space Salcan's leg had slipped into was narrow and too high for us to lift him over to free his foot.

Bokum and Rathay discussed building a series of platforms to lift him onto. They drew plans in the dusty soil near him.

From the far side of the rock, I dug the soil out from under his foot. Just below the surface the distance between the rocks widened, although not enough to free him — until I removed his boot.

Even then it was a squeeze, but he did it. He sat up and massaged his leg and ankle until the movement returned, then stood and tested his weight on it.

Mekroe shook his head. "How come she works it out?"

"Because generally, Mek, the solution is simple," I said.

We stayed in Salcan's camp for a meal and Bokum explained our plan to leave. "It makes it easier finding you like this. Now there's no need to send out a search party."

"I doubt I'll be welcomed back after the incident at the gorge."

Mekroe snorted. "We were slightly more worried about the incident with the water flasks."

Salcan reddened. "I'd forgotten about that. It was just a dye, harmless stuff really. I shouldn't have done it though. But I'll come, if you think I'd be welcome."

Mekroe shook his head in disgust. "If we thought Papa wouldn't want you, we'd have left you stuck in the rock, but you are family. The alternative is to stay here by yourself."

We spent the night west of the caves. Bokum did the first guard duty and I built up the fire to make a hot drink for him and Arbreu, who he had woken to take over.

Bokum talked quietly. "Wake me again when the moon has moved two hand widths, Arb —"

"Bokum," I interrupted. "Mekroe's not a child. He's quite capable of doing his share of guard duty. Rathay and I can help also. With five of us, we can double the guards. It'll be safer."

Bokum reddened. "Sorry Kirym, I know you can help, but I need to be doubly careful. I'm not sure we can trust Rathay now Salcan's back. I will ask Mek, but it's my responsibility."

"Well, no Bokum. It isn't. You can organise Mekroe and Rathay, but not Arbreu and me. You can co-operate — or not, but we'll make our own arrangements. You can do it all for your group, or you can share the load. Anyway, it's because Salcan is back that we can and must trust Rathay."

We did it my way.

Papa was organizing shelter when we arrived. Everyone had evacuated to a high plateau south of the settlement. It was raining heavily, the rain starting soon after midnight. One shelter was finished and overcrowded with children and the elderly. Family chests sat beside a pathetically small pile of possessions.

Another shelter was partially erected and attempts were being made to finish it. Under a rock overhang, Mama had a ground oven steaming and the mouth-watering smells drifted around the area. With the wind blowing, erecting shelters was difficult and almost everyone was wet and irritable.

Salcan was briefly welcomed back and we told Papa about the lakes and the messages we'd sent to Teema.

"Well, I hope he understood them, Kirym. I sent Peet south with a message for them, but if they return on the north path —" he shook his head. "This rain's not helping and it's getting heavier. We can do no more until it stops. Everyone needs a rest. We have a few possessions and we'll make do. We could have lost everything in the earthquake anyway. Now, we've a few decisions to make."

"What decisions?" asked Bokum.

"Well initially, where to rebuild?"

"Why rebuild?" I asked.

"We can't live in the open, Kirym. We need shelter, so the sooner the better."

"Why go to all that trouble, Papa. Let's just leave. The boats are there, we have maps and instructions. There's nothing holding us here."

"Building is a lot of extra work, Veld, and if it doesn't need to be done, why do it?" said Mama. "We'll need to sleep out for a few nights but the weather will improve in a day or so. We can get everyone to one dwelling near the cliffs. It'll be crowded, but that'll only be temporary."

Papa sighed. "We have little food, few possessions, Loul. Summer would give us the chance to replace things."

"If we leave now, we will have the best part of summer to grow crops in a new land, Papa. Anyway, Papa, we can forage on our way to the boats, and while we get everything down to sea level." I pulled my damp cloak close. "If we tell everyone we're going, it'll make it real. It's like underlining something and it's better knowing, having a definite plan."

As Papa considered this, Teema's group with Peet arrived, grateful for the warnings we'd sent.

As Teema told Papa what had been done on the boat, there was a distant rumble. It got louder and louder and the ground began to shake.

Amid the fear of another earthquake, only Arbreu realized what it was. "The lake!" he shouted. "It's breached!"

We dashed to the edge of the plateau to watch.

A vast wall of dirty water raced towards the settlement. It came fast. Whole trees and massive rocks rolled along the face of the wave. The sound was huge, even at this distance. The wall of water lessened slightly as it washed across the flat ground that opened up around the settlement, but that only made the debris more obvious. The trees growing around the settlement splintered into kindling, and with the dwellings, disappeared beneath the water. Soon all we could see was the chimney from our dwelling teetering incongruously above the sea of mud.

After the initial silent shock of seeing the destruction of the settlement, there was a scream of terror. Then as Yanda understood the devastation, she collapsed.

I didn't recognise her. She looked deranged. She was carried to the shelter and sedated heavily.

The water continued to stream across the ground settling into a dirty, debris filled lake of brown and black. The rain got heavier and eventually we returned to the shelters, subdued by the destruction.

Mekrar was in tears. "We could have died. I never thought the land would turn against us like that."

Mama hugged her. "Nothing has turned against us, Mekrar. This is nature. We were warned and we're safe. Kirym realized that something was wrong, Arbreu understood what it was and you had time to warn us. It's a valuable lesson for us, we must always be aware of our surroundings."

As I turned away I bumped into Danth. I was shocked at his look of suppressed hatred and rage. He stared at me for a moment and then turned his back on me.

Four days later, we arrived at the sea cliffs. Some of the men had come ahead and were building a temporary dwelling in the wooded area on the land side of the cliffs.

Once we had settled, half of the men went to the cliff top to work there and on the boats. Mama organised the rest, a few to enclose the front porch of the dwelling with a wall so the children could play safely, high enough so no one could climb over it and with guards on the gate to ensure Yanda didn't get out. The rest foraged, collecting anything that might prove to be useful.

Everyone had been warned about the noises, but nothing could really prepare them for it. Once they got over the shock, most could ignore it.

Not Yanda though. She became hysterical whenever it began and needed constant sedation. She never recovered from the shock of seeing the settlement destroyed and we were increasingly worried about her. She couldn't understand where she was and kept trying to walk home.

The only person she seemed to recognise was Young Harby. I wondered why until Zelriff explained. He was the image of his grandpapa, Old Harby, at the same age.

Nine days after we arrived at the cliffs, Papa said I could spend a day and night on the boat. I would be the youngest person to have gone down. It was very exciting.

Old Harby had warned us that a storm would arrive soon after that.

Papa had decided that everyone would be off the boat during the storm, so the night I was on the boat would be the last anyone spent down there until it had passed. It would be impossible to use the ropes with the amount of wind we expected, especially as the tunnel to the boats had now been cleared. The force of the wind was phenomenal now there was nothing hindering it.

We couldn't enter the cave before the wind dropped, so I waited in the stone shelter we had built when we first came to the cliffs.

The trip down was different now. We were lowered to one of the top ledges and walked the rest of the way. Getting people into the cave could now be managed from inside the cave as well as out.

Sundas insisted on handling the rope. He adapted a harness with extra ropes to keep me safe. It took ages to put it on.

I stepped over the edge and followed Sundas' instruction to lean back allowing the harness ropes to hold me, and walk backwards down the cave wall. It was strange — exciting.

It was icy in the cave, much colder than I thought it would be.

It didn't take long to get to the ledge where Teema and Papa waited.

Teema began to untie me. "How many safety ropes does Sundas think you need? Does he imagine you would try to escape?"

He hooked them to the wall and attached a single safety rope to my harness. "We just won't tell Sundas about the minimal level of security down here," he said.

There were lamps on all levels and on the path leading to the sea. The men had built hand rails all the way down the stairs, and there were areas to stop and rest, if I needed to. A few sections of steps had fallen in the past, the men had replaced them with ramps.

It was dark in the cave, the lamps became small pools of light that seemed to be eaten up by the darkness.

From the bottom of the steps, we followed the handrails west towards the sea, ending at a wide tunnel. A line of lamps went north, and stopped some distance away.

"That's the path to the stream," said Teema.

We walked through the tunnel, and he pointed out a few places where there was still a little debris from the rock fall that had blocked it. I could see the lighter outline of the corner ahead.

Then I saw the boats.

They were massive, much bigger than I'd imagined. I'd studied the engraving on Arbreu's knife but couldn't picture how they'd look in reality. Now, I couldn't see why it hadn't been obvious.

There were now a number of ladders for each boat, put there so workmen weren't held up climbing onto or off the boat. We climbed up one of the on ladders and watched as Bokum and Armos almost ran down an off ladder without even holding on. It was amazing.

The deck was huge. I ran from one end to the other.

Papa laughed at me. He showed me the deck dwelling and the big room where everyone would sleep. "Do you think you could sleep in one of these?" he asked, lifting me onto a hammock.

This was fun.

There was an oven at one end of the room and Teema showed me how it worked so it didn't burn the boat. A store cupboard had been filled with wood, and more was stacked along one wall, and covered with a net to stop it from moving around when we were at sea.

Some of the men had returned to the top of the cliff. The rest of us sat on the deck to eat and discuss the day's work.

Papa was deep in conversation with Armos. He sounded worried.

"It's the path, Armos. I don't understand where it is. The rest, well most of it's easy, or will be, I think. But without knowing where the path is, can we leave? I don't want to go without being sure."

"The instructions are in the poem," said Armos.

"Yes, but it's not complete. I wonder if there was something vital in the bit that's missing. It says 'go west, the path is obvious', but what path?"

"Could that really be the path from the old settlement to the cliffs?"

Papa rubbed his hand over his face. "I don't know, but if it is, where to from here? We can't sail without knowing. What if it was something on the cliff face, a message or … And what if it's no longer there? But even if it is, we won't know until we get out there and it might not be."

"It is obvious, Papa. It's the river."

He wasn't listening to me.

"Papa!" I shook his arm. "It's the river!"

"What's the river, Kirym?"

"The path! The river is the path. When you look at it from the highest point on the cliff, it looks like a path going west. It is obvious, and it's the only answer. It's the one thing that wouldn't change much over time."

He frowned. "It's not that simple, Kirym. The river doesn't keep going. The tides weaken it. It disappears."

"It says 'the path is obvious', and the river's movement into the bay is. Once we're beyond the river current, there will be something else. It doesn't say it'll take us all the way, just to follow it." I couldn't understand why he didn't see it. "Papa, so far, all the instructions have been simple when we looked at them the right way, haven't they?"

He nodded.

"So why should this be different? Why not trust it?"

His frown became a smile. "It's the best suggestion yet, Armos. So simple and I couldn't see it. Yet it makes a weird sense. What do you think?"

Armos shrugged. "I was looking for something far more complicated. It's possible that when the river no longer flows, we'll be in a current and that will take us in the right direction."

Arbreu kept me company while Teema and Papa worked on Dream Seeker. I looked for the chest Papa found when he first came on board. We unbolted it and I ran my hands over the silken surface. Near the bottom, I felt a line in the wood. I couldn't see anything, but Arbreu could feel it too. It went right across the front of the chest and around the side, a hand's width from the bottom.

As I felt for the line along the side, a section of the wood clicked in and out. I explained what had happened to Arbreu and he felt around the other side. When we did it together, a hidden drawer popped out at the bottom of the chest. Inside was a thick folded parchment which I lifted out.

Some things moved at the back of the drawer and I reached in to pull them forward. There were three strange shapes, like dried leaves, but thicker and larger than most leaves.

I lifted one carefully out. "What is it, Arbreu?"

"I think it's a seed pod. I've not seen any so big before, but you can see where the seeds sat." He lifted out the second one. "Look, one of the seeds is still in this one." The small seed looked fragile. Attached to it was a little mass of white downy wisps.

As we had travelled to the cliffs, Arbreu and I had collected useful plants, setting them into pots to take with us. I wanted to take fush grass and lots of harkii nut with us, but I also took a number of the kegrim grasses, borcarn bushes and many of the other healing plants we used. I arranged for Zeprah to care for a set of them on Dream Seeker so if something happened to one lot, there'd be a backup.

Now I took the little seed from the pod and went to where the plants sat. Taking a spare pot, I settled the seed into the soil, adding water.

"It may not grow, Kirym. It's been here for a long time. Many seeds die if they don't find soil after a few seasons."

"But it may, and I still want to try. I've not seen seeds like this before. We may get a pod tree, like the tree in your story."

He frowned. "That's just a myth, Kirym, a story made up to entertain children."

"Most myths are based in truth, Arbreu. We create them to make the facts easier to remember. Somewhere in the past, there's a connection between our families. It'll be written somewhere."

"It's only a story," he said. "My family had no association

with the sea." I shook my head. "You know things about the sea I don't. There's a link somewhere. We just have to find it." I carefully put the pods back into the drawer and pushed it shut. There was a soft click as it became one piece of wood again and we secured it in the cupboard. I slipped the parchment into my shoulder pack and put it on the hammock I was to sleep in.

There were noises on the deck and we went up to join the men as they climbed aboard.

I helped set out food for a meal. "Papa, some of the families who lived here, left and travelled south didn't they."

Papa frowned, thinking. "The memory box talked of groups leaving to build new settlements, and we know trips in and out were made a number of times. It was written, but not in detail."

"We always seemed to know that some of the people who lived with us came from elsewhere, and there was no way over either of the gorges, was there?" asked Kirym.

Papa shook his head distractedly. "Why do you ask?"

"I think I know what happened to them."

Papa stared at me.

I explained about the drawer in the chest and the seedpods. Then I reminded him of the myth Arbreu told us back at the settlement.

"I think it was Arbreu's ancestors who left in the boat, it makes sense and it all fits."

"It's a bit farfetched, don't you think?" Arbreu said.

"You could both be right," Papa said. "As Kirym says, Arbreu, there's often a shadow of truth in myths. It could have been your family. Then again, Kirym, the myth may have come from another family. Someone who joined with Arbreu's family or maybe someone they met. There would possibly have been people in this land before our ancestors came here, and maybe that's why we chose to live between the gorges. It was inaccessible to those around here and perhaps no one else had laid claim to it. But there's definitely a southern connection. The knife Arbreu carries shows that. The knife shows three boats, the journals indicate three, yet only two are here."

"It's a lot to think about, Veld," said Arbreu. "Now I'm less sure of my history than I ever was, but there's no way of proving or disproving it."

"Well not at this stage, it seems, and perhaps never. But the important thing is to get this boat ready, and now we have the idea of a path, we can begin to search for a new land. So eat up and let's get back to work."

During the afternoon, Arbreu took me to the mouth of the cave. I'd never been this close to the sea and was intrigued with the movement of the water. He tried to tell me what he had learned in the past about the tides and the power of the ocean.

One wave came up higher than the others and ran over my feet. I squealed with fright and we both laughed. We played in the rock pools for most of the afternoon. It was sheltered here, although we were warned not to enter the water. The channel that ran out to sea was very deep and teeming with fish, some of them rather large. I could see their dark shapes slicing through the water just over an arm's length from shore.

We returned to the cave and watched the sails being taken down and stored. Everything possible was tied down to ensure there'd be no damage during the coming storm. As evening approached, some of the men were pulled up to the cliff top. Those of us left moved back to Dragon Quest to eat and sleep. It got dark early and the wind gusted through the cave.

Papa woke us before dawn.

We climbed the steps and ledges, getting to the second

level before we heard Tarl shout to us from above.

The lull in the wind was very short and we had trouble with the ropes. They kept blowing out of our reach and getting tangled. Eventually Tarl tied rocks to them to give them some weight and allow him to swing them over to us.

It was raining heavily when we got to the top of the cliff and we were soon soaked.

Papa was last up and although we were eager to get to the dwelling, we stowed the ropes and leather guides safely in the shelter first, to ensure they weren't blown away.

The wind was strong but the dwelling was well protected and waterproof. A food pit had been dug inside, providing hot food and warmth. The storm lasted for two days and nights, short but vicious. We stayed warm and dry for the duration, rested and waited.

All around, excited groups discussed the coming journey. I read through the pages I'd found in the chest and took them over to show Papa. Part of it was a map of land and a harbour. To one side of the harbour was an arched doorway with the words 'Opens With the Tide. Use Not at Night'. Folded into the map was a thin journal.

"It gives instructions for getting into a new harbour, Papa."

Papa brought out the other maps he had. It finally fitted together. "There's a lot we don't know, but we'll find out as we travel," he said. He carefully put the maps and journal with the others he had.

I started to walk away, but then had a thought and returned. "Papa, we need to sort out the situation with Rathay. We put the Judicial Summit off because Halse died and a lot has happened since then, but we need to give him an answer. It's not fair on him to leave it longer. Most people have forgotten about it, but he hasn't and it's worrying him."

Papa went and talked to Old Harby, Raff and Findlow and

then called Rathay, Teema and me over.

"Rathay," he said. "While we've not had a formal Judicial Summit for you, we have been watching and we're impressed by your efforts to fit in. You're making good friends and you've worked hard. So we'll only revisit this again if we need to."

Rathay was visibly relieved when he realised what it all meant. He shook Teema's hand, and hugged me. Then he happily went back to the sleeping area he shared with some of the other single men.

As I turned to go back to my sleeping space, I noticed Salcan. He was in a corner by himself, his back against the wall, just watching. I thought he looked miserable, although there was something in his expression I couldn't read.

I resolved to talk to Papa about him. While I thought about what I'd say, I started to tidy my belongings. While doing that, I checked the tokens.

Slynd's token had changed. The last time I'd looked at it, it was dark grey and black. Now it was streaked with red.

I took it to Papa. "It's been dark since the earthquake, Papa. The change is serious. I think we're in danger."

"What do you think, Loul?"

Mama shook her head. "Kirym's guess is as good as any," she said.

"We need to leave, Papa. As soon as the storm's over, we must to get onto the boats and go."

Papa thought for a few moments, nodded shortly, stood and called for silence. "We've done all of the preparation we can. There is nothing to hold us here now. When the weather settles, we'll start loading people and final possessions. To a large extent, you each have the choice of boat to travel on, although I may change that if numbers or expertise are needed somewhere. Raff, Grenin is in charge of Dream Seeker, but I want you to be headman there. Young Harby, you'll travel on Dragon Quest. Your major responsibility is Yanda." He smiled. "There are a few romances happening in each of the families, and that may influence where some wish to travel."

There were tears. Some decided not to travel with their extended family. Danth insisted his family travel with Raff, and Mekroe's request to join Tarjin was declined. After sulking for half a day they worked out a code with Mekroe's pipe and Tarjin's drum so they could keep contact when the boats were apart.

Danth stopped the practise saying it was a waste of time, but Papa thought it was a good idea and made it their job for the voyage.

Salcan chose to go on Dream Seeker.

Tindra, Bildon, Rathay and Findlow's family would come with us on Dragon Quest.

Each day, there was only a short time to lower people into the cave and Armos thought we'd need five days to get everyone and everything down to sea level.

During the days of preparation, we had made a lot of harnesses to help streamline the evacuation. Papa had a group of men on the top two levels in the cave and another at the top of the cliff. They worked for as long as the wind allowed morning and evening.

A heavily sedated Yanda went down on the third day. She, along with a few older ones and some of the youngest children, were lowered right to the cave floor. It was time consuming but safer.

The lurches and drops that had marred Arbrcu's first trip had been ironed out with the addition of an oiled leather collar. It sat around a rock and the rope was coiled around it a number of times. That acted as a brake making it easier to lower everyone.

A piece of leather was now fastened over the edge of the rock to ensure the rope didn't rub and fray. Most of us were lowered to one of the top two ledges and walked the rest of the way.

All went well until the fourth day.

Big problem! In fact, Papa's biggest problem yet!

Sundas refused to be lowered into the cave.

Papa begged, cajoled, and even ordered.

Sundas sat at the top of the cliff and wouldn't budge.

Findlow and Armos talked to him, but he refused to go near the hole.

I was helping Mama hang the last of the hammocks when Papa came to ask for help.

"I can get him down, Papa, but you must agree with everything I say to him."

Mama shrugged. "I'd prefer not to sedate him, Veld. It'd take a lot to put him to sleep, and he'd fight it. If Kirym thinks she can do it, at least let her try."

I asked Papa to bring up a rug for me. Then I put on my cloak, picked up a loaded pack. I climbed into harnesses and I was pulled up while Papa climbed the levels.

At the top, I went and sat beside Sundas.

He looked wretched.

"I know it's scary, Sundas. Can you think of any other way to get to the boat?"

He shook his head miserably.

I hugged him. "If you can't get down, we'll have to stay up here then, and I'll stay with you. We can remain here or build a dwelling somewhere else." I paused. "Can we stay at the cliffs until the boats have gone? I'd like to see them sail away."

Sundas was horrified. "No! No, no, Kirym! You must go on the boat. It's your family."

I clicked his token. "You're my family too, Sundas. We don't leave family by themselves. If you stay, I stay."

Papa arrived and handed me the rug he'd brought up.

"See Papa brought up my things. Papa, can you ask Arbreu to look after my plants, I'd like to think of them growing in the new land."

Sundas looked stricken. "Veld, you can't let her stay. She's your daughter. Make her go down to the boat."

Papa shook his head. "I can't force her come with us, Sundas, any more than I can force you to. She's right about our rules. No one is left alone. Either she stays with you or we all do. But I have obligations to Findlow, Raff and their families. If Kirym wishes to stay, I have to let her."

Sundas turned to me. "Kirym, please go down to the boat and I'll come later. Tomorrow."

I shook my head. "I'm going to stay here until you're on the ledge or at the bottom of the cave." I sat on the grass and looked mournful.

Papa struggled to keep a straight face as Sundas sighed deeply.

"Kirym must go with you, Veld. All right, I'll go down. But it's so dark in there."

Behind him, I beamed, although when he turned back, I was serious again.

I took his hand. "You'll be fine, Sundas. It's just a short step to the first level. It's not as dark once you're inside the cave. The lamps really light it up." I said. "Papa can ask someone to light more lamps while you're putting on your harness. Bokum and Findlow are waiting for you and I'll be right behind you. We can walk down to the boat together."

Sundas climbed into a harness and sat on the edge. Soon he was out of sight.

While waiting for my turn to go down, I wandered over to look at the sea. When I realized what was down there, I almost panicked.

"Papa, Papa," I screamed. I fumbled at my waist pouch and held out Slynd's token as I pointed back to the edge of the cliff.

Coming up the coast were three rafts, laden with men. While I couldn't see their faces, I knew it was Slynd. His token was a deep venomous red.

Papa took one look, grabbed my hand and raced back towards the hole.

Arbreu and Armos were tying ropes to a pack ready to lower it.

"Who's up here?" demanded Papa. The panic in his voice scared me.

"Just us and Teema," said Armos. "He's over by the shelter. There's not much more to take down, another day should do it, maybe two."

Papa shook his head. "We've run out of time. Slynd is about to find us," he said. "Arbreu, get Teema. Armos, get down that hole and get everyone on to the boats."

As Papa spoke, Armos hauled his harness on and got one ready for Teema. The rope came back from lowering Sundas, and Papa tied it to my harness and pushed me off the cliff. As I disappeared into the hole, Arbreu and Teema came running.

I got to the first ledge and untied the rope, sending it back for those at the top. I explained to Bokum, Findlow and Sundas what was happening.

Sundas, who had been standing against the wall as far from the edge as possible, immediately forgot his fear, and the three of them grabbed the ropes and helped steady Armos as he was lowered to the ledge.

Armos cut his harness off — much quicker than undoing all of the ties — and raced off down to the boats holding onto a safety rope, rather than taking the time to fasten it.

The end of another rope snaked down and Arbreu appeared sitting on the rim of the hole. Bokum, Findlow and Sundas took his weight and before long, he was standing beside me. The rope went back for Teema and Papa.

I pulled Arbreu towards the steps. "Come on, let's help Armos get everyone on board."

We copied Armos and did it without safety ropes. It was scary. Soon we caught up to two men carrying a load of equipment.

"Leave that stuff," shouted Arbreu. "It's not important. Veld wants you on the boat now!" They lowered the bundle to the ground and stared at him blankly.

Arbreu put his foot against the pack and sent it over the edge. It fell, clattering and clanking until it arrived at the bottom. "Run, Man!" he screamed.

They took off like frightened shanym birds.

Teema raced down to join us. He wasn't holding a safety rope. He overtook us, panting out instructions to Arbreu. "Get everyone on board. Get the ropes sorted and ready the sails."

Nine levels down, Teema slipped at the bottom of a set of steps and teetered on the edge of the ledge. Arbreu grabbed his tunic, hauling him back to safety.

My heart was thumping.

We raced on. Gaining the cave floor, we dodged the remains of the fallen packs and ran for the tunnel.

I could hear the others behind me, Sundas urging everyone to take care. Then I was in the tunnel and through the other side.

Already, there were lines of people climbing the ladders

and Teema began to shout instructions up to Grenin and Raff.

Arbreu raced up an off ladder to help on Dragon Quest.

I ran past everyone to the cave entrance to check on Slynd's progress.

Just south of the cave was a line of rocks in the water. Armos called it a breakwater. Even at high tide, it created a barrier that the waves crashed over. The rafts couldn't get across and were putting out to sea to go around it.

We had a little longer to get the boats launched. If Slynd caught us in the cave, it would be a massacre.

I ran back and told Papa and Armos what was happening. Almost everyone was aboard now. Papa shoved me up a ladder. When I got near the top, Sundas leaned over, grabbed me and hauled me the rest of the way.

Everyone looked scared.

The deck was a mess of gear. The men were frantically pushing everything into one area to give them space to work. Mama was attempting to usher the younger children below deck. I slipped in front of the dwelling so she wouldn't send me down also.

Armos raced to the front of the boat, yelling more instructions to Grenin. Dream Seeker gave a lurch and started forward as the blocks that wedged the boat up were pulled from under it. At the cave entrance, she hit the water and continued out of sight.

Papa was last on board, pulling the ladder up after him.

Armos ordered the men to pull the blocks from under Dragon Quest.

The boat stood still for a brief moment and then started to slide down the greased wooden slope into the water. It was a strange feeling.

Dragon Quest hit the water and kept going down. Then the front bobbed up, and the momentum pushed us out into the channel.

Arbreu and Teema were already pulling on ropes to raise the sail.

The wind caught it and Armos turned the nose of the boat towards the top of the breakwater. There seemed such a long way to go.

24

Teema Speaks

The white cliffs soared above us and the cave, which sat at an angle, appeared as a thin dark crease in the rock. Dream Seeker, racing ahead of us towards open water, suddenly lurched and slowed. Their sail crashed to the deck.

A rope snaked down behind it.

"Did it break or did they use the wrong knot?" I asked.

"Possibly not properly tightened, but it doesn't matter, does it?" said Kirym. "They'll handle it because they have to."

Bokum frantically climbed the mast, a new rope between his teeth.

The rafts were paddling along the top of the breakwater. We were not going to make it. Around us, men frantically searched through the gear for bows, arrows and spears.

Bokum reached the top of the mast and was attaching the rope, guiding it through an eye in the mast. Armos manoeuvred Dragon Quest around Dream Seeker and slowed to float between them and the rafts.

Slynd and his men rounded the breakwater and the three rafts spread out across the channel.

"Keep her tight," bellowed Armos.

I sat on the roof of the deck dwelling with Kirym and Arbreu. The wind died, the sail hung limp, and the air felt oppressive.

Kirym rubbed her temples and looked around to the cliffs behind us.

I grimaced, nodding. "I've a headache too. The stress of finally meeting Slynd I guess."

She frowned. "I'm fine, Teema, but there's something else not right. Not Slynd. There's a funny feeling here."

"Maybe it's because we're on the water," said Arbreu. "Would that cause it? I don't know."

"It doesn't happen on the lake," Kirym said.

The rafts paddled towards us.

We looked back to watch Bokum at the top of the mast. He threaded the rope and lowered it to the deck for Salcan to tie it to the shaft that held the sail.

A barrage of arrows thumped into the dwelling around us and we dived for cover. When no more arrows came our way, we peered around the dwelling and saw with horror that they had turned their attention to Bokum.

Kirym grabbed her bow and leaned against the corner of the dwelling aiming in the direction of the nearest raft. Her first arrow went wide, but she snatched another and aimed carefully.

Standing behind her, I looked along the shaft of her arrow. She had Slynd in her sight. She took a deep breath and loosed the arrow.

It grazed his cheek. Blood trickled down his jaw.

He followed the direction of the arrow, spied Kirym and with a roar of rage, grabbed a small axe and threw it.

He was very accurate, but the movement of the waves put his aim off. The axe imbedded in the dwelling wall above Kirym's head.

I grabbed her and pulled her out of sight.

Arbreu hunkered down beside us, and we watched Bokum sort out a knot in the rope.

Kirym cried out as an arrow suddenly protruded from Bokum's shoulder. He arched back, but held on grimly with one hand, ensuring the rope ran smoothly.

I heard the earthquake before I saw it. It was like a huge animal roaring. The trees on the top of the cliffs appeared to jump into the air. As they came down, so did the cliff face, collapsing into the sea.

The impact sent a huge wave racing towards us.

Armos was shouting although I felt I was hearing him from a huge distance. Men rushed to handle the sail and Armos hauled the tiller over.

Yanda screamed. I saw sheer terror in her face as Young Harby, Loul and Zelriff tried to calm her and get her safely below deck.

I pulled Kirym onto the deck as the boat lined up to the waves, Dream Seeker's movements mirroring Dragon Quest's.

Dragon Quest kicked and bucked as the wave hit, but she slipped through and it raced away. It seemed to take forever for the water to settle.

I looked at the land. The cliff face, for as far as I could see, had collapsed and the continued movement of falling rocks created smaller waves that raced towards us.

Kirym's scream brought me back to the present. "Bokum! He's fallen! Where is he?"

I stared at Dream Seeker's mast, horrified. He was no longer there. He wasn't on deck either.

I raced to the side to scan the water.

Kirym was beside me again. "Can you see him, Teema?"

The water was a mass of wreckage. Arbreu climbed onto the deck rail to get a better look. He pointed to Bokum, floating near a heap of debris and men.

Dragon Quest and Dream Seeker turned towards them. Ropes were readied and as we came close, Arbreu threw one to Bokum. It fell a little short and one of Slynd's men lunged for it, kicking Bokum in the shoulder to keep him away.

Arbreu pulled the man in as I threw another rope towards Bokum.

In the water, the man Arbreu was pulling in unexpectedly spun around. He looked bewildered and then he disappeared as if he had been pulled underwater.

He surfaced, screaming, his eyes bulging. There was a swirl of red in the water and a large fin broke the surface. The sharp teeth of a huge fish grabbed his arm. Suddenly the water was a thrashing mass of fish. For an instant, we were frozen with shock, then instinct took over and I started to pull Bokum up to the boat.

Two men swam towards him and wrestled the rope off him. As they fought each other for the rope, they too were attacked.

The rope slackened as they let go and Bokum swam towards it.

Beside me, Kirym was screaming. "Don't splash, Bokum, don't splash."

He must have heard, because he stopped and floated. Three of Slynd's men grabbed the rope, two of them beating off the third. We pulled them towards the boat. Bokum grabbed the belt of one man, but let go as he punched out at him.

There was a swirl in the water and the man screamed as he was pulled under by the sharp teeth of a fish.

Another rope snaked over to Bokum and he grabbed it. As he was dragged through the water, I saw the fin of another fish following him, gaining on him.

I have never worked so hard in my life. It seemed to be forever before Veld and I were able to lean over the side and grab Bokum's belt, hauling him to safety. The fish propelled itself up out of the water towards him, the sharp teeth missing his foot by a breath.

We collapsed on the deck, Bokum on top of us.

Kirym grabbed the rope. "You don't have time to rest," she yelled as she threw the rope to another group of men.

They fought and punched to get it and we hauled three men to the side of the boat. But there was no way to pull them up together.

I yelled at them to let go so we could get them one at a time.

Two of them attacked the third, punching him away from the rope. Three fish surfaced beside them, fighting over the two men, tearing them apart.

I dropped a rope to the third man. He grabbed it and was hauled clear of the water, sobbing and thanking us.

All around us, men were being pulled from danger. The deck was awash with blood and screaming men. In the water, they were still trying to avoid the fish and get to safety. It was horrendous.

Then suddenly it was over.

The water still boiled with fish and bodies, but none lived and the screams only came from those aboard. We had saved all who could be saved and many who couldn't.

Everyone who had healing knowledge was busy trying to stem blood loss and reduce pain. For many, it was too late and their bodies joined those in the water.

Bokum's wounds were superficial compared to most of the others, but he was in shock. He had a long cut on his leg, although he couldn't remember how he got it. The arrow still hung in his back, but it hadn't gone deep, only remaining in because of side barbs.

Zeprah swiftly cut the skin, removed it, cleaned and bandaged his wounds. She gave him herbs to help healing and inhibit infection. Warm dry clothing and a hot drink helped and compared to others he was fine.

Veld turned Arbreu away from the rail. "I want you to keep your head down. Slynd is alive, but he doesn't know you are. That gives us an edge. I want you to keep out of sight but in hearing when I talk to him."

Arbreu nodded and sat on the floor in the deck dwelling.

Veld hunkered down beside him. "Tell me about Slynd's men."

"Most of those saved are his fighters. You can tell the slaves by their clothes," he paused. "If you want to know what's been happening, ask Lanshere." He pointed him out.

There was a flurry of activity as Dream Seeker was rafted alongside Dragon Quest. Slynd's men were brought aboard, the damaged to be ministered to by the healers, the able bodied tied up.

Kirym stood in the door of the shelter and quietly told Arbreu what was happening. She held out Slynd's token, the red dulled now and streaked with black.

Lanshere was brought back to be questioned. He was heavily bandaged, and his wounds were still leaking. He was very pale. Veld sat him on the other side of the wall so Arbreu could hear him easily.

"You're Lanshere?"

Lanshere nodded.

"Why did you attack us?"

"Slynd's orders."

"Why do what Slynd says?"

"People who don't follow his orders have a tendency to die, generally very violently. I was scared. I didn't want to die."

Veld nodded. "How did you end up here?" he asked gently.

"Things got bad this spring when someone destroyed his bridge. He couldn't build another because he'd left his tools on the other side of the gorge."

"What happened then?"

"We went to a deserted settlement. Slynd left on one of his trips. He seemed alright when he returned, but he sat in a corner for a while and then he went berserk. He said you people must still have a path, because you'd been over and robbed him. He was so angry. It was frightening. He accused three of the men of helping you and executed them." Lanshere shuddered. "He called it justice," he said bitterly. "It was a nightmare. He wouldn't let us bury the bodies. We stayed with those stinking corpses for five days. He didn't sleep and he wouldn't let anyone talk. Then one night he set the dwelling alight. Not everyone made it out. He made us walk all night and the next day, but we just went in circles. Finally we found a cave and he decided we'd stay there." Lanshere slumped forward and coughed, holding his chest.

Veld helped him to sit.

"There was an earthquake," Lanshere continued. "Slynd was buried. I was lucky. I was near the mouth of the cave and got out. Enough of the fighters escaped to make us dig him out. It was hard work and the cave roof kept coming down. I thought he was dead — oh I hoped he was dead. But he wasn't. He slept for three days and when he woke, it was like he was a different man. More fixated than ever, but it was different. He said he knew how to get into his land. He made us build the rafts. Today we came into the bay. He was fine until he saw the boats and then he went crazy again. Then the wave came and the rafts overturned and there were those fish."

"Are you carrying weapons?" asked Veld.

"I had a knife, but I lost it in the water. Most of our weapons were on the rafts. Slynd carries knives, one on his hip and one on his thigh and one in his right boot. Sometimes he carries one down his back. It's tied in his hair. Take care though. He's quick."

Veld asked Findlow to check all of the prisoners for weapons. "Be careful and double check the ropes tying them, I don't trust any of them."

Veld turned back to Lanshere. "What were Slynd's plans when he got here?"

Lanshere shrugged. "More of the same. Killing! Torture! He's mad. I wish he'd died in the earthquake." His voice got lower. "I wish I'd had the courage to kill him. But I couldn't — I couldn't kill anyone, not even him." He looked up at Veld. "You've got to believe me." He sounded desperate.

Veld nodded. "I do. Are you hungry?"

Lanshere shook his head. His face was white, he looked strained. "Thirsty though."

Loul brought him a drink and added something to help ease the pain he was in.

He drank, thanked her, lay on the deck and closed his eyes.

There was a roar of anger from Slynd as Findlow removed his knives.

Veld hunkered down by Arbreu. "I want you to face Slynd after I talk to him. Just choose your moment. We'll see how he responds."

Arbreu nodded. "What about Lanshere?"

Veld looked over at Lanshere, noted his shallow breathing and shook his head.

Slynd was brought forward and shoved against the side of

the boat. Amazingly, he was unharmed bar the scratch on his cheek caused by Kirym's arrow.

Veld stood in front of him. "I hear you've been busy, Slynd."

"Don't believe anything that dog says," Slynd snarled. "I saw him talking. You can't blame me for what others did. I just want what's mine."

"What do you want?"

"The land! This land! My birthright! It's mine! Mine!" he screamed shrilly. "Not that you'd admit it."

"What birthright?" Armos snorted. "Your mama left you all she had, a name, which you still have. Nothing else."

Slynd snarled at him. "She was nothing. I said birthright and I meant it. We have the same papa, Veld. Old Parvell wasn't noble enough to join with the woman he took. So I was never recognised." He looked at Veld. "But that makes us brothers and I'm older. I should be headman."

Old Harby laughed. "History disagrees with you, Slynd. You'd seen four moons when your mama arrived here. She stayed for two winters, and then disappeared, leaving us to care for you. She never named your papa. Even so, if you'd wanted to, you could have made the claim to be headman. Anyone can. That position is not a birthright, but we'd never have chosen you. A leader is loyal to his people."

Veld hunkered down in front of Slynd. "A headman doesn't kill his people, so why bring murderers to our land?"

Slynd looked past him as if he wasn't there.

"Why did you attack my settlement, Slynd?" said Raff. "I welcomed you in the past. You ate our food, drank our wine. Yet you killed my people while they slept. You killed my children and my grandchildren. Babies! Leaders don't do that. They nurture relationships with other settlements. We offered food and drink in friendship when you visited. We provided you with shelter, entertainment. I let you play with my grandchildren." He paused. "And you killed them."

"That's a lie," snarled Slynd. "I haven't killed anyone. When I walked into your settlement I was attacked. My men defended me. I didn't attack you."

"Yes you did." Arbreu stood and walked through the door. "No one has ever attacked you, Slynd. You attack at night when people are asleep. You attack settlements with no guards and you boasted of destroying a settlement that held only women and children."

Slynd stared at Arbreu in disbelief.

I could see him trying to understand the implications of Arbreu's presence. Then he screamed with rage and struggled to his feet. "You're dead! I killed you! People I kill, stay dead!" He made a huge effort to calm down, looked at Veld and laughed. "How did this one survive?" He thought for a short time and nodded. "I knew it! There's another path."

"No, there isn't," I said. "We created a path specifically for Arbreu. Then we destroyed it to ensure you could never ever use it. Every path from the surrounding land has gone. You showed us the last one. But now, nature's taken that away too."

Slynd spat at Veld's feet. "You're a fool to trust Arbreu. He planned the killings. He chopped down a tree over the gorge. I stopped him from using it. You should be thanking me. I saved your lives." He stared at Arbreu, frowned and lunged towards him.

Arbreu stepped aside as Slynd grabbed at his face.

"Who gave you a token?" Slynd screamed. "You've no right. You're a slave. How dare you!"

"The cave made that decision. But what's it to you? You don't even wear yours."

Slynd looked almost conspiratorial. "It's with my treasure. I keep it safe, hidden." He paused, his eyes widening. "How do you know about it?" He glanced around the boat and kicked out at Arbreu, his voice rising to a scream. "You! You stole my treasure." He struggled against the ropes binding him.

Veld leaned against the dwelling. "You had no treasure, Slynd. Stealing doesn't make you the rightful owner. What do you really have? Nothing!"

Slynd snorted. "Oh I have plenty, Veld. More than you know. My family!" He gestured around the boat. "My people will rise and support me. My warriors are here," he paused. "I've a woman too." He looked around. "Where's Lantiah? She should be here supporting me." He recognised me. "You, boy! Go get my woman."

I saw Armos tense and prepare to stand. Catching his eye, I shook my head imperceptibly. He nodded and relaxed.

Lantiah had been sitting unseen at the back of the crowd holding Parlansho. Now she stood and moved forward.

I leaned over and whispered in Arbreu's ear. "I wonder if Slynd will notice how much more confident she is. Joining with Armos has been the best thing for her. She looks fantastic."

"You owe me a bond, Lantiah," said Slynd. "I'm claiming it now."

Lantiah spoke very quietly. "I owe you nothing. Stealing my token broke the only bond we ever had. Now you're dead. To me and all of those who knew you, you are dead. I have a new life and a new family. There's nothing between us. You are nothing!"

He looked her up and down. "I've got your token. I own you. You're mine until you die. You owe me." His voice had again risen to a scream.

She laughed at him. "Dead people have no rights. But even if you weren't dead, you'd still have no power over me. I've long since moved on. The token that tied me to you died. I didn't. The connection between us did." She walked away from him.

He was stunned speechless, then took a deep breath and screamed at her. "Without me you are nothing! Nothing!"

"She doesn't need you, Slynd," said Bokum.

Slynd looked shocked. He called out to her. "I still have your token, Lantiah. That proves the bond."

Lantiah turned. A small smile played about her lips as she shook her head. "Show me. Where is it?"

Slynd looked blank.

"You don't have it, do you?" she said. "I gave it back to the cave, Slynd. That bond is dead. But not much of a connection ever really existed, did it?"

Slynd's face worked as he thought over Lantiah's words. "Where's mine?" he snarled. "If you had your token, you must have mine."

A voice came from behind me. "The cave rejected yours. It wanted nothing to do with you. Now your token is just like you." Kirym stepped forward and held up Slynd's token holder.

The token in it was red, streaked now with black and grey.

As we watched, the colour drained from it. It became lifeless, grey and dead.

Slynd stared at it in horror. He ignored Kirym, so she dropped it at his feet. He stepped away and then with a scream of rage, turned and stamped on it, grinding it into the deck.

He turned and yelled at Arbreu. "Who stole my things? Where are my treasures?"

"Your treasures? You own nothing. The things you hid weren't yours. As much as we could, we've returned them to their owners. Only the token was yours and it's there for the taking."

Slynd lunged at him. "You did it. How did you get up the

cliff? How'd you avoid my traps? How'd you get over the gorge?" His voice had again risen to a manic screech.

Arbreu sidestepped him, turned and walked away.

"Tell me!" Slynd screamed.

Food was laid out. Those of his men who could, ate. Slynd refused everything offered him.

We faced a problem — what to do with them. The discussion went on for a large part of the afternoon.

"Let's find a beach up the coast and dump them ashore."

"We can't, Peet," said Raff. "He'd carry on killing at every settlement he found. We can't allow him access to other people."

"Well what do you suggest?" said Peet. "Can we leave him anywhere? I don't want to take him with us."

Raff shook his head. "I've no reason to feel compassion for these men. Why don't we drop them overboard, here or in the middle of the ocean? That still gives them more chance than they gave my grandchildren."

Veld put his arm over Raff's shoulder. "My dear friend, you'd feel the guilt for life. It would eat away at you. Only men like them can kill with impunity. And even they go crazy. If we kill, we're as bad as he is. Slynd deserves to die, but not at our hand. Not unless there's no other option. We're better than that."

"We can't take them with us, we can't leave them behind. There are no other options." Raff looked distressed.

"Papa why don't we give him what he wants?"

We all turned and looked at Kirym.

"What do you mean?" asked Veld.

"Well, he wants the land." She looked ashore. "Give it to him."

I looked at her with a frown and then comprehended what she was saying.

Veld roared with laughter. "It's perfect," he said.

25

Kirym Speaks

It was well after midnight and again I hadn't slept. I couldn't. It had been a long hard day and I was tired. For the third day running, I had scrubbed the decks, finally accepting them as clean and the blood stains I saw, only figments of my imagination.

Everyone else slept as soon as they climbed into their hammocks.

I lay in mine watching the slow swing of the other hammocks in the room. There was a lamp near the oven, turned low, and it flickered on the walls.

Findlow was night watch tonight. He wandered around checking everyone, soothing restless children, covering those who'd thrown off their rugs, or removing heavy covers if it was hot.

He wore the most amazing night robe. It was long, sweeping the floor and had shapes all over it. Unlike his festival robe, the shapes were coloured and had lines linking them. The colours changed so the blues on one shoulder merged into green on the other and the light colours at the top darkened towards the bottom. It reminded me of the paths that led through the trees of our settlement from one dwelling to another.

I liked my hammock being here. It was in the centre of the boat but near the wall. I could see all around the room and yet it was dark here and hard for anyone to see me.

Findlow came over and handed me a flask. He pulled up a set so he could sit close. "Not sleeping again, darling? What's worrying you?"

I shook my head. "I wanted revenge, Findlow. Revenge for Halse and all the other people Slynd killed. I hated him. I still do and I really wanted to kill him. But when I tried, I couldn't. I didn't think it would be like that. It was horrid and all for nothing. All those people died and he hardly got a scratch. It's not fair. He got away with everything."

"You've learned a lesson that Slynd has yet to learn. That revenge never brings satisfaction. It's my impression, Kirym that people eventually get the life they deserve. You know that the land isn't really what Slynd wants, but he's stuck with it and he'll never leave. His men blame him for the hand they've been dealt, although for his warriors, it was the life they chose. They were already muttering about their own revenge when we put them on land. If he makes it to the top of the cliff, he won't be in charge. His life will be a lot harder. You chose not to kill him. That was brave and difficult. Now you must move on. Your life can be as much of a disaster as Slynd's was if you let it. You know, Halse wanted everyone to be happy. Most of all, she wanted you to be happy. You were special to her, so you need to do that for her. We're coming to a new land. It's a new life for us."

"But what if we don't find a new land? What if it isn't there? What if I got it wrong? The sea is so big and an island is so small. We could miss it."

"Who says it's a little island? It might be huge, so big we can't possibly miss it."

"But our ancestors stopped going there, Findlow. What if there was a disaster, like Slynd or the earthquake? What if it's as damaged as the land we've left?"

He smiled. "Sweetheart, if they left because of a great disaster, well there's been a long time for everything to smooth out, and in nature there's always an equalling. It'd be nice to know why they didn't go back, but maybe it was something really simple. Maybe they no longer needed to, because they found the cave here. We will find a new home. There'll be something ahead that's so obvious, we can't possibly miss it. The journals have been right so far, you taught us that lesson. We'll be safe because we're all together and because your Papa is a very very wise man, and he listened to you. You need to relax now and enjoy being at sea."

He pulled my rug up over my shoulders and I closed my eyes.

The next thing I knew, it was morning.

I was getting used to the movement of the boat now. The winds of the last few days had dropped and the waves were smoother. I climbed out of my hammock, a chore that was easier now I knew how to cope with the rise and fall of the boat on the waves.

Mama was dishing up a meal and Mekroe brought over a platter to share with me. "I've already been on deck, Kirym, and today's going to be the best day ever. I wonder when we'll reach land."

I began to feel excited.

I started on my morning chores. Mama insisted that all the work be done before we could play. Some of the hammocks were taken down through the day and they and the rugs used on them were stored on those left up. Soon my hammock was piled high.

Harbs was helping Siba to dress and feed their children so I collected a platter of food for Yanda.

I sat by her hammock and reached out to hold her hand.

She was very cold and she didn't feel right. She felt more solid. Last time I held her hand, it was cold but soft. This was a different cold and her hand wasn't as soft.

"Oh, Yanda," I whispered.

Zelriff was distraught.

Findlow went on deck to tell Papa and Armos and soon after, Mekroe went up to pass the news on to those on Dream Seeker.

This was so unexpected. Everyone was shocked, but strangely it was Zelriff who was the most upset. She sat beside Yanda holding her hand and crying.

Mama sat with Zelriff for a while and then went to organise the rest of the meal. Before she did, she arranged for everyone to take some time sitting with Zelriff through the day.

I went up on deck to watch the sun turn the mist to gold. We had to wear safety harnesses while we were on deck despite the improvement in the weather.

Sundas helped me into one. "Veld says we'll stop the boats and have a ceremony for Yanda when it's warmer. I'm sorry she died before she saw the new land, but maybe she wouldn't have known it was a new land."

As the sun rose, I could see dark shapes in the water and

pointed them out to Sundas. Slowly the mist evaporated. The sea was all sorts of blue and green. The shapes came closer and closer and everyone came to watch. As time passed we realized the fish were huge. When they finally came up to us, the biggest was almost the length of the boat. Their dark grey skin was lighter underneath and there were strange growths on the bigger fish, like lichen on trees. Five big fish joined us, one of them was enormous. There were three babies with them — the smallest stayed close to one of the bigger fish. They seemed to be very gentle, although the two biggest stayed further from the boat. They swam around and climbed out of the water and slapped their bodies down with a huge splash, and yet could enter the water almost without disturbing the surface. Sometimes they went underwater for a long time before surfacing again. They stayed with us while the sun moved two hand spans and then they slowly drifted away.

The sun was high in the sky when Armos had the sail lowered. Teema and Arbreu threw ropes to Bokum and Raff and the two boats were tied together. There were calls of greeting to the friends we'd not talked to for so many days.

Papa and Armos had Yanda's shrouded body brought up. She was placed on a stretcher in the shade. Zelriff sat near her body, more composed now, although she looked tired and sad.

Papa and Armos finally stood and we all moved to the front of the boat. Papa knelt by Zelriff and talked to her quietly, then stood to include everyone.

"Today, we say goodbye to Yanda. Only Zelriff and Harby can remember a time when she wasn't with us. As we say goodbye to her, we have to consider the great knowledge of our family she takes with her. It's sad to lose this with her death, but with each birth we gain more, and with each death we lose a little. Yanda, Zelriff 's sibling and loved by all of us. Special to Siba and Harby, and a special grandmamma to their children. Yanda, we leave you in this unknown place, but we will take you with us in our hearts and memories. You take your memories with you, but you will remain with us always."

Together Papa, Armos, Peet and Young Harby lifted the stretcher and took it to the side of the boat. They sat one end of the stretcher on the rail and lifted the other. After a small hesitation, the shrouded body slipped off the stretcher and into the water. It sank and then bobbed back to the surface again before sinking slowly out of sight.

Siba's sobs broke the silence.

Zelriff put her arms around her. "Come girl, she's gone and it's for the best. She was a horrid old woman. She'll be missed, but in the best possible way. She's been a problem for a long time and I suspect she'd have been worse given half a chance. It's silly to cry over something we can't change and even sillier if it's something we wouldn't want to change."

Siba looked shocked. "Grandmamma, how can you say that? She's your sister. You've spent the last few moons complaining that she wasn't nice to you and you spent the morning crying because she'd died."

Zelriff patted Siba on the arm. "It just shows I can be a silly old woman on occasion. Death shouldn't be an excuse to lie to ourselves. Death doesn't make Yanda nice. It just solves a big problem." She took a deep breath. "I cried because I was scared. Scared it'll be my turn next! I was being silly. My time will come when I'm ready for it. I loved Yanda, but I didn't like her. I'll not pretend any longer and now I don't have to. She was nasty. She told my grandbabies horrid untrue stories about me and I refuse to be sad now she's gone. I'll miss her, but it'll be because my life will now be nicer." She turned to Mama. "When are we eating, Loul? No one's fed me today, and I'm starving."

Mama smiled. "I'll get you a platter right now, Zelriff."

Zelriff looked over the side of the boat. A few bubbles were coming from under the water but they soon stopped.

Sundas put his arm around her shoulder. "I wish she'd been nicer. It's sad she'll be remembered like this."

Zelriff nodded. "We need to live with that thought. You were nice to her, Sundas and she wasn't nice back. She was a silly old woman."

"Oh no!" Siba's stared in horror at the stretcher that now lay against the side of the boat. "Her token! We should have kept it. Isn't that what we do now?"

"Tokens do what they need to do, Siba," I said. "We took the last token to protect it from Slynd. Yanda's is safe with her."

"Kirym's right. I didn't think about it. Our customs change as needed," said Papa.

The two boats sat together and we shared a meal, but all too soon Armos called for the sails to be raised and the ropes between the boats were untied and coiled.

Dragon Quest was the first to get the sail raised and she leapt ahead.

Many of us stayed on deck for the day. Mekroe and Rathay put fishing lines over the side and by late afternoon, they'd pulled eight reasonable size fish aboard. It was a nice addition to our meal and although there wasn't a lot, we all had a taste. Fish from the sea tasted quite different to those from the lake.

As the moon rose, the little ones were taken below to sleep, but the rest of us stayed on deck enjoying the fresh air. The boat seemed to move quite fast and Armos told me that we were in a strong current and had a good wind behind us.

It got cold quickly when the sun went down and I was pleased to wrap up in a big rug with Mekrar, Bildon and Lyndym. As it got dark we could see hundreds of stars. Findlow, Sundas and Arbreu told us about them and the differences in the sky in the places they'd visited. It was strange to think that not everyone saw the same stars and that some of the stars we saw in the new land would be different from those we were used to.

When we went down to sleep, the hammocks had been rearranged and there was no longer a space where Yanda had been. It was the quietest night we'd had.

These were idyllic days. It was a special time that would create stories and memories we'd talk of for generations to come. The night sky was amazing, those sights as wonderful as those during the day.

I often stood by Armos or Papa, asking questions about handling the boat. I particularly wanted to know how Armos thought he would find land.

He pointed out the signs. More debris in the water and land birds flying above us. Some of these were different from those we had been used to. "There were days when we saw no birds at all," he reminded me.

At dawn on the tenth morning, Arbreu sighted land from the top of the mast. We rushed on deck to see it, a dark smudge against a grey sky.

We sailed closer and the details appeared. The sun peeped the horizon, turning the grey of the rock face to gold and red, so different to the white crags we were used to.

We travelled past magnificent rocky cliffs, beaches and an occasional rock enclosed bay. But the coast was rocky and we couldn't get close to the shore.

It was mid-afternoon when we sighted an unusual group of rocks ahead. They seemed, from the distance, to arch over the water.

"There, Papa," I shouted.

Now I understood the map I'd found in the secret drawer of the big chest. I raced down to get it.

There was the arch with the instructions, Opens With the Tide. Use Not at Night.

As we approached, we saw it was made up of two formations that appeared to meet only because of the angle we had seen them from. Beyond the arch was a channel through the cliffs leading to a small bay. The entrance was very rocky and the only way in was through the arch itself.

Dragon Quest's sail was lowered and Dream Seeker came along side.

Armos talked to Grenin and Papa as we crowded around. "This appears to be the place we're looking for. It looks narrow, and it could be tight getting past the rocks but the tide is right. Do we go in now or wait until tomorrow?"

I held my breath, sure everyone else was doing the same.

"It's been done before, and it won't get any easier, Armos," said Papa. "Let's do it."

There was a moment of silence and then Armos grinned and punched the air. "Yes!" He turned to Grenin. "I'll go first. Follow, but not too close. Put Bokum on the dwelling roof to let you know my exact moves. You know the hand signs. Don't crowd me." Then he went into a technical discussion about how to cope with the wash of the tide.

He took the tiller and motioned Rathay and Peet to raise the sail.

The rocks formed a passage through to the bay. There were

jagged stones scattered around the edges and thrusting in towards the centre of the narrow channel. Armos had two men on the sail and another eight on the sides spotting rocks and holding long poles in case we got too close.

Teema stood on the roof of the dwelling motioning moves to Armos. Once we entered the channel, we lost the wind, but the tide boiled through taking the boat with it. I understood why we couldn't go against the tide. The channel ended and we picked up the wind again. We sailed past the tall cliffs and turned into the bay.

It was massive, much bigger than it had appeared from beyond the arch, bigger even than the lake at home. It flowed in behind the cliffs on both sides. The far shore was low on the horizon, even when looked at from the top of the mast.

We settled for the night in the deep water near the southern cliffs. The rock face was wild and inhospitable, but Papa still organised double guards overnight. The deck was strangely still after so long at sea.

Once morning came, we raised the anchor and sailed east. Even from a distance, we could see that the south-eastern end of the bay was inhospitable. The cliffs there rose straight up from the water and we could see the waves crashing against them from a long way off. The bay was deep enough to take the boats quite close to them, but there were no small bays.

The water was wonderfully clear and we could see fish and plants beneath the boat. It looked quite shallow here, but Armos warned us it was extremely deep. When he finally dropped the anchor, he showed us just how much anchor rope we needed.

I was amazed.

Papa climbed the mast to look around before the sun went down, but the northern shore was still too distant, and he could see no details.

He wanted to know if the bay was home to other people. If it was, we wanted warning of them. Contact with Slynd had left us wary of strangers, although we knew that he was an anomaly in life. However, a lot of people were wary of strangers.

We spent the next night anchored near the northern end of the eastern cliffs.

From the mast we could see sheltered beaches, sand dunes and small hills along the northern shore. About a third of the way along, we spied a black line in the water.

Armos sailed close to see what it was.

Sometime earlier, a path of rocks had been laid out into the water. It was well made and worn smooth with use. It was wide enough for four men to walk abreast, coming out into deep water and sitting above high tide. The water was deep enough for us to bring the boats alongside to float even at low tide. There were posts to tie the boats securely. With Dream Seeker seaward of Dragon Quest, the two boats were almost touching.

Suddenly we were tied to the land and the voyage was over. There was a clamour to get ashore.

As Armos tried to field the requests and complaints, there was a bellow from Papa.

He stood by the tiller with his arms folded, frowning. "We're now on land and I'm in charge. So you're all harassing the wrong man."

There was silence.

"No one goes ashore until we know who and what is here," he said. "Armos, we need to discuss the finer points of landing on a hostile shore."

Amid a buzz of comments around the deck, guards were organised and Grenin and Raff were invited aboard.

Teema climbed the mast to see what was on the shore, but it was indistinct at best.

Papa decided to send two small groups ashore to explore the area nearby early the next day. He asked for volunteers. Almost everyone wanted to be included.

After the noise died, he chose Teema, Rathay and Arbreu for one group, and Young Harby, Bokum and Zeprah for the second.

He again doubled the guards overnight.

They left before dawn.

26

Teema Speaks

Arbreu, Rathay and I were the first back to the boat.

Everyone wanted to go ashore and there were half-hearted murmurs of annoyance at the need to wait. Even in the dim morning light, the trees were so green, the sand such an intense shade of yellow. The sky was so blue, and even out on the boats, we could hear the call of the birds and faint cries of other animals waking from their night sleep.

Eventually Harby, Bokum and Zeprah climbed aboard and we told Veld and Armos what we had seen and found.

Veld climbed onto the deck railing and called for silence. "There's nothing to indicate this area is inhabited, so we'll spend some of the day ashore."

Everyone cheered.

"But," he continued, "we will have guards on the landward side, and no one will go beyond the top of the first dune. If you are told to return to the boats, you will do so quickly and without argument."

It was great being on land again. We collected driftwood for a fire and food was brought ashore. We shared our first meal together in the new land and returned to the boats tired but happy for our evening meal.

Salcan did not return.

A furious Veld led the search and we trailed him east and then north, but lost his tracks when he entered a stream.

"He's obviously evading us and I'm not willing to expend any more energy on him at the moment," said Veld, glancing at the darkening sky. "Maybe we'll find him when we search the land. He might just return when he realises how lonely he'll be off by himself. We'll search again later if he doesn't."

No one except Kirym seemed overly worried about him. I tried to reassure her, but she was strange about it.

"I accept that he is capable of caring for himself, but he's family," she said.

I wondered what she meant. "He doesn't want anything to do with us, Kirym. He took himself away from all of us on purpose, and he he's done it before."

"He's still ours," she said.

We were awake before dawn, and once we had eaten, Veld divided us into groups to start exploring the land. He gave us maps to ensure no doubling-up. The maps were based on a map we found in the chest on Dragon Quest. It gave us the shore line, and two rivers, but the internal detail was non-existent.

This was a quick one-day exploration just to get the layout of the local area, and possibly find a place to settle. We would go further afield later when we had evaluated this area.

Kirym, Arbreu and I joined a group exploring the area to the west and inland of the stone path. It was wonderful walking under trees and seeing colours other than blue and grey. The land was rich in animals, vines and trees and we happily collected the early fruits as we travelled.

We found areas of grains that may have been planted, although I was sure that the alignment of the growing area was nature playing with my desire to believe they had been planted.

There were orchards that had definitely been planted because the straight lines the trees stood in were not part of nature. We found olive trees, elderberry, grape, apple, pear, apricot, blackcurrant, orange and lemon.

We also found many plants, fruits, vegetables and herbs we didn't recognise.

Kirym found a few plants that were very rare in The Land between the Gorges, and three she knew only from pictures in the memory box. One of the rare plants she picked berries from, while warning us that they were poisonous in their present state, but would be used for healing when they were dried. It hammered home the realisation we were in a land we didn't know. There were many unknown dangers.

By early afternoon, we were strung along the trail as we each stopped occasionally to explore things that caught our fancy. I was at the rear, trying to keep Mekroe and Tarjin from falling too far behind.

Mekrar and Kirym were in front and were almost at the top of a ridge we had decided would be the limit of our day's exploration. Kirym walked backwards watching Lyndym and Bildon racing towards her.

Mekrar abruptly grabbed Kirym around the waist and dumped her on the ground. She pulled the other girls down as she ran back to Findlow.

It was so out of character, I was momentarily rooted to the spot. Then I raced towards them, Mek and Tarjin thundering behind me. I reached Mekrar as she talked to Findlow.

"What's wrong," I called as I approached.

"Quiet!" she hissed. "There are dwellings over the ridge. I only got a glimpse, but dwellings mean people."

I stared at the top of the ridge.

Kirym, Bildon and Lyndym had disappeared and Arbreu was running up the hill to where they had been.

I sprinted after him.

He veered towards some trees to the north of the path.

I followed him, annoyed to see Kirym leaning against a tree in full view of the valley below. As I arrived, Arbreu had dragged her to the ground and was telling her off.

"You should have waited for us to check the valley first, Kirym. We don't know the danger. What if someone down there saw you?"

He should have looked at her face, he might have been warned.

She waited until he'd finished before standing and quietly cutting him to pieces.

"The dwellings are derelict. The ground is wild. The trees are full of birds. There are two does and three fawns down there, one newly born. The only tracks are animal tracks. Humans leave different signs. The valley is obviously not lived in." She took a deep breath. "There are no people there now, and there haven't been for a long time. I looked carefully and I did nothing dangerous. Stop treating me as if I were a stupid baby."

She turned away and walked down the gentle incline.

Arbreu looked shocked. He'd forgotten this side of Kirym.

I stared at the valley, noting all she had said, although the deer had fled from the area once they heard the raised voices.

She was absolutely right.

The land dipped into a huge valley. The hills on the far side were tall and rose higher as they marched away from the sea. The peaks beyond them were taller again.

Mekroe and Tarjin raced ahead to be the first to the valley floor. Arbreu, Findlow and I followed more slowly, some distance behind the girls.

Arbreu still looked stunned. "She really knew what she was looking at. She took it in so fast, much faster than I did."

Findlow laughed quietly. "You know she's capable, Arbreu. From what I heard, she singlehandedly helped you climb the ledge in the gorge."

"I know, but she's still — well — so young."

"She has a thirst for knowledge. She asks questions and if she doesn't understand, she'll ask again. She could've done this exploration by herself. She passes on the information also. I'm amazed at what she's taught Lyndym."

Arbreu looked thoughtful. "Well it's not a mistake I'll make again. I get the impression that Mekrar has some of the same talent."

I nodded. "She's not as thorough as Kirym, but she's good. They're great company on a trip. Just quietly, they're better than all of the boys in the family, and a few of the men."

We started to explore. It was a big area and we didn't have time to look far.

We were the last group to return to the boat that evening. Veld had waited for us at the end of the rock path and hurried us onto the boat for a meal. He wanted us all to hear everyone's findings. He filled in the big map as we talked. There'd been a lot found to the northwest, orchards, vineyards and what had possibly been gardens. There had been people here long ago, but we had no way of knowing who they were, why they had left, nor how long they had gone.

Then it was our turn. Arbreu outlined the streams, the orchards and other plantings. When he wrote in Mekrar's Valley, Mekrar drew in the dwellings.

We paused to let the importance of the find sink in.

There was a clamour of questions and the obvious objection was voiced. "The valley is a long way from the boats."

"We returned on a different path," I said. "We found a path leading towards the shore and we followed it."

Findlow sketched it on the map and wrote Tarjin's Path beside it.

Findlow and I were discussing the fastest way back to the boat when Tarjin bellowed for us to come. We crashed through the undergrowth in the direction of his voice.

He stood at the head of a narrow ravine, a path that led through the hills towards the sea. It was beginning to be overgrown, but had obviously been cleared at one stage, and a stone path laid. Most of it was easy to follow. The path ended at the bay and we turned east.

The shore line made us doubt the reason for the path. The shore was rough and we had to climb over and around large rocks. This wasn't a path anyone could hurry. I wondered how many bones had been broken in the past, in the rush to get to the stone path.

Again and again Findlow and I slowed everyone down, but despite all warnings, Mekroe raced ahead. He disappeared around a rocky bluff and I was dismayed to hear him scream.

Insisting the others not rush, I leapt from rock to rock fearing the worst. I rounded the bluff and looked for Mekroe.

He was leaning against a large rock, but that wasn't what caught my attention. He stood in front of a huge cave, similar to the cave we had found the boats in.

This was the connection that tied the boats to the settlement. They couldn't easily be provisioned here and that explained the need for the rock path. Now I understood why it had been built.

We outlined the rest of the coast. The path beyond the cave was smooth and the trip was faster.

"There must be an easier path between the valley and the boat caves," I explained to Veld. "The other paths are so easy, we must have missed one from the ravine. If we work back from the cave, I'm sure we'll find something."

The valley would be our home.

Kirym found the perfect place to build the gathering porch. The site was elevated and looked over the wide valley to a lake north and west, an orchard in the northeast, massive hills far to the west and north and a place for the family dwellings below to the east.

There had previously been two large dwellings there, but they were overgrown and falling down. It took the best part of two days to rid the site of the debris.

The foundations were laid for one very large dwelling, and we duly celebrated on the first full moon we spent in the valley.

Arbreu found large flat stones in the stream and these

were collected and brought to the building site. They would become the fireplace that would, as with Veld's original family dwelling, divide the two large main rooms, and four guest sleeping areas. Old Harby was our fireplace expert and he organised setting each stone and sealing them in with clay. He and his helpers took three days to build the fireplace and as they did so, the framing of the walls and roof were built around them.

The ancient floors were hardy and well preserved, and we kept them intact. The fireplace sat across the area between the two old dwellings leaving just a small strip to re-floor. The exterior walls were of wood caulked with clay and lined with woven panels. The wooden walls were thick to protect us through the winter, the rooms big enough to squeeze everybody in if needed. We built wide porches on three sides of the dwelling, a place for our ceremonies even when the weather was bad.

As summer progressed, a variety of other dwellings were built and we began to feel at home.

I was enjoying the late afternoon sun on the northern porch with Arbreu and Sundas when Kirym joined us.

"It's beautiful here, isn't it?" she said.

I nodded and heard sounds of agreement from the others.

"It's nice to be almost settled again."

"What do you mean almost? We are settled, aren't we?" Arbreu sounded surprised.

"No, we can't be settled until we find the token-cave."

In the silence that followed, I realised I'd forgotten about the need to find the cave and I was sure everyone else had also. "I think Veld will want to wait until next spring or summer before we look for it, Kirym."

"We can't wait," she said. "We can't afford to. Bokum and Zeprah want to join and Jorlenta is pregnant. Her baby will need a token. If we wait until the last moment, we'll have to rush. What if we don't find it? We have to look now."

I had to admire Kirym. She always had her answers well thought out before she started a discussion and her arguments were compelling. I was tempted to start preparations to leave immediately, so I wasn't surprised when Sundas agreed.

"I'll help you, Kirym. We can leave in the morning."

I was more surprised at the voice behind me. "I'll come too," said Findlow. "You're right. Some of our priorities are faulty. Do you think it will be hard to find the cave?"

Kirym turned to him with a huge smile. "I knew I could count on you and Sundas. The journals tell us the cave is to the north. Everything else has been where we were told they'd be so it's just a case of finding out how far away it is."

I knew I was fighting a losing battle. "We were lucky finding the bay," I said. "Had we approached from a different angle or at night, it would've been so easy to miss it. The same with this valley and the boat cave. We won't always have that sort of luck."

I was taken aback when the answer came from Sundas rather than Kirym.

"It wasn't luck, Teema. There were lots of instructions and Kirym and Veld studied them and followed them. The writers had done the trip, so it had to work out."

"Armos knew land was close, Teema," said Findlow. "He reefed the sails on the last night, so we hardly moved. We'd have investigated Kirym's arch even if it hadn't been on the map. Once in the bay, well, the rock path would be a magnet and having tied up we'd have searched for somewhere to settle. The valley is less than half a day's walk from the rock path. Even if you hadn't found the ravine path, we would have built here because it's perfect. We'd have found the boat-cave eventually."

I thought about it and knew he was right, but I wondered if Veld would allow the search.

He did.

He called everyone together to plan it.

I talked to Findlow during a lull in the discussion. "I really wondered if he'd allow it."

Findlow shook his head. "He wouldn't encourage Kirym if he didn't think she was right. However she would go even if Veld decided against it, and I would too. She knows more about the caves and tokens than anyone else alive. She's intuitive about them and she's always asked lots of questions about them."

"I remember her asking about my visits to the cave and especially those I'd been to before she was born. She is right about their importance, isn't she," I said.

"She takes care of all three big tokens. She says they require a home just as we do."

Everyone wanted to come along and the trip needed surprisingly few days to plan.

We walked north along the length of the valley between the ridge and the lake.

There were the remains of many dwellings, proof of a large community here at some time in the past.

I wondered what happened to them.

"You know, Bokum, these would be a good base for Raff's settlement if he wants his family to live separate from us. They'd be close while having their independence."

"I'll mention it to him, Teema. I've not heard his plans yet, although there was some talk of them moving nearer the stone path, or even settling at the path and storing and preparing the gear needed for trips. What they do won't affect me though. I'm staying put. Zeprah became part of Raff's family when she joined with Ranot. Now she has a token, she wants to be with us. We're both fond of Raff and Soojee though. In some ways it's sad though because they've lost so much."

"I'm pleased you're staying," I said. "Kirym will be delighted when you tell her, or will you leave that to Zeprah?"

Bokum laughed. "We told her yesterday, but she already knew. She said the decision was made when the cave chose Zeprah. But she says Raff and Soojee are now Zeprah's parents and I should accept them as that. Our children will be their grandchildren."

"Kirym sees things differently. I think she's right. She's always been enthusiastic about family."

Bokum looked speculatively at the buildings. "Maybe we can restore a few of these and use them as a base for fishing and hunting or even just getting away from everyone for a season or two. I'll talk to Veld."

There was a chuckle from behind us. "You'll not be getting away for a long time, Bokum." Findlow joined us, still laughing. "You're joining soon and you'll be lucky to get away for any reason before your first child sees its third season. Even then you'll have to tread carefully."

"Zeprah's quite happy to travel and hunt, Findlow. Why should she change? She'll probably join me."

I stared at Bokum. His face was pale, and his hands shook. For the first time since we had become friends, he appeared unsure of himself.

Findlow roared with laughter. "You're both here because she knows the importance of the cave and a joining token for you both. But you're all the close family she has, Bok, and you'll have to stay nearby for a while. Children arrive and, well women change then. They see different things as being important. Family, security, and other women." He walked ahead chuckling.

Bokum look shocked. "I hope he isn't right. I enjoy my trips away. I like to provide game and fish. We all need to do that." His voice shook.

"You only hear what you want to, Bokum," said Kirym, slipping in beside him. "He didn't say it'd last forever, nor that you couldn't hunt. Just that Zeprah will need you more at the beginning. She lost a lot in the hills, and she'll cling to what she has. That's you, Soojee and Raff. She'll be happy to join you out hunting once she's settled. Overall your life won't change that much."

Bokum nodded thoughtfully.

"Anyway, Findlow speaks from his own experience," Kirym continued. "When Lyndym arrived, Natia demanded a home. Their travels had been strenuous even though she enjoyed them. She happily travelled after that, but shorter trips and closer to home. She collects people around her like a shanym bird gathers its chicks."

"Well they do have an eclectic group with them. Some would call them weird, the rejects of other families. She has found the best in them and she does treat every single one of them as hers," I said.

"She encouraged all of them to come along on this trip," said Kirym. "She saw the importance, and wants them all to learn it."

"Actually, I'm surprised so many women are with us," I said. "Even Zhins is with us and she hasn't been on a trip like this since before her twins were born. That's what, thirteen seasons?"

Kirym nodded. "That's how important the cave is to everyone."

The land here was gentle, although northwest across the lake a waterfall cascaded over a cliff. The far side of the lake was rough and the hills there were very steep. I was glad we were walking this path northward.

By late afternoon, the land we travelled in was far wilder, and we began to look for a sheltered area to spend the night.

Bildon raced after a few of the children who had run ahead and out of sight amongst the trees. She returned with them and news. "There's a lovely open area ahead. I think it would be big enough to set up a camp site for the night."

We followed her to a tree lined grass area by the lake. It was perfect.

Armos had brought along two sails from the boats and we erected them over a frame to create shelters. They made an excellent temporary dwelling and were much quicker to erect than the shelters we'd brought with us in the past.

A group of us threw nets into the water. It was very noisy, and we got very wet. But we caught nineteen large fish and twelve birds. These were prepared along with some of the food we brought with us, for the meal.

"Ahhh, this is the life," I said to Arbreu, as we sat back to watch the sun settle on the horizon while the food cooked.

Veld spread his maps and noted the areas we'd travelled through and those we could see. We decided unanimously to call this spot Bildon's Rest.

She was delighted.

The following day was much hotter. By late afternoon, we had come close to the massive flat-top hill to the north. Again we found a sheltered area by the lake to spend the night.

We called this place Duck Walk, because of the line of

ducks crossing a small finger of land that jutted out into the lake near their nesting area.

It was a warm pleasant evening, but just before midnight it started to drizzle and by morning, it was raining heavily, still warm, but the rain was solid.

Veld joined me as I looked out over the misty water, quite different from the golden glow of yesterday. There were no birds in sight although we could hear their calls in the distance.

"We may as well stay here for the day. What do you think, Teema?" he asked, handing me a welcome platter of hot fruit with a sprinkling of nuts.

"We don't have a schedule to keep and there's no point in getting wet."

Over the morning, the rain grew heavier and our view of the lake was reduced to the area in front of our dwelling. The rain stopped soon after midday, but as everything was wet we decided to stay here for another night. It was pleasant and we relaxed, enjoying each other's company.

Kirym, Bildon, Mekrar and Lyndym wandered off to pick flowers and herbs. They were soon out of sight.

I sat with Veld, Findlow and Arbreu watching the boys attempting to catch fish with their bare hands amid screams and laughter.

Sundas looked worried when he approached me. "I'm going to search for Kirym. It's late and she's been gone a long time. I'll take her cloak in case it rains again."

"I'll come with you, Sundas. Don't worry though, she's quite capable and she's not alone."

He smiled happily. "Kirym is sensible, but she doesn't know this land. What if something happens?"

As we collected our own cloaks we were joined by Arbreu and Findlow.

Arbreu handed me my bow and arrows. "Sundas is right. We shouldn't have let them go off by themselves. We know nothing of the land, and just because we haven't seen other people doesn't mean they aren't here. Bitarn talked of some tracks he'd seen when he went hunting. He said they were massive. We've not seen anything really big or vicious, but it's a huge land, and we haven't looked everywhere. Something could be stalking them right now."

There was a low chuckle from Findlow. "Bitarn could see a mouse footprint and imagine one of Sundas' imantas. I'll believe when I see them. However I'd like to be there when you tell Kirym you want to protect her again. I'll bury what's left when she's finished with you. I'm sure it'll be a small hole though."

Arbreu laughed along with the rest of us. "I'll not make that mistake again, but she'll know we've followed her, and why. I guess we'll be annihilated anyway. All of us, not just me."

That's why I have their cloaks," said Sundas. "I'll tell Kirym I thought Lyndym and Bildon would get cold. She'll appreciate our concern for her friends and she won't think we're worried for her too."

Sometimes Sundas amazed me with his perception.

We came across bundles of herbs, fruit and vegetables Kirym and her group had gathered and left to collect on the way back.

I was surprised at how far they had travelled and I was beginning to wonder if we'd find them and get back before dark. We tracked them to the base of the massive hill.

An animal track went in both directions.

With no indication what direction they chose, we turned towards the lake where I knew there would be edible waterweed Kirym was fond of. Soon we were walking through increasingly deeper pools of the water.

"This is silly," I said, calling a halt. "Kirym wouldn't do it. The weed is easily harvested nearer the camp. She must have gone east."

We retraced our steps. The sun crept lower and I began to feel sick at the thought of Kirym missing overnight.

"We might have missed her when we went the …"

Sundas stopped and held up his hand for silence.

I realised I was holding my breath, although my heart seemed to be thumping so loud I thought Arbreu, standing closer to me, would tell me to be quiet.

Then I heard what Sundas had heard.

Lyndym laughing. It echoed, giving the strange illusion of coming from inside the hill.

We continued around the base of the hill, quickening our stride as we went. Then the path came to an abrupt end.

The long ridge that ran north from the sea, curved around and joined the massive hill we had been walking around.

"They must have returned when we went towards the lake," said Findlow.

"I heard them," I said. "We all heard Lyndym laugh."

He shook his head. "It could have been anything. A bird or an animal along with our desire for it to be them."

"It *was* them," said Sundas.

"Then we missed something," said Arbreu. "We must have. I really think Kirym is close. Closer than the camp, anyway."

He and Sundas turned back, studying the ground for tracks as they went.

"Wishful thinking?" asked Findlow quietly.

I shrugged. "When he said it, I was sure he was right. Just a feeling, but …" I had no real way to explain it.

It looked like a wide crack, as if the hill had been split open with a huge axe. The entrance was covered with undergrowth, and we would have missed it, had the sun not been so low in the sky.

The path curved into the hill. The ground was surprisingly clear of debris, once we were past the entrance. The walls were smooth and towered above us although the path got wider as we walked. It felt dark and foreboding. I realised it would see very little sunlight. Despite that it was very dry underfoot.

"I wonder why no plants have grown in here?" asked Findlow. "It seems to be an ideal place, sheltered and windless."

"No sun, and perhaps little rain," I suggested. I sped up, concerned for the reducing light.

We rounded the final corner of the ravine at a run.

Kirym, Lyndym and Bildon stood in an open grassy basin surrounded by cliffs. But that wasn't what held their attention and ours.

Around the cliff were three caves.

27

Kirym Speaks

Kirym's caves!

Papa drew them on the map and wrote my name beside them.

We arrived at the canyon as the midsummer moon rose. This time when I entered the canyon, I was more aware of the huge open area and the walls around it. It was over five hundred steps across and slightly longer than wide. The cliffs went straight up, towering over us.

The top rim of the cliff was marred only by a huge gash to the north that came half way down.

It was very dark until the moon peeped over the cliff. Then we could see the canyon clearly. The caves were black against the dark rock face.

We were dressed in our festival clothes and cloaks. With ground rugs to sit on, we prepared to stay for as long as needed.

I had carried the tokens in the pouch until we came into the canyon, but now I nestled them onto a woven platter covered with flowers and sweet smelling herbs. The tokens glowed when we approached the middle cave.

We'd made no decision about how we were to enter, and when we got to the entrance everyone was reluctant to be the first.

Finally Papa called for silence and gave lamps to Bildon, Zeprah and Sundas and told them that as new members of the family, they should lead us in. I followed them with the tokens, Papa came next with everyone else behind him.

All around me I could feel the excitement of being in a token-cave again. It was different though, I felt contented, as if I had finally come home.

Inside it was quite different from our previous cave. It was made up of a number of interconnecting areas around a big open space. There were lots of ledges and low rocks we could use as seats.

All around me were ooh's and aah's as people spotted massive twisted columns in some of the areas off the central space.

The shapes of the rocks were magnificent, but I concentrated on the coming ceremony, which I knew would take place in this central area. Right in the centre of the cave was a flat rock that stuck up like a tree stump. I sat the platter holding the tokens on it.

We placed our rugs on rock ledges and around the walls and waited.

As the lights dimmed, the tokens began to glow and then pulse. The rhythm got faster and faster until the whole cave seemed to quiver. The cave lit up for a moment, then plunged into darkness and lit up again and again. Small tokens glowed from the walls and roof of the cave.

Then the lights went out. From high in the roof, there was a whispering sound sort of like the wind passing on a message.

The large green token sent a beam of light to connect with my jewel. From there, it shot over to touch Teema, then Arbreu, Bokum, Zeprah, Sundas, and Findlow, zigzagging around the family and finally connecting to Papa, Mama, Teema's and my blue tokens, and then on to the large blue token.

A ray of white light gleamed from each of the two large tokens to the rainbow token. We were all briefly connected then the light danced over to an outcrop on the wall where a large yellow token lit up. The connecting light beams disappeared, leaving the large tokens glowing in the dark.

A shaft of light from my two tokens connected to the blue, green and rainbow tokens, and finally reached out to include the yellow. Three white rays shot out of the rainbow token searching around the cave, pausing on cracks and crevasses. Slowly, almost reluctantly they died and disappeared back into the token. They flowed out again, but this time as they returned they changed colour, now orange, red and purple.

The connections between the tokens disappeared, but the large tokens continued pulsing gently. One by one, the tokens we wore joined in.

I could feel mine throbbing on my forehead. I watched and listened to the tokens as they linked again. It was almost as if they were talking to each other. I felt my tokens reaching out and connecting to them again.

I glanced over to Teema and Arbreu, sending them the message I felt.

We're home!

Then I felt an empty space. Something was missing.

Somewhere more tokens were waiting to be found.

THE END

If you have enjoyed The Caves of Kirym, please leave a review on the website of the seller you purchased it from. Good reviews are the life blood of independently-published authors, so please take a few moments to let others know what you thought of the book.

Thank you for reading.

Do look for further adventures as
The Token Bearer's series continues.

www.wordlypress.com

www.ingramcontent.com/pod-product-compliance
Lightning Source LLC
Chambersburg PA
CBHW021236060726
47590CB00005B/1782